Between Courting AND Kissing

#3 A Gentleman's Guide to Courtship

BY

CHARLIE LANE

WOLF PUBLISHING

Between Courting and Kissing by Charlie Lane

Published by WOLF Publishing UG

Copyright © 2024 Charlie Lane
Text by Charlie Lane
Edited by Chris Hall
Cover Art by Victoria Cooper
Ebook ISBN: 978-3-98536-268-4
Paperback ISBN: 978-3-98536-269-1
Hard Cover ISBN: 978-3-98536-270-7

WOLF Publishing - This is us:

Two sisters, two personalities.. But only one big love!

Diving into a world of dreams..
  ...Romance, heartfelt emotions, lovable and witty characters, some humor, and some mystery! Because we want it all! Historical Romance at its best!

Visit our website to learn all about us, our authors and books!

Sign up to our mailing list to receive first hand information on new releases, freebies and promotions as well as exclusive giveaways and sneak-peeks!

WWW.WOLF-PUBLISHING.COM

Also by Charlie Lane

A Gentleman's Guide to Courtship

The Duke of Clearford has five marriageable sisters, and none of them are wed. But his Gentleman's Guide to Courtship will ensure success for any suitor... *unless* his sisters refuse to be wooed. *Unless* their secret reason for refusing proves too scandalous.

#1 Never Woo the Wrong Lady

#2 How to Romance a Rogue

#3 Between Courting and Kissing

#4 First Comes Courtship

#5 Court a Lady with Care

#6 Dukes Court for Keeps

Between Courting AND Kissing

Chapter One

April 1820

Trapped. The candlelit ballroom, a gilded champagne bubble of a prison. No hope of escape. But Lady Prudence Merriweather desperately needed one. Three exits out of the cursed ballroom, and all of them guarded as if by dragons.

Before door number one, her brother, the Duke of Clearford. He held one of her suitors, the heir to the Earl of Heinsford, by the upper arm and scowled about the ballroom, no doubt looking for her. The Heir, as he must be called since he introduced himself in no other way, seemed resigned to his fate. He wore the placid expression of a small puppy dragged about by a determined young girl. He'd quite surrendered all hope.

Before exit number two—the double doors which led out to the garden—stood another suitor, Viscount Norton. A handsome enough fellow with lovely white gold hair and a soft smile. His clear green gaze traveled about the ballroom, looking for her, too. But not at all seeing her. They stood rather close. His gaze seemed locked on her face. She waved. Still, he failed to register her existence, his eyes remaining foggy as if she were a bit of glass he looked through to something more interesting beyond. A tiny pang between two ribs. She rubbed at it, reminded herself to embrace her habitual invisibility. She must consider it a boon. Particularly tonight.

Because she had much to do in a short time, and because her greatest adversary, sharper eyed than the others, stood before exit number three. Another suitor. The American, Mr. Benjamin Bailey. He stood wide-legged at the entrance to a parlor off the side of the room, as if he knew she might seek out less crowded climes. If he caught her, he would say something he'd learned from her brother's Guide to Courtship. *Guide*. Ha. The blind leading the blind. Her brother had never courted a woman. Prudence had never read the blasted book, but it likely included only dubious advice. No kissing until betrothed. No flowers. Encourage competition. Silly maxims, and they'd moved Mr. Bailey no closer to success in his courtship of Prudence.

Neither did his costume. Climbing boy? To begin with, he stood a head above the other men in the ballroom, his shoulders wide enough to sit comfortably upon. Boy? Ha. A burly, bearded beast of a man entirely out of place here, better suited to somewhere men wrenched survival from a pitiless land with their bare hands and sharp teeth. And with the soot all about him, his long honey-colored hair held back loosely with a black ribbon, tangled as if he'd just dropped out of a tight, unpleasant place. Was that a rip in his sleeve? She'd give him a mark for accuracy. But a *sweep*? Bad taste. Particularly when she found the practice of using children for such dangerous tasks so unsavory. Put him in the negative, that did. Not that the other suitors had accumulated marks enough to tread water. They were all drowning.

Not their faults, really. She did not wish to be courted. They swam toward a goal which didn't even exist—marriage to her.

The American's sharp, blue eyes caught her looking, and his beard rearranged itself into what might be a smile if he knew a good barber. He'd caught her. Those eyes glittered with purpose, and he took one powerful stride toward her, his body rippling into predatory life.

She darted behind a woman wearing a wig and dress from the previous century. Thank heavens for the lazy during masquerade balls.

The woman's reluctance to find a costume anywhere outside of her own attics proved useful. But Prudence couldn't stay safe behind wide panniers and sky-high powdered sausage curls for long. She pulled her pocket watch from her skirts. A quarter hour till midnight and she'd still not managed to leave the ballroom. If she did not do so soon, tonight's poetry reading would never happen.

Poetry readings, particularly of the sort Prudence helped organize for Miss Cora Eastwood, required a careful touch, an eye to detail. No one could know they even existed. Except for the right people. Women of the *ton* who liked their poems a little naughty.

They needed a common place of congregation for their audience—balls. And they needed an abandoned room inside the residences where those entertainments occurred. Prudence relied on gossip to discover the locations they would commandeer for their next readings. Made them difficult to find in the middle of the night.

Would be easier to do the sensible thing and hold a select and private salon in broad daylight, but Cora's muse demanded certain details be met before delivering. Namely, anonymity. High noon and the bright light of the waking world would not suffice.

And now Prudence was crunched for time.

Her feet tapped. She'd be late. If she didn't find the room *and* Cora, who would ensure the candles were perfectly lit? They hit against her legs in her skirt pockets. Cora had the pocket tinderbox secured beneath her stays. Useless without Prudence's candles. And if Prudence never escaped, who would place the discreet markers along the path to the room so the brave women of the *ton*, out for a little entertainment, could more easily find it? Most importantly, who would take up guard in the hall to ensure no one discovered their little meeting?

No one but Prudence. Cora may be Prudence's closest friend, but not even friendship hid the poet's faults. A mind like holey cheese. Unable to hold on to the small details which *mattered*. Cora could metaphor with the best poets London had to offer. But her little enterprise, the secret midnight poetry readings at balls, had lacked finesse until Prudence had decided to help her. Now they ran like a well-turned clock.

Not tonight, though. Because Prudence couldn't escape the blasted ballroom. She inhaled, exhaled, hard little breaths to pound down the frustration rising up her neck, making it difficult to breathe.

Then behind her, the comically wide skirts rustled, and the woman's neck twisted. "Prudence, dear? Is that you bumping my backside?"

Prudence jumped as the wigged woman turned, her panniers knocking over a potted palm. Aunt Millicent. She blinked at Prudence and held up a quizzing glass to her eye, magnifying that orb as well as the beauty patch shaped like a heart stuck just at its corner.

"Aunt! What a surprise."

"How so? I'm your chaperone."

"Ah. Yes. I mean... I didn't see you when you arrived. What a magnificent costume!"

"Your grandmother's old gown and wig."

"Don't you think it a tad..." Prudence did not drop her gaze to her aunt's bosom. "Risqué?"

Millicent adjusted her stays, pushing even more of her pale flesh into view above the gown's bodice. "Not nearly enough, dear. Where are your suitors?"

Prudence peered around the edges of Aunt Millicent's wig. "Everywhere."

Oh, but Lord Norton no longer stood before the garden doors. Retreating outside was not the best option. If she went out, she'd have to come back in. Created an entirely new problem. But... needs must. Because if Samuel and The Heir did not find her, the American would.

A fan smacked the side of Prudence's head.

"Ow!" She scowled at her aunt.

"You should be dancing, dear," the woman said, snapping open her weapon.

"I'm feeling a bit fatigued." Prudence stepped sideways toward the open doors. "I'll just pop out for a moment..." Another step sideways.

Aunt Millicent fluttered her fan. "His Grace wishes to see you. I told him I'd send you his way before retiring to the card room."

Her brother. "I'll find Samuel. I promise. You have fun, Aunt Millicent. Good luck!"

Her aunt narrowed her eyes, seemed to realize Prudence's easy agreement to speak with her brother was too neat a victory. But then she shrugged, the motion nearly popping one breast out of her gown. She caught it, though, before disaster, and chuckled as she turned to push her way through the crowd. She folded her fan and waved it above her head. "You have fun, too, dear!"

Prudence made slow but steady progress toward the outer doors where the ballroom spilled into the night-shadowed garden. She kept her head down and made herself small. Not hard to hide when no one looked. Those she passed thought her nothing more than an evening draft from the garden. As usual. Prudence quite blended into the background. A pane of glass to be looked through, not at.

The doors, already open to combat the warmth of the crush inside, welcomed her, and she stepped beyond them and into—

"Prudence, there you are."

She groaned, rocking back into the light of the ballroom. So close. She sewed a smile onto her face and turned.

Samuel stood behind her, back stiff, shoulders wide, dark hair perfectly and fashionably coiffed over a handsome face and serious, gray eyes. The only concession he made to the masquerade was a narrow domino covering his eyes. If he knew what she planned to do this evening, he'd pack her off to the country and never let her leave.

"Suitors," he said in an even tone, "are not out in the gardens."

"Perhaps they are."

"Suitors are in the ballroom, Prudence, dancing. As *you* should be. With them."

"I will. It's merely too hot in here. I'm melting, Samuel." She gazed longingly toward the garden.

He flicked the black veil framing her face. "I'm in all black, just as you are, and I'm perfectly fine. Not melting at all."

"Then you have a talent for wearing black. I, apparently, do not." That much was true. She'd pushed the front of the veil back over her coiffure, hiding her dark-blonde hair and giving herself space to breathe.

"But you do have a talent for dancing, Sister." He wrapped an arm around her shoulders and guided her back toward the ballroom. "I've seen you. You have the ability to captivate any suitor with your light step and grace."

"But I do not want to captivate anyone. How many times must I explain? I wish to be—"

"A spinster. Liar. You're scared."

She gasped, tugged from his embrace. "Am not!"

"Then dance." He waved an arm toward the dancers, toward—blast it all. The Heir stood waiting nearby, blinking at Samuel. Awaiting, no doubt, His Grace's instructions. "You wish to dance, Tallsby, do you not?"

Without looking at Prudence, The Heir nodded.

Samuel guided her toward him, stopped her just before the man who did not quite fit his name. Perhaps he did stand tall. When he did not stoop.

She bobbed a curtsy. "Good evening."

Finally, he looked at her. His eyes widened as if she'd appeared out of nowhere. "There you are, Lady Prudence. Would you dance with me?"

She glanced at Samuel, wide-legged and grim-faced, and she leaned close and whispered, "Where is your knife? Come. I know you have one on your person."

His eyes narrowed. "Why do you wish to know?"

"I would like to stab you with it." The words ground between her teeth.

Samuel nudged her toward Tallsby. "I merely desire you to be happy."

"Look to your own happiness, Brother," she grumbled, but she took The Heir's outstretched hand.

"You have only just arrived, Lady Prudence?" He swept her out onto the dancefloor to await the first notes of the music with the other couples.

"I've been here an hour at least."

He took her hand in one of his and put his other hand on her back. "Are you well this evening?"

"Yes." She placed her remaining hand on his shoulder.

"And what are you dressed as?"

"Midnight." She spoke without looking at him, her entire attention on Samuel, who watched from the edges of the ballroom.

Tallsby watched Samuel, too, as the first chord of a violin wavered into the air. "Ah. How... creative. Have you seen your sister tonight? Lady Noble? All in gold." He sighed. "A picture of beauty and elegance." As he swung her into the first turn of the waltz, he finally looked at her. "Perhaps if I may be so bold as to make a suggestion, you should have worn gold. Or blue. Something more delicate. Black, I'm afraid, does not suit you."

"I shall take that under advisement."

"Do you know, I courted your other sister one Season—Lady Andromeda. Mrs. Kingston now. Such a sweet soul. I would have liked to court Lady Noble, but her beauty rather intimidated me. Mrs. Kingston possesses a less fearful beauty, but she seemed too serene and peaceful to be disturbed with masculine interest."

"I'm not sure I take your meaning, Lord Tallsby."

"You, however, my lady, are perfect for me. Not so terribly beautiful as your sisters, nor so angelic. And unlike your younger sisters, there is only one of you. I'm not quite exotic enough to enjoy the idea that there's a copy of my wife running about England."

"Thank you?" If only he hadn't approached her. But then, he hadn't really. He'd approached Samuel. Or Samuel had approached him, dragged him toward her, as if Prudence couldn't attract her own suitors.

But then... she couldn't, could she?

"I'm afraid I'm feeling indisposed." Did she look pale enough? Black washed her out. The truth—her stomach a bit sour, and her jaw so tight it shot pain straight up to her temples.

"Heavens, Lady Prudence. You must sit." Tallsby guided her off the floor and toward a row of chairs near, thankfully, the garden doors.

"Lemonade?" she asked, popping open a black lace fan.

He jumped. "Yes!" And he disappeared toward the refreshments.

She wasted no time slipping into the night air with a deep breath, her shoulders relaxing. Escape the ballroom—done. Excellent. Her spirits lifted a bit, that sour sting in her belly dissipating a bit. Now onto the next task. Nothing better for low spirits than arranging every-thing just so.

First, she must re-enter the house. She put her hands on her hips and frowned up at the edifice. Bellingham House was rather old, and London crept closer to it year by year. The Marquess of Bellingham resided here, an old friend of her father's before he passed away. And now of her brother. Perhaps Bellingham was more of an old friend to the Duke of Clearford, whomever that duke may be. No matter. He possessed excellent trust in mankind; almost every window and door thrown open and lovely little balconies on the first floor. Trees, too. Good for climbing onto those balconies.

Cora's maid had said they could meet in a first-floor parlor in the midst of redecoration. But which room was that? Impossible to say from the outside.

Choosing the location for the poetry recitation always proved the most difficult bit of their enterprise. They couldn't stride into the planned venue and demand to know what room would prove most isolated and abandoned. They relied heavily on details gathered through the strongest information network known to the world—the servants. Information cleverly gathered as gossip from Cora's maid. Or through Prudence's younger sister, Isabella. She knew, somehow, every-thing that happened in London.

But which window would prove easiest to climb into? Prudence walked back several steps and bumped into something.

A giggle.

Not something. Someone.

"Apologies," Prudence mumbled, flipping her veil down over her face. The woman and her beau, shepherd and shepherdess, ran off into the bushes, and Prudence tilted her head back to study the house's façade.

"Lady Prudence?"

She cursed. She knew that voice floating out from the ballroom. Lord Norton. She spun on a gasp and fled into the garden. Dressed as midnight, the dark would conceal her. As long as the gold thread sewn into her skirts and bodice and veil did not catch the moonlight or the light spilling out of the house, she'd remain well hidden.

But no closer to her goal. Oh, for the chance to wail her frustration skyward. She'd have to schedule a good scream in the garden for tomorrow afternoon.

She dashed away from a Greek god chasing a goddess down the lane and ducked behind a row of prickly hedges. Had the entire ball-room decided to hold court outside? The masks likely gave them all greater courage to cavort how they pleased. And with whom they pleased.

"Lady Prudence?" Norton followed still, looking for her even though he never looked *at* her.

Bent over to remain hidden behind the short hedges, she darted between Queen Elizabeth in a stiff ruff and a swan with a little orange beak attached to a domino.

"Lady Prudence?" Lord Norton's ever-patient voice.

She could not hate him. Such a sweet temperament. Always accommodating. A man who followed the rules of gentlemanly conduct with absolute perfection. And whose continued interest began to make her thighs and back ache. She could not much longer hold this posture, knees half-bent, stooped over behind a bush. She floated to a crouching position, her skirts billowing out around her knees. A bit of relief for her thighs. Though this position also would not last long.

How had it come to this?

If her thighs ached any more, they'd burn holes right through her skirts. She had to move soon or lose all feeling below her waist. She found her pocket watch, the silver warmed by her body, and pulled it out. In the light of the moon, she could see its white face clearly. She should be in the room already. Her schedule in ruins.

"Lady Prudence?" Norton's voice so close now, right over the other side of the hedge.

She clapped her hands over her mouth, stopped breathing, lost her balance, and toppled backward. Her arms flew wide, and she gasped, a startled gurgling sort of sound. The house rocked out of view, giving way to the night sky, and she slammed her eyes closed as her head slammed into the ground. She waited for the running footsteps, the worried query as to her health.

But they never came. Lord Norton must not have heard her fall.

Now her chance to run. Surely, he'd ambled off deeper into the garden. She could throw her veil down over her face and make for the house, dart back into the ballroom—easiest route—and just elbow whatever suitor stepped into her path out of the way. She needed to be on schedule, to make sure everything was just right for Cora. Because without just right and on time, there existed only chaos. Lists and schedules kept the world from falling apart, and Prudence would stick to hers, no matter what plagues terrorized London.

Despite the tender lump pulsing at the back of her head, she opened her eyes, ready for battle.

And looked right up into the scruffy face of the American.

Mr. Benjamin Bailey. Dash it all. She'd been discovered.

Chapter Two

Benjamin Bailey usually enjoyed the sight of a pretty woman on her back. But the garden was too crowded for amorous activities, and the woman staring up at him with wide eyes was not for him. He only pretended to court her, after all.

The veil had flown away from her face during the fall, and Lady Prudence scowled up at him, her pale face bearing clear signs of her ire —brows pulled into a deep V, mouth pinched thin, blue-green eyes sparking in the moonlight. A few tendrils of her hair—a forgettable shade between brown and blonde—escaped its tightly controlled coiffure beneath the veil.

He held out a hand to her.

She smacked it away and rolled to her hands and knees, pushed to her feet on her own. Only to grab his wrist and yank him down, bending his body in half at the waist.

"Devil take it, woman," he hissed, shaking her grip away and shooting up tall once more.

She grabbed his shoulder this time and yanked him down again, whispered in his ear, "Either leave or remain hidden, Mr. Bailey. I'd rather not be caught."

"I already caught you."

She sighed, world-weary. "*Again*. I'd rather not be caught *again*. Besides, you're going to release me."

"Catch and release? Will I?"

"Yes, as soon as I can be certain Lord Norton will not latch on next."

Ben straightened as much as she would allow and peeked over the shrubbery that hid them. There, in the moon-brightened shadows— Norton's light hair, his angled profile soft as he gazed down at a veiled woman. He reached for the edge of the woman's veil, where it fell just above her lips. The woman pushed his hand away, keeping her secrets.

"I don't think you have to worry about Norton." Ben ducked down once more. "He's occupied."

"Occupied?" Lady Prudence straightened all the way, her head bouncing above the top edge of the shrubs. "Oh!" Then another gasp on the pathway of a slow, deep inhale. "Oh *no*." The two words joining the sound of an exhalation.

He peeked over the edge again. Norton now kissed the woman, their lips locked beneath the veil's edge. "She's wearing the same costume as you." Black everywhere, the silk embroidered with golden stars and moons. "What are you supposed to be?"

"Midnight," Lady Prudence said, the word barely audible. "We should stop him!"

"Don't think either of them would appreciate an interruption."

The veiled woman clutched at Norton's lapels, pulling his body against hers. They stumbled back several steps until her back hit a tree trunk. Then Norton trapped her, pressing his palms against the tree beside her head and parting her legs with his knee. She groaned.

Ben's body tightened. The show grew more salacious by the moment. He glanced at Lady Prudence. She bit her bottom lip. If he could see her eyes in the sun's bright rays instead of in the moonlight, he'd be able to tell—did they darken with confusion or with arousal?

She gasped, her hand flying up to catch the sound, to muffle it.

Ben looked back to Norton and his catch. His now nearly naked catch. The viscount had torn the shoulder of the woman's gown, and her bodice gaped low, revealing stays and the thin shift beneath. Norton had freed one small breast.

And Lady Prudence still looked on.

Devil take it. Her brother would not approve. Her brother would scatter knives about Ben's body if he knew.

He cupped her shoulders and tried to turn her. She would not budge. "Back to the ballroom with you." Once more, he tried moving her.

"I should say something. We should stop it." Her voice, hazy and monotone. Her gaze never once wavered from the picture before them —Norton dropping his head to the woman's breast, licking her nipple, teasing it with his teeth. Lady Prudence bit her lip again. Aroused. Definitely aroused. Slowly, her teeth released her lip, leaving it swollen and plump. What color, though? The usual pink or a tortured red? He'd need more than moonlight to tell. Her chest rose and fell, and the low bodice of the black gown strained, small, pretty breasts testing its limits. He'd never seen Lady Prudence like this—tempted and tempting, curious and blooming.

His body tightened further, his cock leaping beneath his fall. An erotic show just beyond the hedge. A pretty-enough lady aroused at his side. Hell. How else was his body supposed to react?

Dangerous indeed. He'd no desire to become target practice for a blade-happy duke.

"You are leaving. *Now*." Ben stepped between her and the bush, blocking her view.

The arousal drained from her face. If her brother threw knives from his fists, she threw them from her eyes. Just as deadly, too. Yet he found himself wanting to chuckle. Lady Prudence proved a spitfire.

He leaned low enough that she could hear him as he whispered, low enough his lips almost brushed her cheek. "That show is not for you, my lady. It's not for any innocent."

She leaned infinitesimally closer, her lips whispering against his ear, "If there is one thing I detest, it is being called an innocent. I do as I please, and I will not abandon my—"

"Cora Eastwood!" The name rode a feminine shriek into the night air. It hadn't come from Lady Prudence. She seemed just as startled by the shriek as he was—her eyes wide, her lips open on a silent gasp.

On the other side of the shrub, the woman in black jerked,

ducked her head into Lord Norton's chest as if the veil did not hide her well enough. Norton yanked her torn sleeve up her shoulder, tried to fix her bodice, and when he could not, stationed himself in front of her as he turned to confront the possessor of the shrieking voice.

An older woman dressed all in white feathers stepped onto the stage.

"Oh no. Oh no, oh no, oh no." Lady Prudence's dismay sounded much too loud.

Ben clamped a hand down over her mouth, and she *let* him, her head shaking slowly. Perhaps shock gripped her enough to let him drag her from the scene.

"Quiet," he hissed as he tugged her toward the house.

She would not be tugged. Her feet had grown roots.

"I'll throw you over my shoulder," he threatened.

She did not seem to hear him, her attention fully on the events unraveling beyond the hedge.

"Cora, how could you?" The feathered woman's generous bosom shook as she wailed.

Norton remained like a wall before the woman he hid against the tree. "This is not Miss Eastwood."

"I know my daughter." The feathered woman—Mrs. Eastwood, it seemed—stamped her foot.

And the hidden figure dressed all in tattered black moved away from her protector, lifting her veil as she did so. "Good evening, Mama."

Norton turned still as stone before spinning into life, whirling around, and tipping Miss Eastwood's face up to the moonlight. "M-Miss Eastwood?"

She nodded.

"N-not Lady P—"

"No." Miss Eastwood ripped her chin from his light hold and marched up to her mother.

Lady Prudence trembled. Ben wrapped an arm around her shoulders and pulled her closer, gave her a bit of his strength. She was friends with the caught chit, wasn't she? And the lady P-something

Norton had almost named... had it been... Lady Prudence *had* been attempting to avoid him.

Some emotion hard and fast as lightning ripped through him. Norton didn't seem like a wolf. He'd been a vicar once. But he'd clearly just compromised a lady. A lady he'd thought to be the one sheltered beneath the wing of Ben's arm.

Devil take it.

"We're leaving," he hissed.

"But Cora needs me."

"There's not a thing in hell you can do for her right now. Only Norton can save her, and he will if he's a gentleman."

Her cheek hollowed as she bit the inside of it. She closed her eyes. This time when he tugged, she moved, flowing into step with him as easily as if he led her in a practiced dance.

"I must tell the others," she mumbled, casting a backward glance toward the shrubbery.

"You must tell the others what? And *what others?*"

"Nothing. No one."

Like hell. He'd been watching this woman closely for months now, waiting for her to slip up. She rarely did. She hid her secrets well. But when she finally made a mistake, he'd be there to see it, to find her secrets when she finally left the door unlocked. Then he could spill them into the duke's hands and be free of the debt he owed that man.

The glow of the ballroom brightened the black ropes of vines near the doorway to a vibrant green, and as they stepped across the threshold from moonlight stillness to candlelight chaos, he said, "Dance with me."

She tripped, ripped her arm from his grasp. "Do what with you?" Yes, her lips redder than he'd seen them.

He almost couldn't look away, and his brain had slowed. It took much too long to push through the mire of sluggishness and find a word to offer her as answer to her question. *Red* the only word he found, red the only color. He ripped his gaze away, looked at anything else but her lips.

"Dance," he coughed out.

She blinked, shook her head as if she'd still not heard. Was she hard of hearing? Perhaps that explained why she never responded to any of his queries, or to those posed by any of her other suitors. He leaned closer to her ear—she smelled sweet, more like a treat baked in a kitchen than a flower born in the sun—and yelled, "Dance!"

She bounced away from him, hand flying up to cup her ear. "You don't have to scream." She looked left, then right, sighed, and pinched the bridge of her nose.

Everyone looked at them, curious eyes skating across his skin like hot coals. Or scalpels. They did, after all, attempt to cut, to peel away, to dissect and observe.

She darted away from him.

He lunged after her. "Where are you going?"

"To my sisters. Cora needs us."

"Miss Eastwood can handle her own ruination. With Lord Norton's help. Are you distressed it was not you? Are you"—God, he hoped not —"heartbroken?"

"No!"

"Then dance with me."

She swung around. "And why should I? You've not even *asked*."

"I've asked twice now."

"You've *demanded*. It's not at all the same thing."

With more force of will than he'd known he possessed, he did *not* roll his eyes. "Lady Prudence, will you honor me with your hand in the next dance?"

"No." She darted away once more. "Oh, there's Lady Templeton. I must tell her. Everything is off." Her words muffled but still clear. She spoke more to herself than to him.

But he could not stifle his curiosity. In fact, it was his job not to stifle his curiosity when she did odd things. He caught up with her, pushing through the crowd just behind her, so close her skirts brushed against his legs. "What is off, Lady Prudence?"

She stopped with a hop, swinging around. They bounced off one another, and he grabbed her arms to keep her from falling.

"You're still here?" She blinked. "Mr. Bailey, you should know, I'm in no mood to be courted at the moment, particularly by an insensitive brute like you.

"Insensitive? What the h—" More eyes glanced their way, and he swallowed his curse, lowered his voice. "What have I done that's insensitive? I've merely done my best to keep you from being compromised."

Her gaze raked over him from face to shoes and back up. "Your costume is in bad taste. The climbing boys are pitiful creatures, tormented by circumstances beyond their control, taken advantage of by evil men. You should not mock them for entertainment."

What the hell did climbing boys have to do with anything? "I'm not wearing a costume."

Her defiant, lifted chin sank a bit, and her gaze flitted over his shoulders, down his sleeves. "But you've got soot all over you, even in your hair, and your clothes are torn. As if you've climbed a chimney."

He looked down at his clothes. Devil take it. He was a mess, even for his standards. His hair had fallen out of its queue, too, and hung lanky around his face. He slapped his hand on his back, his shoulders, but found no ribbon. Lost another one. Damn. He pulled one of the extra, thin, black ribbons he kept on his person from his pocket and tied his hair back before pinning Lady Prudence with a glare. "That's not soot, that's ink. I came here directly from the printshop." He owned several with Mr. Kingston, Lady Prudence's brother-in-law.

"And you didn't think to change first?"

He should have. Clearly.

"Whatever else you are, Mr. Bailey, you are consistent. And that, at least, is admirable." Her veil rippled as she turned once more and slipped through the crush.

He didn't follow this time. Felt suddenly... absurd. The two men chatting next to him wore fine silk and crisp, snowy linen. Their jaws were clean and their hair fashionably styled. The women dancing nearby wore gowns so white the tiniest speck of dust would ruin them. And they'd throw them away or hand them off to a maid and buy all new ones. White as innocence but more disposable. Two nearby wallflowers, neat as pins, caught him looking and gave him their backs. Snubbed by the snubbed.

Hell.

He didn't fit here. Lady Prudence knew it. He knew it. Everyone did. If his clothes didn't give it away, his voice did. Less American than it had been over a decade ago when he'd first crossed the ocean to live with his grandfather. But still different. Still too flat in places, too hard.

Usually, it didn't bother him. But he'd left the printshop and come straight to a ball without even thinking to change his clothes. Why the hell had they even let him through the door? Because of his grandfather, Baron Brightly? Because everyone knew he'd befriended the Duke of Clearford years ago? Connections counted.

Ben shook himself, discomfort flicking off him like water from a wet dog. Where was Clearford? Ah, there, with Lord Noble and Kingston. Naturally.

King saw Ben first and raised a brow as Ben joined their circle.

"You look more like hell than usual, friend," he said. "You battled a printing press, I assume. And lost." His friend's dark hair was longer than fashionable, and a shadow of scruff hung about his jaw, but his clothes were pristine, perfectly fitted. A black domino ringed his green eyes.

Ben eyed King's drink. "I need to keep a change of clothes at all the shops. I keep forgetting. What're you drinking?" Ben needed something strong.

"Lemonade. Want it?"

Ben curled a lip. "Keep it."

"I've not seen you dance with Prudence tonight," Clearford said.

"She's been busy. There's about to be a scandal, Clearford."

The duke's brows drew together. "Where is she?"

"Not Lady Prudence," Ben said. "A friend of hers. I saw the whole thing just now in the gardens. One of Lady Prudence's suitors compromised her. Lord Norton. I think he thought the lady was your sister."

Clearford's hands became loose fists, the kind that could easily wrap around the hilt of a dagger and fling with precision. "Where is she?"

"She might be with Lottie." Noble pushed off the wall he leaned against. Better dressed than all of them together and more flamboyantly. He'd traded his usual somber colors for a gold waistcoat. His domino gold, too. Both matched his hair.

"What are you supposed to be?" Ben asked.

Clearford took a strict step forward. "Now is not the time to—"

"Midas," Noble said with a smirk. "You should see Lottie. Dressed from head to toe in gold. Like a king with a golden touch has had his hands everywh—"

"If you finish that sentence," Clearford said, "I'll put a knife in your gullet."

Noble laughed. "I'll find Lottie."

Kingston stepped away from the circle with him. "I'll help. I'm ready to return home to Andromeda anyway. Only came here to get Bellingham's support for an investment."

"When is she due?" Noble asked as they turned away.

"Two months now, the doctor says." Kingston beamed brighter than the candles above.

"Let's hope it's a boy," Noble said with a shiver.

"I'd rather a girl."

"And end up like Clearford? With all those ladies to marry off?"

"Better that," Kingston said, "than coaches burnt to a crisp in Hyde Park. Have you ever cleaned piss off a doorstep? I have." He shivered. "I'll take a girl, please."

Noble shrugged, and both men disappeared into the crowd.

The duke's attention had not wavered from Ben. "Anything else I need to know, Bailey?" He'd crossed his arms over his chest, and one wrist flinched in a steady rhythm, as if beneath his arm, his fingers rubbed his ribs. Or perhaps the knife hidden beneath his waistcoat there. "You've not seen the twins dancing in a fountain, perhaps, or Felicity dressed as a lad and sneaking about the mews?"

The twins were more of the duke's sisters. Felicity too, likely, though Ben couldn't remember all their names. There were eight of the chits, after all, three still in the schoolroom.

"No. I've nothing new to report. Other than what I already have. And Lady Prudence wasn't involved. We saw it all, though. And I'm positive Norton meant to seduce her instead of Miss Eastwood."

Clearford's jaw worked, clearly chewing through several words he could not say in a ballroom. "I trusted Norton. And Prudence... what can she be hiding?"

"She ran off into the gardens on her own. But that could be because she was running from Norton."

Clearford's eyes flashed. "Scared?"

"No. Annoyed." He chuckled. "Very annoyed." And then aroused. Ben's chuckle died.

"She's hiding something. All my sisters are, but I can't seem to figure it out. They're always one step ahead of me."

"Have you tried asking them about it?"

"Yes. They went all wide-eyed and sad looking. Then enraged. Like I'd questioned their honor. Wouldn't speak to me for weeks afterward."

"Could have been worse."

Clearford scowled. "Prudence can give no good reason for not wishing to wed. Spinster? Ha. There must be something holding her back. I want to know what it is. I need to know." His eyes darkened, and his jaw tightened. "How else am I to protect her? All of them? How am I to keep them safe if they insist on keeping things from me? If they have husbands—solid, dependable husbands—I need not worry so much." Usually, the duke wore a cloak of cool confidence, but tonight a shadow tore at that cloak, revealing the doubt, the fear, beneath it.

"I'll figure it out, Clearford. Don't turn watering pot."

"You're right. You will figure it out. Or I'll keep my shares, Bailey."

"You needn't remind me. Hard to forget my oldest friend this side of the Atlantic has turned blackmailer."

Clearford's eyes bounced from side to side, looking for anyone near enough to hear. He leaned close and whispered, "Desperate times, Bailey, desperate measures. The sooner you find out my sister's secret, the sooner I'll sell you my shares of London Life Prints."

"I told Kingston not to let you invest." But the small printshop in the middle of the bustle of Fleet Street had been one of the first they'd procured, when they'd possessed more ambition than the blunt to fuel it. Kingston and Clearford had supplied the ready cash, and Ben had supplied the knowledge of printing he'd gained at his father's side in Boston.

Ben had wanted the shop, needed it in his very bones, from the moment he'd laid eyes on it. Narrow and easy to overlook with tall windows, a hanging sign, and a blue door. It had looked so much like the printshop his parents had run, an instant bout of homesickness had swamped him, drowning him like the icy waves of the Atlantic. Made it hard to breathe. The only way to get the building and its presses had been by partnering with others. His grandfather was well-off, but not so much he could finance a business. So, he'd partnered with Clearford and Kingston, but now...

Now it was time to own it for himself. Time to resurrect Boston's Bailey Prints in London and honor his parents' memories better than he had so far.

Clearford sighed. "We have a *deal*, an arrangement. It's hardly blackmail."

"You could just sell me the shares without demanding alternative payment."

"I could. I'm sorry." And he rather looked it, too, refusing to meet Ben's gaze, those gray eyes stormy.

Ben himself couldn't find the ire to be terribly fussed about it. Would be more convenient were the duke to do things the usual way. But he didn't mind helping with the sister, finding out what kept the chit unwed and making sure she did herself no harm. A favor for a friend whose countenance had begun to look a bit bruised.

"Are you making no progress with Prudence?" Clearford asked.

"None. She's too smart to discuss her secrets with suspicious suitors."

"You need to be more believable. Women talk to men they trust."

"She shouldn't trust me. You really want me to gain your sister's trust through underhanded means? I'm already lying to her."

Clearford winced. "She doesn't want to marry. You'll not break her heart."

That, the only reason Ben had been able to keep guilt at bay all this time. If there'd been a chance he'd hurt her with all this...

He couldn't. He may look like a beast, but his father had taught him how to treat a lady, and his grandfather had reinforced those lessons.

"What if she ends up wanting to marry me?" Ben asked.

Clearford tapped a finger on his dark sleeve. "Then... excellent."

"Now you're sacrificing me?"

Clearford's jaw ticked. "For some causes, a man will sacrifice anything. Look. Noble and King are returning. *Without* my sisters."

"They don't look happy." Both men's faces were scored with grim lines.

"We'd best see what's happened."

Ben clapped his friend's shoulder. "You'd best see. Not my problem, old man." Ben left before hearing Clearford's reply. He left the ballroom, and he left the house, and he left the *ton* he didn't really belong to. He'd been born to a printshop owner in Boston, had learned the trade at his father's knee. Had taken over after his parents' deaths, running every aspect of the business and running himself ragged. And ultimately running the printshop into the ground.

He'd failed to keep his parents' dream alive; authors of political pamphlets wouldn't trust a fifteen-year-old boy with their work, and less than a year after he'd spilled dirt on his parents' coffins, he'd sold the shop and boarded a boat to England.

Well, he wasn't fifteen anymore, and he'd have his second chance—a shop just like his father's, the door painted just the shade his mother liked, a bell that rang when anyone entered, the scent of paper and ink heavy in the air, and Bailey's Prints on the sign above the door.

But first he had to discover Lady Prudence's secrets.

Chapter Three

May 1820

Prudence marched from one end of the room to the other, holding her crisp, clean list before her. "Wedding in half an hour. Then the ceremony. Then the wedding breakfast. We will remain by your side until you are forced to leave this room. Then I will sit as close to the front of the church as I can. During the breakfast, I will observe your every move so you have support when you need it." She stopped her march in the middle of the room and looked up at her audience.

Her sisters—Lottie, Andromeda, and the twins Isabelle and Imogen—stood with Cora in the large window of Cora's bedroom. The sun poured in behind them, haloing their pastel gowns with bright morning light. Lottie looked like a blue-eyed angel, Annie an imp. The twins seemed like faeries from another world. And Cora, in all her dark beauty, resembled nothing less than a queen.

No wonder Prudence found herself overlooked. Who could see plain Pru when the others gave off such light? No matter. Better the gift of anonymity. Particularly when one did not wish one's activities to be discovered. If she were beautiful, it would be harder to hide.

"You are not alone, Cora," Prudence said, taking her friend's hand. "We are with you." She did not try to hide from the guilt that pinched at her sides. Norton had been after Prudence, and he'd caught Cora. Because they'd been wearing the same thing, had been wearing veils to hide their differing hair. It had been, partially, Prudence's fault Cora found herself betrothed to a man she'd barely exchanged two words with.

Cora attempted a smile, failed miserably. "Thank you, Pru. It's a thorough plan."

"Thorough though it may be, it does not keep Cora from having to marry that man." Imogen fell with a *harrumph* into the window seat behind them.

Isabel sat next to her. "*That man* suggests Lord Norton is a scoundrel. A cad. But I've heard nothing nefarious about him. In fact, there's no gossip at all about him but for what he and Cora produced together. Which suggests he's as boring as they come."

"He kisses like a scoundrel," Cora said, her voice breathy. Her hand, covered in a white lace glove lifted to her lips, hovered there, then dropped heavy to her side. "But he's been a gentleman ever since that night in the garden. Three weeks, and every day he's shown up here with a bouquet of flowers. And not much conversation."

"I'm so sorry, Cora." The list fluttered to the floor, abandoned, as Prudence hugged the bride. "I wish it were me and not you."

Cora hugged her back, laughed. "Liar." She pushed out of Prudence's embrace and stood before the full-length looking glass. The mirror's edge glinted gold, as did almost every surface in Cora's chamber. The Eastwoods were wealthy merchants, and their style tended toward the opulent. Cora pinched her cheeks. "You would be crying right now if it were you."

"Would not," Prudence grumbled.

"No." Andromeda elbowed Prudence's arm. "You'd have run away the night before."

"That sounds more like Pru," Lottie said, sitting on Cora's bed. She picked at the rose-pink quilt. "Cora, should Annie and I tell you what's to happen tonight? When Norton comes to your bed?"

Cora turned around, all wide eyes. "What happens? In bed? Whatever could you mean?"

Silence. Then an eruption of laughter.

"If I didn't know better," Isabella said, "I'd have believed you."

"But I've read your poems." Imogen clapped her hands. "The last one was brilliant, Cora. You must consider publishing them."

"The world is not ready for poems like mine." Cora turned back to the mirror, head tilted, studying her reflection.

Lottie snorted. "Poems about women enjoying the marriage bed? No indeed, the world is not ready. But they should be. How are young ladies facing marriage, without the knowledge we have, to know a thing about protecting themselves? Let alone enjoying themselves." Another snort.

Another bout of silence.

They were lucky to know what they did. But it was a secret knowledge that came with heavy risk. Should anyone discover what they knew... how they knew it... their reputations would not survive. Annie's experience two years ago and Lottie's experience last year proved that. They'd both narrowly avoided ruination. Because of the books.

Prudence's mother's books, the ones they'd discovered after her death, were naughtier than Lord Byron on a particularly promiscuous day. She'd quietly loaned them out to her married friends among the *ton*, running a naughty little lending library those friends had been eager to see continue after her death. So, Lottie and Andromeda had continued. Then Prudence and the twins had helped when they'd discovered the enterprise, demanded to be part of it.

What a shock to walk into Mother's old sitting room and find Lottie and Annie poring over a ledger with a stack of forbidden books nearby. And how thrilling to be tasked with keeping the door locked after that. No one ever accidentally walked in on them again. Not with Prudence in charge of the key.

What a disappointment when Lottie and Annie had decided to marry and give it all up. Not Prudence. The key was hers, and she'd clutch it till death if she must. When they'd given control of the library to Cora Eastwood, the shadowy erotic poet who kept her identity secret, Prudence had arrived with the books. Whether Cora had wanted her or not. Fortunately, Cora had wanted her.

Cora's reflection paled in the looking glass. "I do not know if I can continue. With the books. With my poems. Norton may very well find me out."

"Husbands can be a nuisance," Lottie said. But she grinned, every line of her face falling into softness. She clearly did not mean what she said.

"But what if Norton does not mind?" Annie asked.

"In what way?" Cora picked up a hair pin and stuck it through a braid in her coiffure, pinning it more tightly to her head.

"How many ways are there not to mind?" Imogen asked.

"He could not mind *me*. At all," Cora said. "That is the preferable outcome. He ignores me. Lives in the country while I haunt London all my days."

"I mean," Andromeda said, "what if he *knows* and does not mind. Tristan knows and loves me for it. The books have proved... instructional. The only reason I cannot continue with the library is because his reputation could not abide a scandal. Nor his brother's, should it be discovered." She nodded at Lottie. "And Noble knows as well."

Lottie smoothed her skirts, studying them. "He does. He also did not make a fuss upon discovering the library's existence. But I'd rather read and discuss with the other ladies than organize the whole thing these days."

Words stuck in Prudence's throat, mixing together, turning to mush, and sliding into her gut.

"Do you want to stop, Cora?" Her question ripped through the air like an angry bird's squawking.

Every gaze swung toward her.

"No," Cora said. "I do not want to, but I am afraid it is inevitable."

"But my mother ran the library." Prudence fisted her hands in her skirts. Wrinkles hardly mattered. No one would notice her or her attire. Especially since the suitors would not be in attendance. "While married."

"Perhaps Father knew," Lottie said.

"And did not mind," Andromeda added, her hand resting over her swollen belly. "They did produce nine children."

Lottie stood and rubbed a hand up and down Prudence's arm. "It's a risk. And risks should not be taken lightly for too long a time. We have taken this one for seven years now. If mother's old friends—"

"Our friends now," Prudence insisted. "They came to Andromeda's aid when she needed it. And yours, Lottie."

"Our friends." Lottie's voice as soft as her fingers fixing Prudence's curls at the sides of her face. "If they wish to continue with the books, perhaps they should do so for themselves."

Prudence turned to Cora. "Do you wish to be done with it?"

"No." A slight shrug of her slender shoulder. "Not at all. Circumstances have rather... trapped me."

Guilt churned like a stormy sea in Prudence's chest.

Cora whipped around, her cheeks a sudden, mottled red. "No. I will not let this sham of a marriage change who I am and what I do. I'll not stop."

Hope rose like the sun.

"Then you must practice caution. More than usual." Andromeda stood straight as a soldier, a single brow arched gracefully, commandingly over an eye. "Until we are certain about Norton."

Cora nodded. "But in many ways, it *is* safer now. There will be less talk if I am discovered. I will be a married woman. Oh, it shall rile everyone up a bit, but they will say, *remember how she got married to begin with*, and chuckle and go on to meatier gossip."

"Perhaps." But Andromeda's eyebrow remained raised, unconvinced.

"Prudence," Lottie said, and Prudence did not wish to hear what would come next.

She backed away, holding her palms up. "Do *not* command me to stop. I will not. I do not wish to. You cannot make me." Though it was not the library itself which called to her. It was... that it gave her something to do, something to schedule, something to plan, something to make sense out of the chaos. She enjoyed being *busy*, having *purpose*.

Lottie swung her attention to the twins.

They rolled their eyes, sank lower into the window seat, their knees bunching up around their torsos.

"We barely participate now." Imogen propped her chin on the top of one knee.

"I circulate news." Isabelle wrapped her arms around her knees. "And listen for rumblings of danger in Town gossip."

"And I only get to write to Bashton," Imogen grumbled. "It always seemed more glamorous and exciting when you were doing it, Annie."

The Earl of Bashton was an old friend of their mothers. He was nearing sixty and lived in Cornwall. And he supplied them, as he had their mother, with new erotic books to loan to the women of the *ton*.

"The ladies who meet don't even know *we know*!" Isabella said.

"All the better," Lottie snapped. "Trust me."

Across the room, Cora had gone entirely still. Prudence crept up to her, stood by her side. "This is all my fault. It should be me marrying Norton, not you. He thought you were me."

For a breath, Cora's body seemed to freeze to the very core. But then she shook herself and offered a wan smile. "We cannot change what happened. Now, what time is it?"

Blast. Prudence had nearly forgotten the schedule. The pocket watch was warm beneath her fingers when she pulled it from her skirts. "Oh! We must go. Now. Or you'll be late."

"To my own wedding." Cora's laugh seemed thin, fragile as eggshells. "Can't have that."

Andromeda pulled the twins to their feet and headed toward the door. "I'll take them home." The wedding in a quarter hour's time would be a small gathering. Of the sisters, only Prudence would attend. Lottie and Cora joined them at the door, and a tangle of arms wrapped around a bevy of bodies. Hugs and whispered reassurance as Prudence's sisters took heavy steps into the hallways, finding reasons to come back to Cora for one more word, one more hug.

"You are beautiful today," Lottie said, squeezing Cora's hands. "And your life will be beautiful. You will find a way to make it so." She kissed Cora's cheek, then disappeared behind a closed door.

Leaving Prudence and Cora, the guilty and the damned.

Prudence swallowed hard and checked her watch once more. "We must be on our way." Easy words, too difficult to push out.

"Of course." Cora straightened her shoulders. Each move, a minute and difficult click into place that transformed her from frightened to determined, at a measured and deliberate speed. One trembling second, she was a woman awaiting her death, and the next steady moment, she was a soldier, battle hardened and ready.

Prudence crumbled. "Cora I'm so—"

"I know. You needn't be. I let him kiss me. I kissed him back. I did not stop him when he did... other things. You did not make those decisions, Pru. I did. Now"—she smiled, but it did not reach her eyes—"it is time to get married."

"Yes, yes." Prudence ran around the room, gathering all they might need—her list from where it had fluttered to the floor, Cora's silk-trimmed bonnet and gloves, the small bouquet of roses tied round with a pink ribbon. "I've everything."

"Thank you," Cora said as they stepped into the hall. She donned her bonnet and gloves as they descended the stairs. When they'd settled into the coach seats, she rested the roses on her lap. Her gaze fixated on the blooms. "From Norton. They appeared this morning. With a note. *Cora, for you, Norton.*"

"How... ardent."

"Prudence, I'm scared." Cora's eyes slammed closed like heavy iron gates. "We leave right after the wedding." She shook her head. "In a week's time at most. To go to his country residence."

"So soon? The Season's not yet come to an end."

"There's been... talk. Because of how quickly we wed. Because he'd not been courting me. Mother thinks it best if we disappear until the *ton* finds better fodder for their gossip. We are not to return until next Season. I'll be alone with him until Christmas. Entirely alone with a man I do not know."

Prudence moved across the carriage to sit next to her friend and laid her head on Cora's shoulder. She could not offer apologies anymore. Cora did not want them, but they clogged up behind her lips, choking her.

"Will you come with me?" Cora asked.

Prudence lifted her head slowly from Cora's shoulder to look into her face. Her eyes were open now, watery.

"Will you come to the country with me?" she repeated. "And with Norton, of course. I'm afraid having you near will pain him, but... but I do not care. I want you near. It will comfort me, and I'm afraid I care more for my comfort than for his pain."

Prudence nodded, her head bobbing like a baby duck on a pond. "Yes, yes, of course I'll come. Though you must not think he's... in love with me. He never exhibited signs. I've seen signs. In my sisters' husbands. He never acted like that—intense and soft at the same time. He was always just... pleasant. I do not know why he sought me out in that garden, but—"

"I don't care if he's in love with another woman." She swung her head in a sharp angle to look out the window of the rolling carriage. "I don't care."

"Of course not." And more softly than before, "Of course not."

They sat like side by side statues guarding a doorway—silent and still and separate.

Prudence folded her hands in her lap, and paper crumpled. Ah, her list. She folded it, sharpening the new edge with pressed fingers before folding it again and making it smaller. When she slipped it in her pocket, her hand froze. More paper, there, warm from her body. The letter. She gave a half sigh, half grumble and pulled it out as she left the list behind. Three communications from him in a week. All of them short, all of them equally irritating, and all scrawled on the same paper, as if he didn't have the time or care to find a new piece. She might have started that, though. She'd not cared enough to use a new piece to respond to his first epistle. Had jotted her response below his and sent it off. Now five messages occupied the same space.

What in heaven's name could Mr. Bailey be thinking, writing her to begin with? More poor advice from Samuel. Or perhaps just poorly interpreted advice from Samuel. She held the paper flat against her thigh, leaned back into the squabs, and read the strong strokes of Mr. Bailey's handwriting as it charged across the paper.

. . .

Dear Lady Prudence,

I do not have time to visit you today. A meeting ran late. But I had a moment to jot down these lines. I hope your day is a good one.

Mr. Bailey.

She'd replied:

Mr. Bailey,

I did not give you leave to write me. Please do not commandeer such familiarity when there is no reason for it. My day has been passable so far. But I only tell you as a courtesy since you asked.

Lady Prudence.

And within two days, he'd sent another note. Impertinent, impossible man.

Dear Lady Prudence,

Your brother's book gave me permission to write. Not in so many words. It recommended that when a gentleman courts a lady, he creates some sort of "safe intimacy" with her. His words, not mine. What better fits that description than letter writing? Especially when I have no time to visit you—it's a hell of a week. Mr. Bailey.

She should have ignored the letter, fed it to the fire, and told him with her silence how welcome his attentions were. But... she'd not been able to help herself. She'd sat. She'd written. She'd sent.

Mr. Bailey,

You should not curse in correspondence with a lady. And my brother is a fool. "Safe intimacy?" Intimacy, by its very nature, is dangerous, a risk. Only

fools flirt with it. Why are your meetings always going over or running late? Your schedule does not seem very well managed.
Lady Prudence

And he'd responded. Though not promptly. Not that she'd wished for a speedy response. The letter was the one currently burning a hole through the skirts draped over her thigh. With slow, careful fingers she unfolded it, read.

Lady P,
Time slips away from busy men. I've much to do if I wish to make a name for myself. I cannot tell you about the risks of intimacy as I've never attempted intimacy, of the emotional sort, with a woman. But I am familiar with letter writing. A well-turned sentence can convince a mind to do anything, can't it? I assume you're going to Lord Norton and Miss Eastwood's wedding tomorrow. I was not invited, and even if I had been, I wouldn't attend. I somehow scheduled three meetings within the same hour. Shouldn't mention it. You'll read me a lecture. Perhaps I'll stop by your house sometime in the afternoon after the wedding breakfast. Make sure you are well.
Mr. Bailey.

She'd not yet responded to it. Too many shocks in that single letter to think through all at once. Shock number one: He'd scheduled three meetings within the same hour. She shivered, *such* a mismanaged schedule. He needed a secretary, clearly. Shock number two: He wanted to make sure she was well. As if he cared about her. She snorted. Cora looked up at her, a curious brow raised. Prudence patted her friend's hand and returned her attention to her own hands, to the letter. Third shock: The bit about a well-turned sentence convincing a body to do anything. That made her shiver, too. A different kind of rustling through the body. Prudence couldn't quite define it.

She wouldn't respond to the letter. It would only encourage him further.

The coach jerked to a stop, and Cora rose quickly, not waiting for the footman to open the door. Prudence followed her onto the pavement outside the church. Silently, they parted at the church door, Prudence joining the other onlookers in the pews. She sat next to Cora's parents, Mr. and Mrs. Eastwood, shooting to their feet as a duke's sister joined them. Mrs. Eastwood wore the wide grin of a delighted mother. Her daughter had caught a title.

Prudence nodded, polite and calm, trying to shake away the bitter thoughts. Just because Mr. Eastwood did not have a title did not mean he or his wife were after one. Yet, why else would Mrs. Eastwood grin when her daughter looked so grim?

Did Mr. Bailey seek to marry a title, too? What other reason would he have for courting her, for writing to her? His reasons did not matter. The only worry worth holding to her heart at the moment—her friend. She tried to lend her strength from a distance, tried to steady her hands with positive thoughts as Norton fit the ring onto it. Tried to outfit Cora's voice with steel, so it did not shake when she recited the vows. And when Cora marched back down the aisle with a new husband at her side, Prudence prayed for her friend to have smooth steps.

The ceremony over, the guests moved into the sunlight, blinking. The world seemed the same, though her friend's life would never be the same again. Seemed heartless. Something should have changed. The sky turned pink, or London's streets turned to rivers. Anything to signal Cora's loss.

"Something pinching you, Lady Prudence?"

Prudence gave a little scream and clutched her newly pounding heart as she whirled around and spotted...

Mr. Bailey, leaning loose and scruffy against the church wall. The languid pose of house cat, hands stuffed into pockets, clothing rumpled, queue coming undone. But the restrained power of a tiger, muscles sleek and ready to pounce.

Chapter Four

Prudence tried to shove her heart back into her chest. It fairly suffocated, lodged as it was so high in her throat. "Mr. Bailey!" She rubbed the hollow of her neck as rubbing her chest seemed inappropriate, too much like what she'd seen in the garden—Norton's hands on Cora's revealed skin, his lips there, too. "Are you trying to frighten me to death?"

Mr. Bailey tipped the brim of his hat up, revealing more of his face, more of a wide grin—white, even teeth, behind a bushy, unkept beard—and blue eyes that sparkled, only the slightest bit, with mischief. "Not at all." He drawled the words out as he popped off the wall and sauntered over to stand in front of her.

"What are you doing here?" she asked, her heart finally relaxing into a regular rhythm. Mostly regular. He stood so *close*. And that did something to her. Made her squirm.

"I realized I didn't have time for an engagement this afternoon, after the breakfast, so I thought I'd walk you there."

"I'm taking a carriage."

"I'll go with you."

"You are *not* climbing into a carriage with me. Alone," she snapped.

"You've not answered my letter."

"You'll ignore me? Pretend not to hear my very reasonable state-ment about riding alone in a carriage with a strange man?"

"*You've* ignored my letter. Besides, I can't be strange to you anymore. Not after what we witnessed in that garden. Together. Many married couples never experience such... intimacy." He chuckled. "Not the safe kind, was it?"

Her bones seemed to be trying to leap out of her skin. She couldn't look at him. What they'd witnessed in the garden... It stole her breath, just the memory of it. So much skin. And in such a public space. And to think... Norton had been after her. It could have been her breast open to the night air, her nipple Norton had kissed. She shivered. The image had been arousing, but the idea of Norton doing the kissing... all wrong. She'd not yet met a man whose lips she could imagine *there*. Whose touch she'd welcome.

But Mr. Bailey had wrapped his arm around her then, a partner in her voyeurism. She'd not minded it. But had *he* ripped *her* bodice open, she would have had to find something nearby to brain him with.

She paced to the side of the carriage, spoke with the driver, and sent him home. Without her.

Bailey lifted a brow as she came to his side. He offered her his arm. She ignored it. Clearly a glutton for punishment, she started down the street toward the Eastwood's London home. Bailey matched her steps easily, shortening his strides and letting her set the pace. Why had she agreed to walk with him? Merely because she felt the need to move? That squirminess he sent rippling through her had latched on to the shadow which had settled over her during the wedding. Something inside her might snap if she didn't put her body into motion.

Or because she'd known, *known*, that if she'd stepped up into the carriage, he would follow her as surely as if he had the right to. She was too tired to argue him back down onto the pavement. Better for her in all ways to walk, to let him walk with her.

"You owe me a letter," he said.

"I do not. Writing one another is not at all proper, not without an understanding of some sort. If I write to you—"

"You've done so twice." A cheeky grin, barely visible, winked out from behind the bristly hairs of his beard.

"If I continue to write to you, and we are caught..." They could end up like Cora and Norton this morning. Wed. And unhappy about it.

"I don't think you're scared of the impropriety." He rummaged in his pocket, pulled out a cheroot, twisted it between his fingers, the other hand lazy in his coat pocket. "You barely reacted to the scene in the garden. At least not with the sort of shock a gently bred young lady should show. I think what upset you more, then, was your friend's position. Maybe shock that your friend would do such a thing. Not the intimacy itself."

She snorted, a sound to cover up her fear. She'd not been shocked so much as intrigued. She'd never seen such a thing in real life before. She'd wanted to know how it compared to the pictures in the books she'd read. So very different. No comparison. The pictures possessed no sound or movement, no scent. The pictures were dead, but the moment between Cora and Norton had been so very alive. The music floating from the ballroom, the wind rustling the leaves, Cora's little sounds of surprised pleasure, Norton's heavy breaths and unintelligible, deep-voiced whispers. She'd thought herself immune to passion.

But that night in the garden, her body had awakened to life as well, heat pooling between her legs, her breasts heavy and tight, each breath more difficult to take than the one before.

"I think," Bailey drawled, "you're scared of something. But it's not impropriety. What, though?" He tapped the cheroot against his thigh. "What?"

"Nothing. I've nothing to hide, so I've nothing to fear."

He lifted the cheroot, swept its length across his upper lip, and inhaled deeply, closing his eyes for a moment. "Then write to me."

Impossible man. "I am not averse to smoke. You may light it if you wish." She nodded at the cheroot.

He held it upright, holding its long length at the bottom with long, ungloved fingers stained with ink. Some blotches old and fading, others new and stark against his skin. Strong, capable fingers, and they held the cheroot with a gentle touch. "I don't smoke anymore."

"Then why carry one about?"

"I still crave it." He snapped the cheroot back inside his pocket.

"Then why don't you smoke?" She slipped a hand inside her own pocket, feeling the smooth, calming curve of her pocket watch.

"My grandfather cannot abide smoke. Makes him ill." He hunched his shoulder's forward, focused on his boots. "Takes too much effort to refrain when I'm with him if I'm too used to smoking them. Better to abstain all the time. Easier."

"You have a grandfather?"

He laughed. "Doesn't everyone?"

"Yes, but..." She'd rather thought he'd raised himself in the wilds of the Americas. Or perhaps he'd been orphaned and raised by bears or some such untamed thing. "Do you see him often?"

He winked. "Ask me that question in a letter, Lady Prudence. Then I'll answer it."

She huffed. "You're incorrigible."

"You're scared."

"I. Am. Not." Each word as crisp as a snapped sheet. "There's nothing intimate about your letters. All you do is reveal the utter failures of your scheduling methods."

He shrugged. "I get confused. I forget what I've already scheduled, especially if I don't write it down. And I often forget to write it down."

She clicked her tongue against the roof of her mouth. "I should not be surprised. You are absolutely without purpose in every other part of your life visible to the onlooker. Why not this area as well?"

"I'm not without purpose, Lady Prudence." His voice possessed a dark edge which challenged her to continue, promised she'd regret it. "It's the exact opposite. My purpose drives me. I don't have time for things like lists."

Her own list burned a hole in her pocket. "I could help you, teach you." That put a bounce in her step. Of course, she didn't necessarily want to spend any time with this man, but the thought of putting his life in order—oh yes. To take a man who embodied chaos and organize him—how marvelous.

"Oh no, Lady Prudence." He turned on his toe and walked backward with longer steps, studying her face. "I know that look. You want to *change* me."

"Not you. Just your schedule."

He turned back around to walk at her side. "I've resisted change since I stepped foot on this island. I don't think you'll have much luck."

She shrugged. "I won't try anyway. You are not worth my skills. Whatever I sought to teach you would bounce right off your hard skull. Besides, you're Kingston's partner. He should whip you into shape."

And she'd meant it when she'd said she would not seek to change him. Not only did that seem an entirely futile project, but also an unnecessary one. He was chaos, but he was also... Well, he made her feel rather *safe*. Any footpad would think twice, three, four, a handful of times before attacking her with Mr. Bailey by her side. He possessed a rather wild quality which she found... appealing? No, surely not that. But perhaps then... comforting? Yes. Better, that. Who knew, of course, what he looked like beneath the hair and the beard, but it didn't matter. Because this man showed the world exactly who he was, and to hell with what they thought. And she admired that. She needed no second moment to figure out *that* feeling. A third point in his favor —he quit something he craved for the sake of a man he rarely saw. He loved his family. She understood that quite well indeed.

Yes, the man could stay as he was. The schedule...

"Perhaps," she ventured, "you might keep a small notebook and pencil in those pockets instead of a cheroot. The former will help you. The latter, I fear, only torments you."

"I like the smell of it."

"Be that as it may, a notebook—"

"I'll consider it. If you write to me. Then I'll have more to compose in the notebook than just my obligations." A grin flashed through the bushy beard.

Was he trying to charm her?

"What advice from the Guide are you following now?"

"Cultivate safe intimacy. I told you. Is it working?"

She sighed. Why not let him write? She'd be in the country soon enough, and his letters would not reach her for weeks. She could deal with them when she returned. "Very well, you may write to me."

He swung in front of her, stopping her, and she had to rock back a step to keep from bumping into him. From this position, he seemed bigger than before. He always seemed rather small, perhaps because his clothes were much too big for him. But now, towering over her, she understood the true size of the man. He blocked out the sun. She had to crane her head back to look at his face, and his shoulders seemed twice the width of hers.

He did not seem disposed to moving out of her way, either. In fact, his fingers found her wrist, bare and warm against the sliver of her skin revealed above the edge of her glove, below the hem of her sleeve. "And you'll write back, Lady Prudence?"

Her stuttering heart shook up her simple answer. "Y-yes." Eventually.

He leaned low, narrowing the world to them two. "And you'll spill all your secrets?"

At her wrist where his fingers lingered, her pulse raced uncontrollably. What was this? She'd never felt so shaken before, so much like she stood on uneven ground and the slightest wind might topple her. Right into his arms.

Which, now she understood the breadth of his shoulder, she trusted to catch her easily.

Blast.

She stepped away from him, around him, and raced down the street.

"Is that a no on the secrets?" he called after her, a laugh throwing his words sky-high.

She ran until she was certain he did not follow, slowing and looking behind her once she rounded a corner. He'd left her alone. Excellent. Yes, quite. The Eastwood's house was around the next corner, and she did not wish to arrive at his side. Cora would have questions.

She managed a more sedate pace, drawing in slow, calming breaths with each step until she reached their doorstep. The guests were all inside. She saw them through a window. No large smiles and revelry there. Bodies as still as paintings, faces as somber as a funeral.

She leaned her head against the door before knocking, closed her eyes. At least this renewed deluge of guilt washed away the undefinable, shaky, wild feeling Bailey had left her with. Neither feeling good, though.

She rolled and leaned her back against the door. Why did Bailey so insist on writing to her? Did he truly enjoy her company? Truly wish to marry her? Impossible. No man wanted that, not without ulterior motives. And why did he continue to ask about her secrets?

Did he... *know?*

Her heart kicked into a race again. Blast, it might never settle down. Because he was a newspaper man, and she had secrets, and he wanted them. Everything clicked into place. Her sisters had the right of it. She courted ruin with every book she handed off to another woman, with every marker she set up guiding them toward a dark room and Cora's rich voice rising high with naughty words. Did she care? Did she wish to be infamous, all her marriage prospects gone in an instant? Just as they had been last summer when Lottie's reputation had hung on the precarious edge of Lord Noble's good will.

No, she did not want that. She did not particularly wish to marry, but she did not want to lose the option entirely. She did not wish to ruin her family, bring shame to her brother, irritating as he could be. He'd only ever tried to do his best without their parents to guide him.

But could she give it all up? The intrigue, the excitement, the *purpose?*

Her head shook on its own, giving her an answer. She could not give it up.

So, she must be safe. And that meant distancing Bailey, taking precautions. And both could be achieved by making Cora happy and following her to the country. A boring, tame proposal.

No. An opportunity. She would use the time to devise a new, safer business model, to prove to Cora and her sisters that the library and the poetry readings did not have to die. They could live on. With the right organization and system. And that, more than anything perhaps, would give Cora back a bit of happiness.

And Prudence owed Cora much more than momentary glee. She owed her a life. And that's just what Prudence would give her.

Chapter Five

Kingston would kill him. Ben had missed another meeting. No way but the sun to know he'd missed it, though. His watch had fallen from a hole in his pocket a week ago when he'd been walking toward Fleet Street after his brief stroll with Lady Prudence. It had seemed an omen. She'd declared his schedule broken, declared he needed help, and his watch had slipped from his pocket as if seeking escape from his incompetence. Then he'd smashed it beneath his boot when he'd gone back to retrieve it. Hell. Should have bought a new one days ago.

The sun above his only timepiece now, and it mocked him. Late, late, late.

No. Missed entirely. He might as well set his steps toward Mayfair and hound the woman who hounded him.

Why had Lady Prudence refused to return his letters? She'd said she would. How could he probe for her secrets without her full epistolary attention?

He rounded the corner, bringing the door of the duke's residence into view. Another man stood on the doorstep. Norton.

Ben picked up his pace, not quite running to reach the man's side before he could knock. He caught Norton's wrist just before he slammed it onto the door.

"What the devil?" Norton, flustered, ripped his hand out of Ben's hold.

"Precisely my reaction to seeing you here, Norton. You're a married man. Leave Lady Prudence alone."

"I'm not here for her." He smoothed his lapels and straightened the angle of his hat. "Well, I am, but not in that way." He knocked, and the door opened swiftly. "Good afternoon, Mr. Jacobs. Is His Grace receiving visitors?"

Mr. Jacobs' thick black brows somehow loosened. "Lord Norton. A delight to see you again. Yes, His Grace is receiving visitors. Do come in." He stepped aside, opening one arm wide in welcome.

Norton stepped in, doffing his hat and greatcoat.

Ben tried to do the same, but Mr. Jacobs blocked his way.

"Mr. Bailey," he said, "what brings you here today?"

"I'm here to see Lady Prudence."

"She's not in."

Could be the truth. She seemed a busy chit. But she also possessed a devious mind. Wouldn't mind lying to your face, that one. He didn't feel like arguing, though. "I'll see Clearford, too." He could fish about for other ways to earn the woman's trust, see if Clearford's guide held any better advice than *cultivate safe intimacy*. Whatever that meant. Ben rather agreed with Lady Prudence on that one—intimacy of any sort held risk. But... with the right woman. At the right time. Worthwhile.

Mr. Jacobs sniffed, did not move.

Ben flung the edges of his greatcoat back and placed his hands on his hips. "I know he's in. You've just let Norton through to see him."

"Mr. Norton is a gentleman." Jacob's gaze lowered over Ben's frame, from the limp and loosely tied cravat to the too-large greatcoat, wrinkled clothes, and scuffed boots.

Ben rolled his eyes. "And I'm Clearford's friend. Must we have this argument every time I'm here?"

"Someone must retain the high standards of a duke's household. If the duke will not."

Ben cracked his knuckles, stretched his neck side to side. "Must I really move you? I've not had my exercise today, and I admit I'd like the challenge. Heft a fully grown man across the entryway. I think I can manage it."

His face twisted into a deep-lined scowl. Mr. Jacobs stepped to the side. But Ben received no welcoming, outstretched arm as Norton had.

Ben didn't need one. He bounced inside and smacked Jacobs on the shoulder. "Good choice." Then he and Norton followed the butler down the hall.

After a brief knock, and a muffled yet terse "come in" from behind the closed door, Jacobs opened it, ushering Norton and Bailey inside.

Where the duke stood poised on one side of the room, one arm raised slightly above his head, and in his hand a blade. "Have a seat." Said without looking their way. A breath before he went statue still. Then a flick of his wrist, and the blade sailed across the room, hit a square of wood hanging on the wall with a thwack.

"Not dead center that time," Bailey said.

Clearford grunted. "Wasn't aiming for the center."

"Fair enough."

"Tea, Jacobs," Clearford said, sinking into a chair behind his desk.

The butler bowed and closed the door behind him, and Norton and Bailey took seats on the other side of the duke's huge desk.

"That was inspiring," Norton said, his gaze still on the board across the room, a knife still vibrating within it. "Where'd you learn how to do it?"

"My father." Clearford wove his hands behind his head as he leaned back into the seat. "What brings the two of you here? And at the same time?"

Norton leaned forward, speaking before Ben could put words in the right order in his muddled mind. "I've come to petition for your approval."

Before Norton could finish his sentence, Clearford was shaking his head. "I already told Prudence no. If I'd known you prone to seducing young women in gardens, I never would have allowed you near my sister to begin with. You've ruined her friend."

"I've married her." Norton's jaw tight as his body moved out of the lean, spine stiffening.

Ben's hands tightened around the ends of his chair arms, clawing fingers over clawed wood. "Told Lady Prudence no to what? Petition approval for what?"

Norton's gaze remained trained on Clearford. "My wife wishes the comfort of her friend as she grows accustomed to her new home. You'll deny her that?"

"Your wife must have friends other than my sister." Clearford looked up to the ceiling, as if the conversation bored him.

"Would you two slow down?" Ben grumbled. "You're at the finish line, and I've not even started yet."

With a sigh, Clearford dropped his gaze to Ben. "Lord Norton is taking his new bride to the country, and he's invited Prudence—"

"My *wife* has invited her." The words ground between clenched teeth.

"To come along as well," Clearford finished.

"Like hell she will." Ben stabbed a finger into the desktop. "She can't go."

"I'm aware," Clearford said, unfolding his hands from behind his head and refolding them across his abdomen. "I've already denied the request. Prudence is not pleased. It has been a battle of wills all week long." He sighed. "She's begun a campaign of silence. Refuses to speak to me unless I give in."

"Please." Norton held his hands out, palms up. "You must relent. Cora wishes Lady Prudence's presence above all else. It is the only wedding present she desires."

Ben exploded to his feet. "You thought your wife was Lady Prudence in that garden! And you think the woman you wanted to begin with should accompany you and your new wife away from all her family?"

"Precisely why I've denied him, Bailey," the duke said. "Do sit down. No need for dramatics."

Ben dropped back into the chair. "Says the man who throws knives for fun."

Clearford turned to Norton. "You see quite clearly why I will not allow it."

Norton stood, hands clenched into fists at his sides. "You think I mean to take advantage of Lady Prudence during her stay in my home? You impugn my honor."

"You impugned your own damn honor in that garden." Ben stood once more. His hands could make fists, too, but he kept the knuckles loose. Better to show control when another man vibrated with rage.

"We'll have no duels," Clearford said, coming to his feet.

The door opened, and a maid appeared with a tray. She set it on a low table near the fireplace and scurried away. The duke swept toward the steaming tea, welcoming Ben and Norton to join him.

Neither man did, but Clearford didn't seem to mind. He dropped into a chair, stretched one leg out long, and poured his own tea. That right there—one thing Ben had always admired about his friend. He never let others do for him when he could do for himself, no matter his lofty title.

The duke studied them, raised a brow. "No? Very well then. Do as you please." He settled back into his chair with a sigh, holding the cup before his face and inhaling deeply.

He sat just beneath the portrait of himself hanging large as the gods above the fireplace. In it, a much younger Clearford, before he'd become the duke, stood behind his sisters and beside his father in a field, looking at something in the distance. He appeared young and carefree and lacked the lines of worry that currently bracketed his mouth, radiated from the outer corners of his eyes. All eight sisters peered down at the three men in the room, and Ben spotted Lady Prudence among them all with ease. She'd been posed a bit to the side, away from the rest, and she looked out on the world with something like disgruntled distaste. For what? Had she disliked standing still for so long. The Lady Prudence he knew never seemed to sit still. And even when she did, her leg bounced up and down, and her thoughts whirred like a factory full of machines behind her eyes. Always moving, doing. He admired that.

"You're right to keep her home," Ben said, holding the painted Lady Prudence's gaze. "Keep her safe."

That seemed to unlock Norton. He rushed forward, swinging himself into the chair opposite the duke, leaning forward, elbows digging into his thighs as he held his palms out once more. "She would be safe with me. I swear it. I was looking for your sister that night, Clearford. I admit it. Your revision to the Guide suggests a single kiss to test the waters."

"In a sunlit drawing room," Clearford drawled before taking a sip of his tea. "With a distracted chaperone nearby. All perfectly proper."

"Yes, well, that always felt a bit awkward. Some things are easier done in the dark." He dropped his head and ruffled his hands through his hair. "They were wearing the same costume, Clearford. And your sister"—he looked up, opening his palms once more—"was wearing a black veil to cover her hair. They're the same height, similar figures. I had no idea. I didn't even know there was another woman dressed in a black gown that night. I thought—"

"And that's why Lady Prudence can't go with you." Ben marched forward, stood as a third corner of their triangle. "You wanted her, but you didn't get her. Now you'll try another means of—"

"No!" Norton jolted to his feet once more. "I'm not some tormented villain!"

Clearford sighed, rolling his head to the side as he rolled his eyes.

One of Norton's fisted hands tapped Ben's shoulder, a warning. "I want only my wife, Bailey. Do you understand? I may have set off looking for Lady Prudence that night, but I discovered... I discovered—" His voice cracked, and he cursed, a word he whispered into his shoulder. "Suffice it to say I want only my wife. She has my loyalty, and I must now earn hers. I was a vicar once, you know. I do not take marriage vows lightly."

"Sit down the both of you." Clearford took another sip. "Are you sure you don't want tea? It's calming."

"No." Ben began pacing, from the fireplace to the knife-tortured board at the other end of the room and back. Did Norton speak the truth? Or did he lie to gain convenient access to the woman he truly wanted? Shouldn't bother Ben. But after following the chit around so much, writing to her so often of late, he felt rather... protective.

Norton sat, rubbing a palm over his face. "I merely wish to make my wife happy, Your Grace. Please."

"The question," Clearford said, "becomes whether I trust you're telling me the truth. I'm inclined to believe you."

"Clearford!" Ben's pacing took him more quickly than before to the tableau before the fireplace. "You can't be serious."

"I am."

Norton scooted closer to the edge of his chair, closer to Clearford. "You are invited, too, Your Grace. Come and see that I speak the truth. I wish for your sister's presence in my home only in that it brings joy to Lady Norton."

Ben crossed his arms over his chest, tried to see what Clearford had found so interesting about the ceiling earlier.

Clearford ran his knuckles up and down his jaw. "Hm. An excellent suggestion. Yet... I cannot leave my other sisters unattended. The twins are slippery. And the younger ones... no. I'll not leave them. I cannot, Norton. But"—his gaze slid to Bailey, the corner of his mouth tilting up—"Bailey might attend in my stead."

"Me?" Ben bellowed. "Me?" Louder than before. A bit of spittle on his beard.

"Why not? You're courting her. And a house party is the perfect moment to cultivate intimacy. *Understanding*."

Understanding of the chit's secrets.

Hell.

"It will also take her out of the range of other suitors," Ben said, each word feeling heavy on his tongue.

Clearford shrugged. "What does it matter?"

"You wanted your sister to have *options*, Clearford."

"Yes, well, you seem to care rather fiercely for her safety, Bailey. Perhaps *you* are the best option."

Ben tore around a small sofa facing the fireplace and sat, small blue pillows falling to the floor. With Norton here, he couldn't very well scream the words tearing at his throat. *I'm not going to marry your sister, and you know that!* Clearford no longer cared about marriage. Not in this very moment, at least. Tired of being in the dark, he wanted information. He expected Ben to supply it by any means necessary. Including marriage. *That* not a means Ben particularly relished. Nothing against marriage in general. Ben fully intended to fall in love one day. No idea who would look at him long enough for him to take an interest. Every woman he met turned up her nose, unwilling to look past his appearance.

"You're her most ardent suitor, Bailey," Clearford said. "And I trust you as a friend to guard her reputation. Lady Norton will act as chaperone. But... if you have other plans. Work, perhaps. In one of you printshops."

Damn Clearford to Hell. His message clear as a well-printed letter with fresh ink. Ben must follow Prudence, or the duke wouldn't sell.

"Very well." Ben's hands curled like claws around the sofa's arm. "Perhaps I am the best option." Because he had no other options, not if he wanted to make Bailey's Prints a reality.

Silence.

Then, with the halting tones of hesitation, Norton said, "Ah, um, yes. You are, of course, welcome, Bailey, but... excuse me for pointing this out, but... Lady Prudence has always seemed as enamored of you as she has been of me. That is to say... not at all." He blinked at Ben, then leaned forward to pour himself a cup of tea, hiding himself from Ben's response in the task.

Clearford did not hide. He held Ben's gaze, tilted his head, eyebrows raised, waiting.

"I think," Norton continued, "she might be intimidated by you. I only say all this because it's clear to me now you have real feelings for the girl. You care for her safety. I admire that. But..."

"Yes, Norton?" Clearford prodded. "You're a fount of wisdom, and I wish to hear what you have to say."

"I don't," Ben grumbled.

"He appears rather terrifying, doesn't he? With the hair and the beard. And the clothes." Norton slanted a quick glance at Ben before returning it to the duke. Apparently, men who flung knives for fun were less terrifying than an American with a beard.

"This is ridiculous." Ben draped his arms across the back of the sofa. "Lady Prudence is not scared of me." Not at all. She rolled her eyes at him, shrugged him off, lectured him. If he were to identify a feeling she had for him, it would be something like annoyance. Not fear. Besides, she'd said she wouldn't change him. Just his schedule. He coughed to hide an unexpected chuckle.

"But she will not let you close when you look like that." Did Norton's words sound like a snort? As if he, too, rolled his eyes, as if he had no fear of Ben's fist finding his face.

He should.

Ben tapped a finger on the back of the sofa. "And you know how to get close to women, don't you, Norton?"

Norton's jaw ticked, his muscles bunched. Those hands—fists again. The man proved surprisingly easy to rile.

"Norton has a point, Bailey," Clearford said.

"What?" Ben's finger stopped tapping as his hands clenched the back edge of the couch.

But Clearford stretched out, made himself even more comfortable, a sly grin stretching his lips. "You do not look the picture of a suitor. And that is exactly what you are supposed to be. Perhaps that's why you've made no progress. How can my sister trust your intentions when you're clearly not attempting to impress her?"

"What are you trying to say, Clearford?" Ben growled.

"That you're a mess. In fact." He rose and ambled toward his desk, opened a drawer, and pulled out a notebook. He opened it on the desk and dipped a pen in an inkwell. "I should amend the Guide. Make sure there's a section on personal appearance."

"I'm not changing how I dress to please a chit, Clearford."

"Then you'll not win the lady's approval, will you, Bailey?" Norton looked irritatingly smug.

"Shut it," Ben growled. He stood and found his way to the other side of the duke's desk, steepled all his fingers atop it as he leaned forward. "Listen here, Your Grace. I don't need to shape myself into a certain foppish figure to please anyone."

Clearford looked up from his book, blinked, stood up straight. "Very well, then. Don't. I'll find another man to help with Prudence."

"*Help* with Lady Prudence?" A quivering question in Norton's voice. "What does that mean?"

Clearford returned his attention to his book, the pen flowing across the blank page, filling it up. "*Court*, Norton. I meant *court*. Naturally."

Ben straightened. Perhaps he should let Clearford choose another man. But if he did, Ben would not get his printshop. Changing his hair, his clothes, shaving his beard—those changes would last for a short time only. Resurrecting his parent's legacy would be well worth the hassle.

"No. No other man," Ben said. "I'll do it."

"Excellent." The duke spoke without looking up, but his hand froze, his pen hovering just over the page. "Do you... know how... to dress fashionably?"

"Bloody hell!" Ben stomped toward the door. "I think I can manage it."

"Surely. But I'll send my valet to you this evening. Just in case."

Ben ripped open the door but stopped in the frame. "When do we leave, Norton?"

"Tomorrow."

Ben nodded. "And where?"

"Norton Hall, near Cambridge."

"I'll see you then, Norton." As he swept out of the room, he heard the viscount's voice, quizzical and low.

"Bailey must love your sister quite ardently to agree to such an improvement."

Didn't hear how Clearford managed to answer that one without fumbling about for a believable lie. Ben spilled onto the pavement before the house with a scowl and a determined stride. Bond Street. He'd find what he needed there. He possessed fancy clothes. But it had been years since he'd bothered to wear them. They got in the way of his work in the printshops. Doubted they still fit. He'd put on a bit of muscle since he started working on the presses, learning how to fix them. The clothes at the back of his wardrobe had been fitted to a younger man, a boy really, just off a boat and intent on pleasing his grandfather.

Styles had changed since then, same as his body. He'd need new clothes entirely. Bloody bother, it was. But what brought him closer to Lady Prudence, what encouraged her to spill her secrets into his ears would also bring him closer to Bailey's Prints.

Chapter Six

Prudence preened. What a success. She'd thought all hope lost for a handful of horrible days when Samuel had refused to let her accompany Cora to Norton Hall. But in the end, a civil conversation with Lord Norton had convinced him all would be well. Her plans could have continued in the country without her presence, but she preferred them not to. They were her plans, after all.

And looking at the smiling faces gathered in Norton Hall's library, basking in the sounds of their cheerful conversations, she could not help but think again—what a perfect success. Cora beamed from her place on a chair near the large windows, sunlight flooding in and lighting her dark hair. Lady Templeton fussed with a tea set nearby, Mrs. Garrison flipped through the pages of a book, looking for a particularly salacious illustration, and Lady Macintosh lectured on the best words to use for a man's member. *All-dissolving lightning bolt* appeared to be her preferred term.

Though Prudence found it difficult to believe a man would wish his lightning bolt to dissolve.

"Cock is much preferable," Lady Templeton argued, filling Cora's cup. "Has a nice serious ring to it. Good for waking one up."

Lady Macintosh chuckled, then shook her head. "I much prefer shaft. More descriptive. My William looks nothing like a rooster."

Mrs. Garrison snorted, raised a fiery red brow. "Are you suggesting your husband has nothing to crow about?"

Lady Macintosh's brows knit together, then they flew up her forehead. "He's plenty to brag about, thank you."

Prudence made her way across the room and sat next to Cora on the sofa. "It's perfect, is it not? Here, we can converse about things that we should not, all day long if we please, and no one will discover it. If all goes well in the next fortnight, we can hold house parties for the library women two or three times a year. We can invite more next time once we know how everything will work. No exchange of paper in Hyde Park, no London gossip. Select guests invited to a secret house party. It's much safer than anything we've done before. And Cora"—she grasped her friend's arm—"just think of the poetry readings we'll have."

Cora grinned. "It does seem, so far, to be an excellent plan. Different from the enterprise your sisters organized for years, but not worse because of it."

"Indeed not. We do not have to stop, Cora. But we can be careful. And this"—she looked around the spacious room with its high ceilings and book-lined walls—"is the answer."

Cora's grin faded. "But what about—"

"Cock, I say!" Lady Templeton slammed her teacup down, sending a wave of tea over the brim. "How can you be so foolish as to suggest gherkin? Gherkin! Of all things! It sounds like you're choking on something."

Mrs. Garrison snorted a laugh. "Perhaps she's choking on the said gherkin, darling."

Cora shook her head and turned to Prudence once more. "But what about Lord Norton? He lives here, too. Surely, he will notice all the talk of gherkins and cocks."

"I've not seen him once since he arrived."

"I haven't seen him since yesterday. He sent a note saying you would be able to attend me after all. Then nothing."

The man had no interest in his wife. Prudence swallowed a lump in her throat. An inauspicious beginning for her friend's marriage. She patted Cora's hand. "Think of his absence as a convenience. He won't be about to discover our conversation, books, or recitations."

Cora took a deep breath. "You're right, of course. It's a boon. Everything is perfect, and you are brilliant, Prudence. To find a way for this to continue but away from London's prying eyes."

"It's merely a test."

"But one that is going wonderfully well so far."

They picked up their still-steaming teacups, clinked the rims, and sipped.

A knock on the door.

The ladies did not hear, and over their protestations of what to call a man's appendage, Cora called, "Come in!"

"*Shh.*" Prudence leaned into the group of older women. "*Shh.* We've company."

They quieted quickly, gazes flying toward the door.

The butler, Mr. Pickings stepped through, bowed. "My lady, another guest has arrived. What room shall I put him in?"

Silence hung like doom above them all.

Prudence began counting its length, her mind unable to grasp anything else. Five seconds, six—him—seven, eight, nine—*him?*—ten, eleven—

"Excuse me, Mr. Pickings." Cora rose from the sofa, shattering the silence with her soft voice. "Did you say... *him?*"

"Yes, a Mr. Bailey has arrived."

Prudence jumped to her feet with a yelp. "Mr. Bailey?"

The butler nodded.

Prudence paced forward. "Surely not *my* Mr. Bailey."

The butler raised a brow.

"*Your* Mr. Bailey?" Lady Templeton's voice behind her.

"Has there been a change of heart we are uninformed of?" Mrs. Garrison asked.

Prudence swung around. "Oh, you know what I mean. He's been courting me." She turned back to the butler. "What does Mr. Bailey look like?"

Cora stood beside her. "I know of only one Mr. Bailey, Prudence."

"But he and Lord Norton are not friendly. I know that better than anyone." They'd competed against one another for her hand since the previous Season. "Come, Mr. Pickings, what does Mr. Bailey look like?"

Mr. Pickings' cheeks flushed. "Tall? Yes, rather tall. And broad."

Two words which could very well describe the Mr. Bailey who'd haunted her steps the last year.

"And unkempt?" Prudence asked, dread pooling in her gut.

"Not at all, my lady. Quite well-dressed. Dashing, even."

Relief flooded through her. She pressed a hand to her hammering heart. "You terrified me, Mr. Pickings, but I see now it is not the same Mr. Bailey." That would ruin everything. Lord Norton cared nothing for how his wife spent her hours, but Mr. Bailey, her Mr. Bailey, would follow her about like a puppy dog. Thankfully that thorn in her side remained conveniently in London.

Cora patted her shoulder and spoke to Pickings. "Please have the bluebell room prepared and show him to the garden drawing room until it is ready."

The butler bowed and left, and Cora turned to the rest of them, head tilted, brow furrowed. "I wonder who this Mr. Bailey could be? I know none of Lord Norton's companions. I suppose we're about to meet one of them."

"Will he cause us problems?" Lady Macintosh asked. "I was under the impression this would be a select and private gathering, perfect for our purposes. I left the London Season for this."

"It is!" Prudence assured them. "This new guest will not wish to keep the company of women all day. We will have to suffer his attentions during and after dinner, but we did not think to have those times to ourselves to begin with. No, nothing has changed. Everything is perfect. We will proceed as planned."

But my, what a scare. Her heart still stuttered.

Cora opened the door to the hall. "I should greet our new guest. Do you think he's related to your Mr. Bailey?"

"He's not my Mr. Bailey."

"Your own words, girl," Mrs. Garrison said. "Cora, dear, do you have any whisky?"

Cora leaned low and whispered before leaving the room. "Don't let them near the whisky."

"I don't even know where it is." Prudence settled back into the circle of her friends, her mother's friends.

"What do you think, Prudence?" Lady Macintosh asked. "What is your favorite word for a man's member?"

Prudence scrunched her face. "Not *member*. Member of what? An exclusive club? A religion?"

Lady Templeton chuckled. "Sometimes God is called on. You'll learn one day."

Prudence reached for the teapot, poured, took a sip. Cold, but no matter.

"What's that, girl?" Mrs. Garrison tapped her shoulder. "Sit up and look us in the eye." Her husband was an admiral, and she possessed some of his... leadership qualities. "Why did you just crumple like that?"

"I didn't crumple," Prudence protested.

Lady Templeton tsked. "Evasive maneuvers if I've ever seen them. And I've seen plenty. Thurston employs them anytime I ask about his quest for a wife." A bitter edge to her voice. Thurston was Lady Templeton's son, a man she deemed too good for most women, including the Duke of Clearford's sisters. But clearly Lady Templeton was reaching her edge of patience with his continued bachelor status.

"Pruuuudence!" Rapid footsteps running closer down the hall as Prudence's name rose into the air on Cora's distressed voice.

They all four jumped to their feet right as Cora swung into the room, breathless. "Prudence... It's... it's..." Each word punctuated by a heavy breath.

Mrs. Garrison's tall, slender figure rushed across the room and pulled Cora farther inside. "Breathe deep, girl, and get it out. What's happened?"

Cora breathed deeply, and her wide eyes sparking with panic fell on Prudence. "He's *your* Mr. Bailey."

Prudence fell back into her seat, her legs no longer working. She shook her head. "No. He can't be. Mr. Bailey, *my* Mr. Bailey is not... he does not... well, he does not fit your butler's description!" Something cold seeped into the skin of her thigh, and she looked down. The teacup she'd been holding had entirely spilled its contents when she'd fallen into the seat. Her green gown, pale and pretty a moment ago, was ruined, a large brown splotch spreading across her leg.

"It is him," Cora panted. "But he's all"—she waved her hands up and down her body—"different. Prudence." Her face drained of color, every expression fleeing alongside the usual roses in her cheeks. "He's *shaved.*"

Shaved. Mr. Bailey, *shaved?* She couldn't imagine it. Yet... she needed to know, to see. Her legs decided they could work once more, and she floated to her feet and out the door.

"Where are you going?" Cora hissed, hurrying at her side down the hallway.

"To see him."

"Should he know you're here?"

"He'll have to know," Lady Templeton said from Prudence's other side. "They're staying in the same house."

"But why are they staying in the same house?" Mrs. Garrison asked from nearby, her voice a whisper. "He should not be here at all. What game is Norton playing?"

From behind them, Lady Macintosh said, her voice hushed and somber, "Does he... *know?*"

They all stopped at the exact same moment. Everyone looked at Cora.

"I didn't tell him!" she hissed. "We've barely exchanged a word. We haven't even—" She snapped her mouth shut, glance at the door slightly down the hall. "We can't all go in at once, gawping like he's a performer at Astley's."

"Can too," said Mrs. Garrison. "It's what we call an ambush. Not a particularly secretive one, but—"

Cora swung in front of them, held out her arms, palms flat like walls to keep them at bay. "No. This is unacceptable. No ambushes."

They parted around her like the Red Sea.

"Bother." Cora scurried after them as Prudence put her hand on the doorknob.

Why was he here? And why had he shaved? He'd fairly rippled with rage the other day when he'd thought her desirous of changing him. But he'd *shaved*.

And what did a shaved Mr. Bailey even look like? Curiosity more than anything shoved her through the door and into the room.

A man stood near the window, his tall, broad-shouldered figure outlined by the sun filtering through the glass. The sun blinded her, and she could not see him clearly enough. He remained a silhouette against the light, and then he moved, walking slowly toward her, growing larger in her field of vision, the shadows the sun had strewn about him dimming until... there he was, towering above her—an Adonis.

Difficult to focus on one change with all of them pummeling her at once, but once her gaze struck across the lower half of his face, she could not look away. Lips. The man had lips. Quite interesting ones, full and sculpted and not at all covered by an inch of scruffy beard. An... interesting shade of subtle pink she'd never noticed before. How could she have, hidden as they'd been?

"Do I have something on my face, Lady Prudence?" His voice, deep and low and harboring a touch of humor. Familiar, too. At some point, his voice had become familiar.

"You have nothing on your face!" She'd squeaked it. She'd yelled it. She'd squealed it? No matter. The sound possessed a horrifically humiliating quality, loud yet terrified.

He scratched at his jaw, interrupting her view of his lips with his knuckles. "I shaved."

"I see." Her tone better that time. More controlled. His fingers in the way of those lips still, but... fascinating discoveries awaited her down its length. The wrist attached to the hand scratching his jaw possessed a pristinely pressed cuff of dark-blue wool, a hint of snowy white linen peeking out. And those fingers—no ink. She stepped back, forcing herself to take in the whole of him. No matter how blinding.

Start at the top. Long, sun-bleached blond hair gone. Mostly. It waved backward from a fine forehead, which sloped into his sharp nose, which didn't seem quite so lethal anymore. His eyes remained as blue as ever. But without the distraction of the beard and messy hair, they shone almost too blue. How *dare* they. Did the coat bring out their color? She shook her head, looked away, trailing her gaze downward, making a to-do list of the man and checking off each bit.

Cravat—snowy and crisp instead of wrinkled and loose.

Jacket—perfectly tailored, likely brand new.

Linen—unstained.

Waistcoat—slightly lighter blue than the jacket, perfectly cut. The fit of it almost too perfect. The buttons strained against the flat width of his abdomen.

Her throat went dry, but she pressed on.

To the trousers. Those, too, perfectly tailored, lovingly hugging his thick thighs and—

She swung around, giving him her back. Cowardly, yes, but her face had become a fireplace.

The gazes of her four friends, she now saw, were glued to the man behind her. They all four possessed slack jaws, and Lady Templeton's head tilted as her eyes dipped down the length of Mr. Bailey's frame.

Mrs. Garrison whistled.

Lady Macintosh hissed in a breath of appreciation.

"I did not know," Mr. Bailey said from behind Prudence, "it was to be a large party." Were the notes of his voice more refined? What sorcery was this? What nonsense? More accurate still... what *trickery*?

For it could be nothing else.

Prudence swung back around. "What are you doing here, Mr. Bailey? You were not invited."

He ran his hands down his form. "No compliments for my improved appearance?"

"I've a compliment or two," Lady Macintosh mumbled.

"For his tailor, especially," Lady Templeton hissed. "Those *trousers*."

Prudence looked at said trousers. So very... tight. "But where's your cigar, Mr. Bailey?"

Lady Templeton elbowed her in the ribs and whispered, "Good one. But open your eyes, girl. His cigar's right there. Have to be blind not to—"

"No." Mortification made her skin so hot it threatened to melt right off. She could barely look Mr. Bailey in the face but certainly couldn't look at his trousers again. She settled on the ceiling. Nothing embarrassing up there. "The cigar you keep in your pocket, Mr. Bailey. Because you like the scent."

He chuckled, and the warm rumble made, somehow, the ceiling a source of mortification as well. She tried her toes, the points of her slippers peeking out from beneath her skirts. Nothing to heat her cheeks there.

"I didn't wish to crush the cigar," Mr. Bailey said. "I've been forced to leave it in my trunk."

"Why not smoke it?" Mrs. Garrison asked.

Prudence shook her head. The conversation went entirely in the wrong direction. She ignored the women behind her. Ignored the trousers, too. "This is a private gathering. Isn't that right, Lady Norton?"

Cora stepped forward, taking up arms at Prudence's side. "It is. But..." She offered Prudence an apologetic grimace, a shrug. "It is Lord Norton's home, and he may invite whomever he pleases."

"But why did he invite *him*?" Prudence jerked her head toward Bailey.

"Have you quite forgotten your manners, Lady Prudence?" the man drawled.

"Ha!" She stalked toward him, skirts swinging round her legs. "You're one to speak of manners. This is the first I'm seeing of them from you."

He shrugged. "It's never too late to learn."

"How long are you staying here?" she demanded.

He leaned forward until no more than a few inches remained between their noses. "Why do you want me gone?"

She glared.

He grinned. Then he straightened. "Norton invited me for company and for my own sake." He looked over Prudence's head at Cora. "I do apologize if my presence is a surprise. I thought your husband would have given you some warning of my arrival."

"It is no bother, Mr. Bailey." Cora glided forward. "Please, sit. Would you like any refreshment?"

He sank into a nearby chair and folded his hands in his lap. "No, thank you."

Everyone else sat, too, in a neat little circle around Bailey. Lady Templeton even dragged a chair from across the room to join them when there proved not enough seating.

Mr. Bailey became a spectacle. Every eye on him. He knew it, too, shifted from side to side, hiding a grimace.

"What do you mean for your own sake?" Prudence asked.

He seemed ready to melt in relief. She'd broken the silence, and now he could breathe easy. "I have realized I must learn to fit in. If I wish to woo a wife. Norton has agreed to help me navigate the waters."

"Why do you need a wife?" Mrs. Garrison leaned forward, her eyes sharp with strategy.

"Doesn't every man?"

She leaned back, nodding as if she accepted his answer. Those sharp eyes, though... she would not be so easily pleased.

"You understand, Mr. Bailey," Cora said, "I am pleased to have you as a guest."

Prudence sniffed.

"But," Cora continued, shooting Prudence a warning look, "we, the five of us, were not expecting to entertain a gentleman. We have our own activities and occupations planned, and I am quite certain you will not find them diverting."

"Not at all," Lady Templeton said. "Things like knitting."

"And pressing flowers," Lady Macintosh added.

"And a bit of rifle target practice," Mrs. Garrison said.

They looked at her.

She shrugged. "I enjoy shooting."

They glanced at Mr. Bailey.

"Oh." Mrs. Garrison's eyes went wide. "But I, uh, do not like an audience. My fragile female nerves are too timid to shoot under the expert male gaze." Her jaw tightened, and Prudence could see in the fine lines at the corners of the woman's eyes—she strained to keep from rolling them.

Mr. Bailey smiled, a charming little curve of enticing lips. "Please do not worry about entertaining me, ladies." His gaze settled hot on Prudence. "I'm quite certain I'll find something to occupy my hours."

The door swung open, and Norton stepped in, swiping a hand

through his hair. "Ah. Here we all are." He paced to Cora and dropped a hand to her shoulder. She flinched, and he yanked the hand away. "I see you've met our new guest, Cora."

"You could have told me you invited him." Her words sounded sweet, but a bitter edge floated just beneath the surface of her soft voice.

"Ah, apologies. You're correct. I'm unused to sharing my plans with others. But I'll do better next time."

Cora stood, almost jumped to her feet, and Prudence and the other ladies followed suit. Cora led them like ducklings toward the door. "We will see you for dinner, then." She nodded and left, head held high. She led them back to the library, and once they'd all piled inside, she closed the door, locked it, collapsed against it with a huff, her gaze settling on Prudence. "Well, this complicates things."

It did. Oh, it did. Because Prudence did not believe Mr. Bailey's claims for one second.

She grasped for a chair and sank into it, her hand lying on the large tea spot marring her skirts. Bother. She'd forgotten about that. She'd stood before him looking a mess when he looked...

"There's only one reason a man turns himself from beast to prince like that," Mrs. Garrison said. She paced the length of the room and back, hands folded behind her back.

"He's not here for Norton," Mrs. Templeton agreed.

Prudence traced the outline of the stain. "He's here for me."

But what he wanted from her, *truly wanted* from her, she could not guess. The only thing she knew for sure? It could not be her—plain, tea-stained Prudence.

Chapter Seven

As soon as the door shut behind the ladies, Ben tugged at his cravat so violently his hair went wild, whipping over his eyes.

"You're ruining the effect!" Norton slumped into the chair his wife had so recently vacated.

"She's not here to see it."

"You don't act like you want her to marry you."

Ben *didn't* want to marry her. Couldn't say that, though. "Despite what that blasted Guide says, there's more than one way to court a lady. Besides, why are all of you following the duke about when he's never conducted a successful courtship?"

Norton pinched his nose, closed his eyes. "He's a keen, analytical mind. And there's precious little other practical advice on the matter. We're simply supposed to know how to do it. We don't. I don't. You clearly do not. What else are we supposed to do?"

Ben sank into a seat across from Norton. "Feels like a great bloody experiment. With us as the subjects."

"But I need it to work."

"Don't see why."

"Would you like to exist in a miserable marriage?" Norton grumbled.

Ben yanked at his cravat again, succeeded in pulling loose an end of it. "You want to court your wife?"

Norton stared out the window, arms limp on the arms of his chair. "Have to, don't I? Or else—"

"Misery."

"Precisely. Stop messing with the cravat. You'll tangle it."

"Too late for that." Ben had somehow conjured a tight knot before his throat. "You didn't have to follow me about the last twenty-four hours like I'm some damn child who can't be trusted to take care of himself."

"Clearly you can't be trusted." Norton rose and ambled toward a cupboard in the corner of the room. He opened it up and pulled forth a bottle half-filled with amber liquid. "Brandy?"

"Can't be trusted? Just because I don't preen like a peacock?" Ben grunted. "Yes, brandy."

"Can't be trusted because you don't take the clear steps to obtain that which you desire. You just sulk about wishing someone would pick you up when you're a burnt, mangled tart, last batch of the day, and you do nothing to make yourself appealing."

"Are you calling me a tart?" Ben's eyes narrowed.

"Yes. In a metaphorical sense." He poured a few fingers each in two crystal glasses and returned to his chair, handing off a glass to Ben before he sat.

"You and Clearford are addled. Here I am stuffed into clothes so tight I can barely move, and did Lady Prudence fall into my arms?" He grunted. "No matter how attractive I make my *tart*, she would boot me out the front door if she had the power to do so. Toss me to the dog because he's been a good boy. Why they hell are we using the metaphor?"

"Because it's about pleasing others so they wish to have you. That's what this"—he waved at Ben's naked face—"is all about. Tell me, did you really detect no difference at all in her demeanor toward you?" Norton sipped his brandy.

Ben scratched his chin. "I wouldn't say that." She'd seemed shocked, her eyes larger than he'd ever seen them as her gaze flitted up and down his form before finally settling just south of his eyes. On his lips. Or perhaps she'd been mesmerized by his smooth cheeks and jaw. Surely that, because a well-bred duke's sister would not stare overly long at a man's lips.

But this duke's sister had secrets. So perhaps this duke's sister did.

"Who are these other women?" Ben asked. They'd been staring at him like he was a piece of meat, and they hadn't eaten in a fortnight. Like he was the last tart baked by an expert chef. Like he was a buxom tavern wench, and they were the randy farm boys. Everyone had treated him differently, looked at him differently, since he'd chopped off his hair, shaved his beard, scrubbed off the ink. He was the same damn man. Just like a well-made tart tasted the same no matter what it looked like.

Everyone else was ridiculous. Mad.

But perhaps Norton had the right of it, though, because Prudence had looked at him anew as well. If the new clothes led to new developments, it wouldn't be a waste of time.

"They are Cora's friends," Norton answered.

"Friends? Not her mother's friends? They appear... more mature."

"Cora asked specifically for those women to stay with her for the next few weeks. So, I cannot think they are her mother's friends."

"You know precious little about your wife."

"She wasn't going to be my wife a month ago."

Ben raised his glass in concession. "They don't want our company."

Norton finished off his brandy and snapped the glass onto a nearby table. "Doesn't matter. They are not here for us. They are here for her. And you are here for Lady Prudence."

"Your point?"

"What are you doing here with me?"

Ben shot the rest of the brandy down his throat and placed his glass beside Norton's. "Damn right. I'll be going, then."

"Do you have a plan?"

Ben stopped just before the door, ran his hands down the length of his body. "*This* is the plan, remember?"

"You can't just shave and think that will win the woman."

"Then why did I shave?" Ben growled.

"To catch her attention. Now you must keep it."

"When did you become a bloody expert?"

Norton grabbed his empty glass as he stood and refilled it at the cupboard. "I'm far from it. But I have the Guide, and I trust that will help."

"You trust Clearford, and I'll trust..."

Norton grinned over the rim of his glass. "Trust what?"

"Shove it." Ben stormed into the hall. Which way had she gone? He stood still, held his breath, heard faint voices down the hall. He followed them to the very end where double doors sat tall and closed. He pressed an ear against the crack between them, and the voices became easier to discern. A tiny bit. The tones were furtive. Only a few words came through with crisp clarity.

"—books, but..."

"We should go back to London. We'll..."

"Hyde Park? Too dangerous. But—"

"Then what?"

"*Shh.*"

"This was supposed to be—"

"... locked doors."

He straightened. Locked doors? He gave the handle a try. Didn't budge. What in hell were they up to?

Silence inside the room.

He knocked. Perhaps banged was a more accurate description.

Still, they clung to their silence, like the besieged awaiting their fate behind a weak castle door.

He knocked again, this time with less force.

"Ye-es?" a voice said. Lady Norton's.

"I was wondering if I could have a word with Lady Prudence."

"I'm occupied!" the duke's sister said. Well, yelled.

Ben tried the handle again, though he knew it would produce no different results.

"We're busy!" Five female voices clamored together.

"I'm not." Ben crossed his arms over his chest and planted his feet. "I've got all day. Several days. How long is this little house party?"

Silence again, punctuated by little audible grunts and gasps, the constant chatter of furtive whispering then, "No!"

That voice belonging to Prudence. Ben chuckled, waited.

More whispers and grumbling.

Then silence.

Then the doors flung open, and there she was, a forced smile pulling her lips tight. "Shall we take a walk through the gardens?"

"Yes." He held out a crooked arm.

She blinked at it. No, not at it, at him, somewhere north of his arm, at his—

"Hell." He tugged at the tangle of a knot at his throat. "Forgot about that."

"Did you encounter a wolf in the hall? Did you fight it?"

"No. We are walking. Are we not, Lady Prudence?" He held out his arm.

She took it after a slight hesitation, and he all but dragged her back to the parlor. Norton had left, and Ben pulled her through the doors, into the garden he'd been admiring before they'd arrived to gawp at his transformation.

"Did you encounter a snake, then?" she asked. "A big one that wound around your throat and—"

"No." He tugged her onto a path which meandered through some trees.

She shook him loose. "If you won't delight me with the tale of what happened to your cravat, perhaps you can tell me what you brought me out here for."

His tongue felt as tangled as his cravat. He tugged at the linen, made it worse.

"Stop." She swung in front of him, and if her word had not alerted him before her body moved, he would have crashed right into her. She peered up at him, her hands hesitant as they rose between their bodies. "Let me?"

He scowled. What did she mean? But when her fingers brushed against the mess of his neck neckcloth, he knew.

"Yes." His voice surprisingly gruff, rough in his own throat. A woman had never neatened his cravat before. Felt odd to have someone so tiny so close, untying the strip of linen that covered his throat. Uncovering him. The air washed his hot skin as her knuckles brushed his chin.

"Stubble already. Did you shave this morning?"

He nodded, and there again, that brush of his chin against her hands, undoing the work the wind did to cool his throat.

She wound the cravat back up again, tied a serviceable knot, and stepped away, placing her hands on her hips and tilting her head as she studied her work. "Not as intricate as you had before, but better than the mess you made of it. And in such a short time." She *tsked*.

"You like pointing out where I make messes. My neckcloth. My schedule."

She shivered. "Do not remind me of that abomination. Tell me, what meetings are you missing currently which you've entirely forgotten existed until now?"

He swallowed a curse. There was one. Two? He had forgotten. Damn. "None. I made sure everything was taken care of before leaving London."

"You're lying." She patted his cravat before starting down the shadow-dappled lane once more.

He caught up. "How did you know?"

"Your eyes tell the truth when your lips do not." Her gaze flashed to his lips. "Why have you done this, Mr. Bailey? The cut hair and shaved chin, the new clothes?"

She could read truth in his eyes, apparently. No use lying. About this. "For you."

A hitch in her step. Her cheeks flushed in an instant. "W-why are you here?"

His turn to round her, to stop her in her tracks. She could not meet his gaze, so he placed his knuckles beneath her chin and lifted it. Still, she would not look at him. The changeable eyes above her rosy cheeks searched for something to land on, anywhere but him. Did he fluster her?

He liked her flustered. He didn't mean to do it. His thumb moved without a single conscious command, swiping across her lower lip.

Her gaze snapped to his. Finally. And her knees buckled.

But he caught her, held her tight and upright against his body as her arms wrapped around his neck. Her breaths came hard and fast, and her eyes darkened. Her lips, usually thinned in disapproval, softened. Pink and velvet. Impossible to look away.

Yes. Yes, he liked her flustered very much.

"Like that, my lady?" he clung to her, keeping her upright.

She clung to him, too, unbreathing, eyelashes fluttering. "I…" A gurgle strangling whatever words she'd meant to say.

This gentleman thing came with power.

"Shall I kiss you?" he asked.

She melted against him. Hell. She'd let his lips ravage hers this very moment.

But that moment didn't last.

She snapped upright and out of his arms, pacing away from him and smoothing her hands down her skirts. A large, brown stain marred one side of her gown. How… unusually untidy of her.

"Did you get into an altercation with a teapot, Lady Prudence?" he asked with a chuckle. "I find it difficult to believe that for once you are more rumpled than I."

She whirled around to face him, waving her hand at his face. "I dislike all this."

He stalked toward her. "I was teasing. I did not mean to offend."

"Not that."

What then? Ah. "The touches. You dislike it when I embrace you. Because you *like* it, perhaps? More than you wish to."

"No." She stiffened her arm in front of her, muscles rigid, palm flat, a wall to stop his progress toward her. "The change in your appearance. Because I thought you did not care what others thought of you. I thought you beyond such peacock preening. Yet here you are." Her arm dropped heavy to her side. "Looking like that. It's a disappointment if you must know." Her shoulders slumped as she turned from him and continued down the path. Her pace sad and heavy.

His own heart, curious thing, stuttered, unsure how to beat in such extraordinary circumstances. He'd disappointed her. By shaving. He rubbed his chest over that organ, trying to soothe it, but it grew impatient. And Lady Prudence grew farther away. And Ben's limbs jittered along with his heart.

Until he ran to catch up with her. He grasped her arm to tug her to a soft stop, to frown down into her scowling face. "Beards grow back, Lady Prudence." He laughed. Mostly because he didn't know what else to do. Couldn't name that feeling coursing like a rapid current through his body, tangling and untangling every inch of him. "I was just trying to please you."

She lifted her chin, a defiant little thing. The chin and her. He expected her to rip her arm from his hold, but she did not, and she wore no spencer or shawl to cover the long, slender length of her arm, the elegant crook at its bend. But he wore gloves. So even though he wondered, oddly, what texture and temperature her skin would yield beneath his fingertips—velvety or silken, warm or cool—he did not know. Damn those gloves.

What an odd thing to think, to feel.

Would be odder still to rip them off right now, toss them to the ground, wrap his fingers round that soft-looking arm once more.

"If you wish to know how to please a woman," she said, lifting that pointy little chin impossibly higher, "you should ask *her*."

He hitched the corner of his mouth up before speaking, hoping he might set her at ease. But any movement of his mouth seemed to push her closer to falling off an edge. She blinked and turned from him, and before she could bolt, he folded her arm with his own and pulled her to his side, set them both strolling together down the path.

"You set my mind at ease, Lady Prudence. Had I known you admired any part of me, I would not have changed all of it. Seems I don't have to try so hard to win you."

She huffed. "Why do you even want to win me?"

Answering that would take some delicacy. He had to walk a tightrope between appeasing her and not making her fall in love. At the end of all this, he couldn't be the reason her heart lay in pieces.

He took a deep breath, remembered, for some odd reason, the giant family portrait in the duke's study. "Because I think we could be friends."

"What makes you think that?"

In the portrait, she'd hovered on the edge. All the other women crowded to one side, the duke and his heir standing tall above them.

And Prudence balancing the lot of them to one side, sitting with her legs curled beneath her, tall and straight and not looking directly at the artist. Almost a bloody afterthought.

"We've much in common," he said.

"Such as?" Her arm in his embrace stiffened.

"We both feel like outsiders sometimes." A risk, that. He couldn't assume her position in the painting meant anything other than the artist's sense of the ideal composition of so many people. But he'd watched her skirt the edges of ballrooms, sneak off into the shadows. He'd seen her hovering silent but observant around the edges of her gathered flock of sisters. They turned to her occasionally, and she did not demand more attention than that. But that did not mean she was idle. Always moving, Lady Prudence, always bright-eyed and busy. "Maybe we both feel like we have something to prove."

Her steps hitched, and she swallowed hard.

"You don't have to prove anything to me, Lady Prudence," he said.

She stopped and tugged on his arm to stop him, too. When he looked down, she reached up, a flash of courage in her eyes. They seemed dark green in the dappled shadows cast by the branches above them. But all sense of color and surrounding snapped out of existence when her fingertips brushed against his jaw. On purpose. No gloves. Up the hard edge to his ear, then down to his chin. Her fingers lingered there, and the edge of her fingernails brushed against the light dusting of newly grown hair there.

"Nor do you have anything to prove to me, Mr. Bailey." Her gaze dropped to his cravat. She patted it, then she unfolded from his light hold, dragging her arm away from his, and set down the path away from him.

And bloody hell, if she'd been a losing general, he'd have followed her into a battle that surely meant death. He trotted after her, and when his brain caught up to the fact, he didn't really care.

"Where did you learn to tie a cravat?" he asked when he caught up with her. Because he could not say, *you're the only human in existence to think me better off in beard and ink stains, and that right there makes me feel more different from any haircut ever can.*

Hell. He needed some distance from her. He didn't want distance from her.

What the hell was wrong with him?

She tilted her face to the sky with the purest little grin. "My sisters and I used to put on little plays, home theatricals, and after Samuel grew too old, he refused to participate. Well, that left us without a man, you see. And we had to have princes and gentlemen and such. So, I asked my papa to teach me how to tie a cravat."

"He sent you to his valet?"

She shook her head. "He learned from his valet and then he taught me. I was in charge of tying the cravat of any sister who needed it."

He wanted her to tie his cravats. Every one of them.

Hell. Another inexplicable, rogue thought. Was he ill? The air at Norton Hall was clearly unhealthy for him, driving him mad. He needed the smog of London to think clearly.

He clasped his hands together behind his back so he did not reach for her, and he asked another question, so he did not give his other thoughts to the air, to her. "What parts did you play? In the theatricals?"

"None. I organized the costumes and scripts and helped my sisters learn the lines. I was in charge of staging, too, and inviting the audience to attend."

"Ah. You organized everything from behind the scenes."

"Yes." Pride in her voice, wistfulness, too.

"Did you ever wish to act? To play a starring role? To have someone else tie your cravat?"

A hesitation clear as the sun above. But then she answered. Quietly. "No. Of course not."

He didn't believe it for one bloody second. He wanted to push, to find the truth. But—hell—he had other truths to discover. And while she was opening up to him so pliantly...

"You prefer operating behind the scenes," he said.

"Yes."

"Just as you do with Lady Norton."

She froze. "With Lady Norton? What do you mean?"

Ah, Prevaricating Prudence. What a horrid little liar she was. She was on her guard now, though. He could push no further. "Nothing. I mean nothing. Just that you seem rather set on ensuring her little house party here is something of a success."

"Oh. Yes." Relief flooded her lungs with air. "It is my fault she's in this position, after all."

He snorted. "It's not. You didn't compromise her. She did that. So did Norton."

"I was the one who suggested we wear the same costume. I thought up wearing the black veil to hide my hair. So we'd look even more alike. And I'm the one Norton was looking for in the gardens."

"You're too smart to believe such drivel." She gasped, affronted. Good. He wagged a finger at her, then sauntered farther away from her down the path, throwing his voice over his shoulder for her to catch. "You didn't yank Lady Norton's bodice down. And you did not let Lord Norton yank down that bodice. He could have stopped, and she could have stopped him. Looked to me like she'd been enjoying herself. Before her dear mama arrived." He whirled to face her, wagged his finger again. "Not your fault."

Her gaze drifted away from him, and she lifted a hand to her mouth, bit her fingernail as her eyes closed. She scowled, as if trying to remember that night. "Perhaps you're right. Perhaps I should not carry such guilt." Her eyes popped open. "But it does not mean I do not wish my friend to be happy. I will do what I can to make that so."

"And who will make you happy, Lady Prudence?" He stepped closer —two, three steps until the breath they exhaled filled the same warm space.

She shivered, wrapped her arms around herself, her shoulders caving in as she met his gaze with eyes like a wary animal's. "Why are you here?"

"For you."

She shook her head. "But why do you want *me*?" Her eyes narrowed, and her thin shoulders became blades, rigid and sharp.

He didn't want her. He *didn't*. But somehow, he had an answer to that question anyway. Not the truth he'd known up until this very second, but another truth all the same. "Because you see me. And I see you. And that's rare."

She took several slow steps backward, away from him, her hand lowering to clench at her skirts. Long, pale fingers, slim and lithe, outlined by a brown stain dried upon her pretty green skirts. The outer edges of the stain were darker, and her hand seemed haloed. What had happened? When had she spilled? Had the coffee or tea or whatever she'd spilled seeped through her skirts, her shift, and burned her?

He scowled.

She backed away another step. "You should leave, Mr. Bailey. I do not wish to be seen."

He whipped his gaze up to hers. "I won't leave. In fact, I look forward to joining the little tête-à-tête with you and your friends. I happen to like knitting. And shooting. I'll make sure not to watch with too much masculine interest. So I don't startle your friend."

And her gaze floated to his lips.

And his trousers tightened. How the hell could any fellow keep arousal a secret in clothes so tight? But she wasn't looking south of his lips, so she wouldn't notice. He wet his lips, and her breath hitched, so he prowled closer to his prey, lifted one hand to brush a wispy bit of hair behind her ear. She shivered.

And he fought a predatory impulse to nip at her earlobe. "Though if you prefer, we can go off together, find a private corner. I have a feeling you like one thing about my lack of a beard."

"Oh? What is that?" Each word wavered.

"You can see my lips now. Would you like to kiss them?"

She inhaled so deeply her small breasts strained against the low bodice that now barely contained them. And his cock strained against the blasted tight trousers. He tilted her chin up, rubbed his thumb over her lower lip. Again. And damn the gloves. Again.

"What'll it be, Lady P? A jolly gathering with just your friends. And me. Or a private corner? Just me"—he leaned closer—"and you, and..." Their lips almost touched now, and when her tongue darted out at the corner of mouth, he almost broke down, almost crashed through the small distance between them to take her right there in the garden, with a dozen windows at least looking down upon them. "Kissing."

His hand still at her chin, he felt her throat bob up and down. "I... I... yes. Yes. A corner. That."

He smirked, stepped away from her, almost lunged back to grab her when her legs went a bit wobbly.

Turning toward the house, he said, "Good. See you soon, Lady P."

No answer from her. He didn't need one. She would comply. No question. She didn't want him near her friends for some reason. Wanted him far, far away, in fact, and would do whatever necessary to make that happen.

Including kissing Ben.

But there would be no kissing. Private corners were good for more than furtive touches. They also proved useful for whispered confidences. And Lady Prudence had shown she could open up to him today. He could earn her trust. And if he earned her trust, he could earn her secrets, too.

No kissing. He could manage that.

His cock disagreed.

Didn't matter what his cock wanted, though, in the end, Lady Prudence wouldn't kiss him. A prim woman like that? Even though she did seem to admire his lips... Never.

Chapter Eight

"I'm going to kiss him today." Prudence strolled the length of the book-lined wall in the library, her finger running down the spines.

Sunlight poured through the windows, and Cora and the other ladies sat in chairs scattered about the room, noses deep in different copies of the same book. *The Prince's Pride*. Prudence had gotten perhaps thirty pages into the book before realizing the royal in question prized his sexual exploits above all else. And he adored recounting them in detail to an innocent miss he corresponded with. The miss was scandalized and begged he desist writing to her. He refused. The scoundrel.

She'd abandoned it last night for work, for planning, for taming the chaos Mr. Bailey had dropped like a hot coal into her lap.

Cora and the other ladies looked up from their books, spearing Prudence with the quizzical expressions of curious puppy dogs.

Cora raised her hand halfway into the air, fingers slightly curled near her ear, as if asking permission to speak. "Kiss whom?"

Prudence gave one stout bob of her head. "Mr. Bailey. It is, I think, the only way to keep him occupied, distracted, so he does not interfere with our activities."

Lady Macintosh hummed. "There are many other ways to keep a man distracted, but... kissing is a rather pleasant one, I must admit."

"As long," Lady Templeton said with a sniff, "as you do not move on to *other forms* of *occupation*. You are not yet married. Other forms of occupation are strongly advised against. Kissing is allowed only with extreme caution."

"If"—Mrs. Garrison said, snapping her book closed and placing it on her lap—"you do move on to other forms of occupation, you will soon find yourself married."

Prudence summoned her patience and clasped her hands before her, used the soft voice she usually reserved for her younger sisters still in the schoolroom. "Kissing, and any other forms of occupation—of which there will be none—would be done solely for the benefit of all of you. Do you mean to say my sacrifices will be punished? That the three of you will tell my brother and demand—"

"Satisfaction." Mrs. Garrison pulled up tall, wiggled her shoulders back into a solid wall of stubbornness.

"That Mr. Bailey do the right thing." Lady Macintosh patted the back of her coiffure and looked toward the mirror across the room. Her hair had gone entirely gray, unlike the two other older women, but it was thick and had a lovely curl, and she seemed rather proud of it. With good reason. It was terribly lovely.

"In short," Lady Templeton said, "marrying you."

"Betrayal!" Prudence crossed her arms over her chest. "All I do, I do for you. I do not believe you would betray me so."

"Without a doubt, we would," Lady Templeton said. "Our disregard of social rules only extends so far." With her lips pinched into a thin line, her round face seemed to shrink, to harden. She meant what she said.

"You do not want to end up like me," Cora warned, her voice small.

"I won't." Prudence placed a hand over Cora's. "There is no danger. I will not have to resort to other means of occupying Mr. Bailey. There is not really any danger of kissing, even. You see, Mr. Bailey does not truly wish to kiss me. He wants my secrets."

"How can you know that?" Cora tugged at a curl just below her ear. "No. I think you're wrong. He changed his appearance and showed up here asking for you. What more could he want from you except your hand in marriage? Nothing else makes sense."

"You should see the way he asks questions." Prudence turned back to the books, choosing one at random and pulling it out by the top of its spine. Her hands needed some outlet for her frustration, some means of moving. "He knows something about us, all of us, and I will remind each and every one of you—he co-owns newspapers with my brother-in-law."

"Yes," Mrs. Garrison said, "and we practically own your brother-in-law. Mr. Kingston owes us. And he well knows it. He would not publish anything in his papers that would harm us."

Blast it all, they had a point. But it would still do to be careful. "What if Mr. Bailey published something without Kingston knowing?" There was always that, and she would not put it past the American to be so underhanded. "It will only be kissing if that. He does not truly want to kiss me. I think he is attempting to manipulate me. But he will not find me so easily manipulated. I will play his game. You will see. If I try to push past kissing to other modes of *occupation*, he will stop me."

She'd made a list of those modes last night. And it burned her pocket now. Touches came first on places of the body not covered by clothes—the neck, the arm, the hand. And then places of the body covered by clothes—the feel of an abdomen or breast through muslin or silk. Then lips touched lips. And then clothes were shrugged off to uncover hidden parts of the body, and those were touched, too, no muslin or linen in the way this time. Just skin and teeth and tongue. She had not been able to decide which would prove more intimate—a man touching a woman between her legs or a woman touching a man there. Still an unknown. But mouths in those places certainly came after hands there. And then came the moment when those two centers of the body were thrust together. The very bottom of the list, that.

She wouldn't even get close to it. Once she set her lips to his, he would run. No doubt about it. Hopefully all the way back to London, then she would not have to repeat this little distraction to keep him away from her secrets.

Prudence clutched the book to her as she faced her friends once more. "While I am occupied, you have a full day planned. I've put the schedule of activities just by the teapot there. You will want for no diversion. It's a full day."

Cora plucked it up, unfolded it, scanned it. "Perfection, but you will not join us at all?"

"I cannot if we are to keep Mr. Bailey away."

"Doesn't seem fair," Cora said. "I should simply demand Norton send him away."

"That will only raise Mr. Bailey's suspicions."

A knock on the door. Then the handle turned, and the door opened, and there he was, unshaven. The scruff just covered his cheeks, not enough to hide his lips. And still *those* fascinated her.

"Good morning, ladies." He bowed. "I was hoping I could join you." He looked at no one but Prudence, a single eyebrow raised. In challenge?

"I am sure the ladies would be delighted by your company," Lady Prudence said, "but I will not be joining everyone this morning. I would like to tour the house. It is quite old, I'm told, and I do love a bit of history."

His other eyebrow joined his first. "Do you, Lady Prudence?"

She found the gap in the bookshelf and replaced the book perfectly where it should be. "I will miss the company though. Unfortunately, the other ladies have already toured the premises, and I shall be alone."

"No need for that," Mr. Bailey said. "If you will allow it, I would like to accompany you. I, too, enjoy a spot of history. Please, Lady Prudence, may I escort you?"

Her heart fluttered. Not because her plan was working, she feared, but because that charming grin on that scruffy face with those well-fitted clothes... blast it all. The combination seemed to be a weakness for her. She should think about his up-ended schedule. His inability to keep a meeting time. Yes, that calmed her heart. Mostly.

"Thank you very much, Mr. Bailey. I would like that." She gave a bright smile to her friends, which they returned with warning glances. She needed no warning. She had a list in her pocket. She knew how far a woman could go, and she knew she would not have to.

"Where should we start?" he asked once they were alone in the hall together.

"There's a portrait gallery I'm keen to visit." Cora had told her it was a rather unvisited and abandoned part of the hall, and it was comfortable for a portrait gallery as well. Apparently, the former viscount and viscountess liked reading there amongst the likenesses of all their ancestors. The current viscount cared nothing for that practice nor for those ancestors, and so he and everyone else avoided the room except to clean it. And that part of the wing was not to be cleaned today, according to Cora. It sounded like perfection.

"Lead the way," he said.

"I don't know the way."

"Well then, we shall wander aimlessly together."

She smiled. A real smile. Was she ill? Perhaps the London fog agreed with her more than the fresh country air. But as they wandered, her steps felt rather bouncy, and she let herself enjoy his companionship.

When they began to climb a flight of stairs, she said, "Tell me about the makeover. I want to know everything about it from conception of the idea to the very final tweak of your cravat."

"Does it need fixing today?" He stopped, one foot on a step higher than the other, and lifted his chin to give her a better view of his snowy neckcloth.

"No. Perfection. You clearly had a valet tie it and have not muddled with it since."

"You've caught me. Mr. Combs tied it. I don't usually have a valet. Norton insisted we hire one before leaving London. And I dare not touch his work. He threatened me."

"With a shaving razor?"

"With the ruination of the only pair of comfortable trousers I possess in this place."

"Dark times, indeed."

He laughed as he continued his climb. "It was your brother's idea. To improve my appearance."

She set her pace upward to his slow, careful steps. "Naturally. But I am surprised you went along with it."

"Nothing else I was doing seemed to open you up. I'm not a stubborn man. I can change when necessary."

Her turn to laugh.

"Not stubborn *all* the time at least," he muttered. "I went to Bond Street to find my grandfather's tailor, and before I arrived, Norton appeared by my side. He insisted we find a *new* tailor, a younger one, and he insisted I use his barber. Eventually your brother's valet joined us, and I quite lost control of the entire production."

"Did it hurt?" She wanted to reach up and put her palm along his cheek. "When they cut your beard?" It had seemed a part of him, like a hand or foot or tooth. "Not physically, of course, but..." Was it wise to suggest this man had feelings that could be cut with blades sharp enough to shave a cheek clean?

His mouth pinched, but it seemed more of a thoughtful expression than an annoyed one. He would not deny his emotions then.

"It was like watching a new man take shape," he said. Oddly, she thought she heard honesty in his voice, as deep and dark as the stairwell they ascended.

They climbed the rest of the steps in silence, but when they reached the landing, Prudence pulled Mr. Bailey over to a window and gave him a hard, long look up and down his body.

"Do you mean to make me squirm?" But he didn't squirm a bit. He hooked his thumbs in the top of his breeches and rolled his shoulders back, giving her a better look.

And she did look her fill. Well-fitted, copper waistcoat, buff riding breeches, hessians, and linen sleeves and cravat as tidy and pristine as she'd ever seen. Gloves covered his hands. Ink beneath them, etched forever into his strong fingers?

She hoped so.

Why did she hope so? That question was not on a list. Led only to yawning chaos. She closed the door on it.

"You say you felt like a different man," she said, "but I do not think you are. I think by trimming the beard away and cutting off the hair, by shrinking the clothes to fit you better, you've given the real man more clarity. Now we can better see him. He only seems new because he's new to us."

"This popinjay is not me." His voice gruff.

"A popinjay? Is that what you saw in the looking glass yesterday and this morning? A peacock preening?"

"What else? Isn't that what you called me yesterday?" He grunted and looked out the window, giving her his sharp profile. Strong jaw, long nose. Finely sculpted lips and bright hard eyes. But without all the other distractions of long hair, ink stains, and scraggly beard, she saw something other than hardness there, too. With the curl of his hair waving back from his fine forehead, beneath his golden brow, she saw doubt. And a fighting spirit to counter that doubt.

How did she recognize it? All those things rolled up into two blue orbs? Because she saw the same combination in the mirror—hard determination and doubt.

"I can admit when I am wrong," she said. "You are not a peacock at all."

"What then?"

"Before, you were a bit of a bear. With matted hair and sharp long claws. The claws remain, but perhaps now you're more of a wolf? A fox? Still a wild animal, no doubt there."

He took a step toward her, his big body pushing her closer to the window, rolling her so her back side hit the windowsill, and she tilted back toward the cold glass pane at her shoulder blades. She swallowed, having to tilt her chin up to look at him. He placed his hands on either side of her hips, gloved fingers clenching the windowsill.

His body, hers, trapped, reminded her why they were here—kissing.

"A predator?" he asked.

She nodded.

"And you would like to kiss a predator?"

She licked her lips.

He dipped low, and oh it was coming, sooner than she thought it would. The kiss. But then he pushed away from the windowsill, away from her, and she melted against it as he strolled down the hall. She pressed a palm to her frantic heart. Blast. What was he doing to her? She conquered her flustered breathing into a steady tempo and marched after him.

He darted into a room. "I think I found it!"

"Well, that was easy, was it not?" She hitched up her skirts, swallowed her heart, and ran to catch up.

The room she entered was long with curtains bordering one wall, presumably hiding the sunlight which would otherwise flood through the windows, to keep the paint on the portraits that lined the other walls from fading. Furniture and rugs dotted the space, clumped near one window, then near another set of paintings. At the very end of the room, a huge painting dominated the narrow wall and beneath it an equally large sculpture.

Mr. Bailey stood before both, head tilted to the side, one arm crossed over his torso and the other scratching at his chin.

She joined him. "Dogs?"

"What it looks like to me."

"I would expect a statue of people."

"Me, too."

"Why dogs?"

"Why one, two"—Mr. Bailey began pointing, counting marble heads with intricately carved fur—"four... six of them?"

"You shall have to ask Norton." She looked up. "Even more dogs in the portrait."

He looked up, too. "Damn. Too many to count. It's a blur of fur and slobber."

"Is that what a group of dogs is called? A blur?"

"A pack, I think. But a blur is more precise. Because of the wagging arses."

She chuckled, changing the angle of her glance, the tilt of her chin, to study him instead of the painting. "See, you're no peacock or popinjay. A more refined creature would not curse in front of a lady. Nor mention unmentionable body parts. But you do so with ease. Very bearish of you."

"I would hate to disappoint you. You know"—he turned fully toward her and placed his hand atop the tallest dog's marble head, then proceeded to scratch behind its ear—"I do not feel as ridiculous as I did before. About my appearance." He dropped his gaze to his boots. "Thank you."

What was that light feeling floating through her? Why did having helped him feel so remarkably good?

"Tell me"—he stepped toward her, his head lifting until she could see his eyes, and those eyes oh-so-heated—"how can I help you? What deep reservations do you hold that I can banish? What secrets can I help you keep?"

Oh. Oh! That man. That was his slant, then? To pretend vulnerability with her so he could gain her confidence? Dreadful beast. She would not be outwitted.

Time to prove him wrong, to call his bluff. She leaned closer, too, fluttered her lashes. "There is only one way you can help me, Mr. Bailey."

"Yes?"

"Kiss me."

He flinched. Ah ha! She knew it. He did not want to. Of course he did not want to. No man did. And in the end, Mr. Bailey would not. If a prickle of grief pinched at her, it was not because she'd wished for it, desired it, had dreamt of it. Not at all.

His hand lifted from the dog's head.

And settled on her waist.

She gasped, a tiny little inhalation of disbelief as his hand slid around her body to nestle low, so very low, on her back. Almost too low. The nerves just there beneath his palm began to thrum, and that thrumming extended outward, everywhere, concentrating most particularly between her legs. She felt... need there. As she never had before. Just the barest flex of his arm muscle brought her closer to him. Just a bit more found her pressed against his body, the pulsing part of her, throbbing now as the lean, tight muscle of his leg teased it between so many layers of clothes. Too many?

No! No, not... what was she thinking? Who knew?

Who cared? His other hand had found her chin, tipped it up, and he dipped low, those fiery blue eyes daring her to pull away.

"You want a kiss, Lady P?"

She nodded. Words crowded in her throat, stuck behind her thick tongue. She wanted a kiss, but he would never. He *wouldn't*. Because that's not why he was really here.

"Are you positive?" he asked.

She nodded.

Something wary flickered in his eyes, and his hand on her back flinched a bit. He *wouldn't*. That flinch, that wariness—he didn't want to. She was safe. She would not have to be the one to back down first. He would retreat, leaving her victorious, and—

He smirked, and those hands resumed their confident press against her body. "Very well." The words said with his lips brushing her ear, his breath hot on her skin.

He would kiss her after all.

She wanted it.

No, she—

"Do you hear footsteps?" she asked.

He didn't seem to hear her, kept his gaze locked on her lips, not a hint of a gentleman there, only wild thing, only desiring. Only no stopping him now.

Oh, out of control. This *looking* not on her list at all. She managed to wiggle her arms between their bodies, to push at his chest. He didn't budge. The footsteps grew louder. Blast it all! They'd be caught. Embracing. She tugged him since he wouldn't release her, lurching backward, pulling him with her, rounding the statue as he blinked into awareness. The door at the end of the room creaked open, and she ducked behind the six dogs, yanked Mr. Bailey down with her.

Lost her balance. Like that night in the garden, she fell with a breathless *thump* onto her back.

Unlike that night? Mr. Bailey fell, too. Right on top of her.

She bit her lips together to keep from crying out as the cold marble floor provided a brutal pillow for the back of her head. But somehow worse than that—the large body falling atop her. Not smashing her, though. His arms flailed wide for one moment, and then he caught himself, hands on either side of her head, a brief catch before his body crumpled fully atop hers.

She cried out again—so much massive weight!—but this time his hand slapped down over her mouth, catching the sound, smothering it. He pressed his mouth to her ear, and they touched everywhere, ankles crisscrossing, knees nestled together, hips pressing, bellies kissing, chest to chest, and chin to neck. This also not on her list—the way two bodies fit together. But it should be.

His lips moved against her ear, barely speaking. "Quiet. Had you not pulled us behind here we could have just bounced apart, and Norton would not have suspected anything at all."

"You would not release me," she hissed.

"He's a gullible innocent sort of chap. But now, here we are stacked one atop the other like paper in a pile. Do not make a single sound. Along with being gullible, Norton is rather prudish. He'll see us married before you can blink an eye. Are you hurt?" His fingers slid between the floor and her skull, cradled the back of her head.

"No." Or she had been, but his touch proved a balm, numbing the sharp pain where, soon, a bump would surely rise.

"*Shh.*"

For someone who had just told her to be quiet, Mr. Bailey certainly possessed a mountain of words.

She slapped a hand over his mouth, bulging her eyes large, hoping he understood. *Two can play this game, sir.* His chest puffed up several times in a row, and a wicked glint entered his eye. Was that muffled laughter? Something wet flicked across her palm. He pressed his own palm more tightly over her mouth. Another flick of wetness. She jerked. The man was *licking* her palm. The brute. The barbarian. The *beast*.

She wiggled. And something hard dug into her belly, stopping every muscle she possessed midmovement. She knew what the *something hard* was. But it took several moments to admit it. His gherkin. Not at all her favorite word for that particular bit of anatomy, but she could not give it a more consequential name. That would be to take it seriously, and she could not.

Otherwise, she would also have to sincerely acknowledge the pulsing which had begun between her legs. And his leg nestled just there, his thick thigh a warm and hard pressure against her middle. It felt good. Oh God, it felt good. She turned her head to the side, needing to hide whatever pleasure flickered in her eyes, and his hand dropped away from her mouth, cupped the back of her head. She closed her eyes and licked her lips.

And then his lips moved against her ear once more. "You like this, don't you, Lady P?"

Too late. She'd not hidden her gaze swiftly enough. He'd seen. But she would neither admit it nor deny it.

He chuckled, and then he pressed his thigh more tightly against her center. He slipped his hand around to cup her mouth once more. Good thing because she'd been about to moan. And when she could not moan, she ground that aching middle of hers against his leg.

"Quiet." His voice a warm whisper on the shell of her ear, so low a mouse would not be able to hear. "Remember what—"

Boot steps clicking down the marble floor, getting closer, silenced him.

"Move all of them." Norton's voice.

"But this has been the family portrait gallery since the very first viscount, my lord," said another man, his voice unfamiliar.

"Yes, but look at the windows." Norton again. "Lovely, perfect view of the lake. But we must always keep them closed because of the paintings. To preserve them. It is truly an illogical place to keep art. Lady Norton could make good use of this room if it were made more comfortable. She'd like the view." Norton's voice lower, more thoughtful for the last bit.

"Yes, my lord," the unfamiliar man grumbled.

The two men continued talking, but Prudence lost focus because every bit of her focus went to the curve of her neck, where it met her shoulder, and where Mr. Bailey had begun to place his nose. He inhaled deeply there, and then—ah, searing pleasure as his lips found her skin, dragged across, kissed it.

Kisses on collar bones. Another item to add to her list.

Too much sensation all at once. She did not want to, but she rolled her hips against his thigh, once more finding the delicious pressure of muscle against that yearning bit of her. His thumb caressed her cheek as his lips sparked fireworks across her neck and chest. He placed soft busses right above the line of her bodice until her breasts ached and her arms moved, curving around his body. Nothing else to do with them, might as well explore.

The soft wool of his coat.

The hard muscle beneath it.

The silky hair at his nape.

The way pleasure was a growl in his throat as she tangled her fingers there.

Not a peacock, this man. More dangerous.

The fireworks he set off across her body made her jittery, made her feel full and needy. She'd read about all of this, had never felt any of it. She *wanted* to kiss him. But he kissed her neck, beneath her chin, the line of her jaw, everywhere but her lips. She bit her lip to tame her desire, moaned.

Mr. Bailey froze first, his head lifting from her neck, his hand slowly moving back over her mouth. She froze, too, biting her lip with more force to stop any more moans from escaping. She listened. The room had grown quiet. How quiet, though? The quiet of men listening after they'd just heard a suspicious sound? Or the quiet of a room unoccupied?

Chapter Nine

Caught. Ben couldn't be caught. And by a moan he'd wrenched from Lady Prudence's lips. The moan made him proud, made him want to return to those kisses he'd been scattering on the gentle swell of her breasts above her bodice.

Thankfully, some sense remained. He pushed to his hands and knees and peered through a crack between two dogs' backsides.

Lady Prudence grabbed his cravat, yanked him back down.

"Like me just here, do you, Lady P?" He shouldn't tease. But teasing came so easily around her, a bit like breathing. No work at all. No thought. Just words popping out of his mouth and her pink mouth settling in an O of shock. If he were the kind of man to think things were adorable, that would be at the top of his list.

Lists. She made lists, and now here he was—composing them as well. An infectious plague of compulsion. One he likely needed to catch. For his own good. He'd miss fewer meetings that way.

"*Shh*!" She pressed her palms flat against his chest, putting distance between their bodies. "I'm trying to keep you from giving us away."

Not enough distance. Their legs alternating on the ground—his, hers, his, hers. His cock burrowing against her softness.

Needed more distance. Now.

He moved to stand. She jerked him back down, her brows settling into a V and her hands busy at his waistcoat. Was she undressing him?

And was he considering letting her?

Hell.

He pushed back onto his heels, ripping from her grasp, and held out a hand. "Norton and his estate manager are gone. We're safe."

She stayed right where she was, back on the marble, face still curled into confusion, eyes on her prize.

"Hell," he mumbled. "Forgot I put that there."

She shook the miniature notebook, its spine lumpy from the small pencil nestled near it inside the book's page. "What is this?"

"You should know. You recommended I procure one."

She scooted away from him and sat up, then flipped through the notebook's pages, her face brightening. "You've written appointments here!"

He sighed. "I always have them written down in my office, but it doesn't help when I'm out and about, so it made sense to keep a notebook. Like you suggested. But I haven't yet remembered I have it. It's singularly unuseful if I can't remember to use it."

Her eyes glowed bright as she closed the book and held it out to him. "I'll help you. I'll remind you."

He shook his head and stood, waved his hand at her. "Will you let me help you?"

She took his hand and jumped to her feet.

"You're bouncy," he grumbled, moving out from behind the statue. Norton had flung open a curtain, and sunlight now flooded the room.

"I am."

"And why's that?"

"Oh, any number of reasons, but the notebook mostly. You took my advice. Remembered something I said after leaving me and acted on it." Standing before him, she sighed and peeled the inside edge of the waistcoat away from his chest, found the hidden pocket there, and slipped notebook and pencil inside. "You remembered me even after I was out of your sight. Who knew something like that would feel so lovely?" Her soft gaze landed on me. "Almost makes me like you, Mr. B."

Mr. B. A tease?

His arms flinched. To run. To her. And drag her into an embrace. And kiss the hell out of her until she moaned again.

Who knew a tease from her would make him feel so... lovely? Her word. Not his. But also his. Where she'd lightly brushed his chest while replacing his notebook tingled. Might never stop. The feeling might spread. Felt like an impending illness.

Ah, hell.

"But," she said, strolling aimlessly down the length of the room, "I'm also a bit bouncy about all those kisses." Her hand stroked down the curve of her bodice, over the swells of her breasts, right where he'd kissed her earlier. Unthinking little things driven by instinct. He'd been a man lying atop a sweet-smelling woman, after all. She gave a little laugh that wrapped about him like chains. The softest chains. Velvet. "I did not think you would go so far."

He strode after her. "You pulled me down on top of you, Lady P."

"An accident." Still, she strolled away from him, her lithe figure and those wispy tendrils of escaped hair melting between sunlight pools and shadow as she passed each window. Her pale-green gown and dark-blonde hair making her a silhouette of spring. Not much curve to her waist and hips, but just enough—he knew now—for a man's hand to find a home.

He shook his head and pressed on. "And you did not think a man courting you would take advantage of such an accident?"

She turned to face him. "Not you."

"Why not me?"

"Because you don't really want to court me. You have ulterior motives."

Well, damn. He opened his mouth. Closed it. Opened again, found half a word, produced a squeak.

She laughed again. "You do not have to waste breath denying it. I won't believe a word. I don't know why you want my secrets, likely for some ugly newspaper article, but—"

"No."

"Do you know, Mr. Bailey—"

"Where'd Mr. B go?"

"I think you are the type of man to allow himself to be compromised if he truly wanted the lady. But you were happy to stay hidden just now. You do not want me." When she turned just her head to look out the window, he realized he'd never paid much attention to her cheeks. Of course not. Cheeks were not universally accepted pleasure points. They were mundane. Ordinary.

Not hers. They rounded more from the side than from the front, giving away her innocence.

"If you were courting me with your heart instead of with your brain, you would have allowed us to be discovered."

He snorted. "And dishonor you?" A good excuse as any, a good argument. But hollow. Because she spoke the truth. If he wanted to marry her, he'd not balk at compromising her. "Perhaps you do not know me as well as you think."

"Always a possibility."

What to do now? The game over or changed at the very least.

"You might as well leave, Mr. Bailey," she said. "There is no story here. Only a woman forced to marry a man and her friends gathered around to comfort her. Lady Templeton, Lady Macintosh, and Mrs. Garrison are here to help. They have experience with... *married life,* you see, and Cora does not."

"Lady Norton possesses a mother. I believe we saw and heard her the night Lady Norton became an engaged woman."

"Yes, well, she was not particularly informative. But the ladies invited here are informative and willing to share their wisdom."

"Then you should not be here. You've no need for information on *married life.*"

"Not yet. But soon. My brother is rather adamant on that point."

"Don't you think a woman's husband a better instructor on such matters than women of an older generation?"

"Not at all. We require knowledge from a feminine perspective."

Was that it then? The nefarious secret Clearford feared? His sister sought out the knowledge provided by older women because some mothers, like Lady Norton's, refused to provide it, and other mothers, like the duke's, were dead. He felt deflated, like an empty water skin. Not nefarious at all. Rather... it made his heart ache a bit. For Lady

Prudence. For the duke, too, who didn't have a father to help him figure out how to court a lady, so he had to figure it out on his own.

And for ladies to seek such knowledge... yes, dangerous. A secret to hide. Particularly from an older brother who likely didn't want to think about such matters. All because they'd lost their mother.

Hell.

Ben found his way to the window and tapped a finger against the glass. The lake beyond resembled a mirror, still and silver and reflecting the clouds above. Deeper, though, it would be alive with the ripples of fish moving through the water, the gentle wave of grass at the bottom, the stirring of silt.

Something in him just as deep stirred, rippled.

"My father taught me how to swim," he said. "And how to fix a printing press. And how to treat a lady." And his father would not be proud of how Ben had treated this one.

"Is he still in the Americas?"

"Yes. In the ground."

"Ah."

"Mother, too. Just like..."

"I am sorry." Soft footfalls. Then she joined him at the window. "I know. What that is like."

"I know. My father printed political pamphlets. And a newspaper. I learned the trade at his feet. We were well-off, but—"

She poked his shoulder.

He looked down. "Yes?"

"You were well-off where?"

"Boston."

"A thriving city. Not the wilds in the middle of nowhere. You probably had a nice house."

"One of the largest in the city." He shifted from foot to foot. "I'm missing your point, Lady P."

"It's just that you traipse around London as if you've no idea how to comport yourself, but... you *know*. How to dress, how to behave. That is why all this"—she gestured to his frame or, likely, more specifically the new clothes, the hair, the gloves, and she huffed—"does not seem so foreign on you. What a trick you're playing on all of us."

"Not a trick," he grumbled. "The way I dress—dressed—is convenient for what I do. I need to be able to move comfortably, not worry about ruining a suit which cost more than one of my workers make in a year. And I don't wish to set myself too far apart from those workers, either. They need to know they can trust me."

"You're a man of the people who prefers labor to luxury."

"I suppose you can say that. My father believed in work, in a man finding his own purpose instead of following blindly a purpose handed him through birth. He left England to find his purpose. I wish to honor him by upholding those values. No matter how much it stains my clothes, my skin, or my reputation, I will follow my own path. My father had only the clothes on his back and a small sum given to him by my grandfather when he arrived in the States. He met and married my mother, and they opened their shop. Bailey's Prints. A thriving business until they fell ill. A fever that spared me but not them. Took too many that winter."

"I'm sorry." Her head popped up, and she blinked. "You have a grandfather?"

"Mm. Baron Brightly."

Her eyes widened. "Baron? I did not know your grandfather possessed a title. I *should* have known that. I've studied Debrett's. Well, I was supposed to study Debrett's, but... other books have occupied my time, and... hmm. I thought you were allowed into polite society because of my brother's affinity for you."

"Likely that as much as or more than my grandfather's influence. A duke's opinion weighs more than a baron's after all." He tried not to sneer the words, but his grandfather was one of the best men he knew, and that anyone could determine his worth less than another man's because of a title he'd inherited... made him want to snap a neck. "But maybe also because"—he inhaled deeply, not wanting to say it, but also needing to say it for her, no matter how little it made sense—"I'm his heir." He winced, the word *heir* a bit like a paper cut every single time he said it.

She snapped out an arm and wrapped her fingers tightly around his elbow, swayed a bit. He steadied her, both hands on her shoulders.

"It's not that great a shock. Don't bloody swoon, Lady P."

She laughed. "It is. It is a shock. I think I might need to sit down."

Fine. If she could partake in theatrics, so could he. He picked her up and slung her over his shoulder.

She screeched as he strode for a nearby chaise longue. But her screeching turned to giggles, then uncontrollable guffaws as he sat on the chaise and yanked her off his shoulder and onto his lap.

"Laugh your fill. Get it out." His words were gruff, but he smiled as she lost control in his arms, her own arms wrapping around her belly and tears dripping from beneath her tightly closed eyes. A lovely lass. He'd never noticed before the masquerade, the garden. She'd always seemed a shadow, hard to pin down, hard to see. He saw her now, joy leaking from her eyes and spilling like sunlight into the air. She was beautiful. And her soft little arse curved against his hip like perfection, and her breasts shook with her laughter above the line of her bodice where he'd kissed her earlier. And he wanted to kiss her now, kiss those pink lips to taste her mirth.

But he also wanted to simply watch her laugh. Because he'd never seen any damn thing in his life so entirely beautiful.

Slowly, her laughter died, and she wiped tears from the corners of her eyes with a soft sigh, a little hiccup, and then her gaze skittered to her upper arm. Where he stroked his fingers up and down below the small puff of her green sleeve. When had he started that? Why didn't he stop? She looked at him, holding her breath.

"Done?" he asked, still stroking up and down her arm.

She nodded, taking halting breaths that he thought had nothing to do with her bout of laughter. "I only laughed so much because I realize one day—" Her lips twitched. "It is only that one day you will be—" Another twitch. "You should not be holding me so, Mr. Bailey. Kissing is one thing. Hiding in a narrow space is one thing. Laps are quite another."

He hugged her more tightly against him. "Spit it out, woman. One day I'll be what?"

"Benjamin Bailey, Baron Brightly." She spilled the four words into the world all at once, then rolled her lips between her teeth, her cheeks twitching, her eyes bright.

He cursed. "I had hoped no one would notice."

"You are going to have to change your name. Far too much alliteration."

"You change it for me."

"I'll make you a list of possibilities."

God, he wanted to kiss her.

So, he did.

As soon as their mouths touched, her arms snaked around his neck. And as soon as those arms had locked him up tight, he parted her lips with his tongue. Not the correct kiss for a first kiss, but the right one for *their* first kiss. Laughter tasted like lemons and smelled like something sweet.

First kiss? It implied more to come, a second and third and a hundred and one. That thought entirely odd. Didn't matter what oddness his brainbox cooked up now because he swept it all away. All of it irrelevant in the heat of her mouth, the clinging pleasure of her fingertips at his nape, the sweet pain of his cock surging against his fall, against her arse.

He kissed her hard until he could not breathe, until the skin-rippling ache of needing more turned into something deeper, something patient, something that could wait. Then he kissed her softly, gently, taking his time, listening to the music of her ragged breathing. He'd made her that way. He grinned and rested his forehead against hers, let her find a rhythm once more, catch her breath as she clung, still, to him.

His mother had told him once, sometime in the year before her death, about the moment she'd known she loved his father. *It was the most ordinary moment. Every word we'd ever said seemed to be a prelude to it. One breath I guessed, and in the next, I knew. Couldn't say it then, though. Needed courage. It's easy to fall in love, Ben, but much harder to own it.*

Why that memory? Why *now*? His brainbox cooked up all manner of odd things today. Must be because his cock had stolen all his blood, and his brain had none to rely on for more a logical cogitation.

Air slowed between them as the rapid rise and fall of her chest gentled.

"Thank you for telling me," she said. "About everything. Your father and grandfather. The four Bs."

"Don't make me regret it. I don't want to hear those four Bs on the lips of every lady from here to London."

"No. Only on my lips." Her fingers floated up, gently touching those lips.

Hell.

He kissed her again, unable to stop himself, each nip and peck more needy than the last. "I don't know why, Lady P," he said between each one, "I can't stop kissing you."

"Don't stop."

He stole her mouth once more, thrusting his tongue deep, biting her bottom lip. "Won't."

She groaned. "We must."

"Make up your mind. No, I'll make it up for you." He continued kissing her.

"This... this feels like it could lead to more."

"Nothing more. Just kissing." Just that. Surely just that.

She wiggled in his arms, ducked out of his hold, scurried away from the chaise, away from him. "We should continue the tour of the house."

He stood with a sigh and an uncomfortably hard cock. Clearford likely would rather Ben not use such measures to achieve his means.

But kissing hadn't been about gathering information. He already possessed that; she'd told him the secret, finally, and it was harmless. Women talking about womanhood, preparing those younger, more inexperienced than them for marriage. She'd spilled her secret, and now he'd completed his task. That kiss... no ulterior motives. He'd merely enjoyed kissing her, having her perched atop him. Teasing her from such an enjoyably close distance. Her lips had moved with the hesitancy of a novice but also with the eager curiosity of a woman who had enjoyed his kisses as well.

They excelled at kissing each other.

"It's not really a tour, remember?" he said. "It's kissing. Was always supposed to be about kissing. Private corners and all that. You, attempting to distract me."

"Distract you?" A nervous laugh. "No. You are the one with unclear motives. You don't really want to kiss me. Remember?"

"Can't say I do remember any such nonsense. Those are your words, your accusations. And entirely contradicted by my actions." His unwise actions. Clearford would kill him, choose an internal organ, take aim, and hit the bullseye with a blade sharp enough to defend a sister's honor.

Lady Prudence smoothed her skirts and headed for the door. "Join me if you wish, but no more kisses."

"Just so, Lady P." He ambled after her.

So much changed. He knew what she hid from her brother now, for one. And that meant he no longer had to stay here. He could return to London today, tell all to Clearford, and return to his printshops.

But ink and paper would keep. Wouldn't spoil with a week spent in the country. Besides, someone needed to teach him how to manage a schedule. And Lady Prudence seemed an expert. Perhaps his purpose required staying longer, participating in an exchange—she could teach him how to run a business on time. God knew he needed such instruction. And he'd teach her how to...

No. He'd not finish that thought (even though the word kiss still rang between his ears).

Because she had the right of one thing—he wasn't the type of man to compromise a lady if he didn't intend to have her.

And he had no intention of claiming Lady Prudence.

The kisses? The mere natural result of having been pulled down onto a soft female body. What man wouldn't be roused by that? The kisses had been nothing more than release. That low undercurrent of wanting to drag her back into the protection of his body currently humming through him? Merely the aftereffects of a good kiss.

Good? Something more than that. Much more.

No matter. The nodcock notion would dissipate in time. His beard would grow back and this urge to kiss her again. And again and again. Would fade. He looked forward to the occurrence of both. Truly he did.

Chapter Ten

Three days of not kissing Mr. Bailey had not proved enough to banish the ghost of his lips from Prudence's own. And three days of waiting for him to knock on their locked doors and interrupt their conversations had worn her down.

Because the knocks never came.

He'd let them be. For three days. Dinner almost approaching on the third, and he'd not sought her out once, not strode into one of their gatherings to poke his long nose about and send them all spinning into a panic.

It should have been a lovely reprieve.

But Prudence sat in a too small chair in a dark corner of the library, legs swung over one arm, back resting against the other, and bit her thumbnail, tore it ragged with her teeth.

The book they'd been discussing lay forgotten on her lap.

She'd never bitten her fingernails before. But if she didn't do that, they'd notice what she'd been doing before—touching her lips, smoothing her fingertips over the remaining sensation of Mr. Bailey's kiss.

She'd been sitting just so in his lap that day, hadn't she? Yes, draped across him as she currently found herself draped across the chair.

What did he mean by staying? But by keeping his distance? He wanted their secrets, and he did not yet have them, so why had he not pushed and pried as he had upon his arrival? She'd seen him at dinner, of course, in the hour before and after when they all gathered for drinks and conversation. He'd been polite, civil.

Entirely unlike himself.

"What trickery is he up to now?" She let her head fall back with a groan.

A book snapped closed across the room. "You've been pouting for three days, Pru," Cora said. "Will you tell us, finally, what happened in the portrait gallery?"

Prudence swung her feet to the floor and hid her face in her hands. She'd not told them because she'd not wished them to know she'd been the one distracted, not him. And after those kisses, he seemed to have gotten what he wanted. And lost interest.

And that bothered her, turned her usually perfectly organized mind into utter chaos.

Three more books snapped shut outside the darkness of her palms. They waited. They'd been waiting.

And she needed them to help reorganize the chaos into order.

She let her hands fall to her lap. "What does it mean when a fellow kisses you, then ignores you?"

Cora cleared her throat. "I'd like to know, too, actually."

The three older women sighed as one, shared looks with sad eyes and raised brows.

"Very well," Lady Templeton said. "Listen up, girls."

"We'll reveal all." Lady Macintosh nodded with the slow, ponderous tilt of the chin downward gained only by years of experience churned into sage wisdom.

Silence.

Then Cora demanded, "Well?"

"If a man kisses you," Mrs. Garrison said.

"Then ignores you," Lady Templeton added.

"It means he disliked the kiss," Lady Macintosh finished. "Or..."

Lady Templeton inspected the cuff of her sleeve. "He liked the kiss so much it scared him."

"Or," Mrs. Garrison said, rising to her feet and marching across the room, "he's not thought about it at all, and it is something else entirely distracting him from what, to you and possibly to him, was a memorable occasion."

"So, none of you have the foggiest," Prudence said.

"That hardly matters." Mrs. Garrison stopped before her, standing tall as a general. "What matters is your answer to this question: Do *you* think it was a memorable occasion?"

Prudence looked away. The rug possessed a rather nice design. Floral, lovely color, thick—

"Do you?" Mrs. Garrison barked.

Prudence jumped, answered without thinking as if the bounce of her backside against the chair had sent the answer flying out of her mouth. "Yes!"

Mrs. Garrison smiled. "Excellent. Now, would you like it to happen again?"

"It should not happen again."

"Not what I asked, girl. Do you want Mr. Bailey to kiss you again?"

She closed her eyes, felt still, the sensation of his large body cradling hers on the sofa in the sunlight three days ago. "Yes, I would like that. But..." They waited a long time for her to continue speaking, and in the generosity of that silence, she found the right fear to wrangle forth. "I've... I've never wanted to kiss a man before." She winced. "I've read all the same books you have, but never felt... motivated by them until... until recently." Until she saw Cora and Norton in the garden. Until she felt Bailey's heavy arm around her, felt his breath hitch as he watched them, too. Only an odd little seedling of an idea then, but one that bloomed full flower as they'd traipsed the stairs together three days ago.

"What changed?" Cora asked.

"I've never felt as comfortable around a man as I do around Mr. Bailey. At first, I did not mind his presence because I knew he did not mean it. To court me, that is. He posed no true threat. And then I grew to understand him better. He's..." She remembered the way he'd scratched the marble dog's head. "Amusing."

Mrs. Garrison marched back to her chair and sat. "Is he now?"

"Yes, but it does not explain why I want Mr. Bailey to think I'm quite perfect, and why I fear he does not." That fear sat like a boulder in her belly. She hated it, wanted it gone. But how did one move boulders? Too big. Too eternal.

"Because his thighs are quite perfect in his breeches?" Lady Templeton asked.

"Because he possesses a perfect smile without that beard?" Mrs. Garrison offered.

"Or perhaps, Prudence," Cora said, her expression unreadable, "because you found his kiss quite perfect?"

Yes, yes, and yes, but not entirely. She stood. "I can stand the uncertainty no longer. He's no doubt attempting to drive me mad so I break down and give him what he wants."

"Marriage to you?" Cora asked, coming to her feet.

"Of course not!" Awakening attraction did not mean marriage. Surely not. If that were so, nearly every young man and woman in London would be engaged before the end of their first ball. Besides... "He has ulterior motives, remember?"

The ladies groaned.

"I thought we were making progress with the chit," Lady Templeton mumbled.

"Are you going to refuse to play his game?" Mrs. Garrison said. "Remain here and unaffected by his absence? A solid strategy, that. Remain behind your defenses."

"No." Prudence strode to the door. "I'm going to confront him."

"Ah." Four voices together, a doubting chorus.

No matter. She needed to see him again to ensure this buzzing feeling he'd put inside her was not fatal. Surely it would disappear once they spoke alone again, once she found more reason to believe he chased her only for nefarious reasons.

A knock on the door.

She'd been waiting for that knock for three days, and now she hardly knew what to do next.

Cora knew, though. She sailed to the door and unlocked it, opened it, revealed Mr. Bailey, grinning with his hands behind his back and his cheeks newly shaved.

His gaze found Prudence like a bird finds warmer climes in the winter, and he looked only at her as he spoke. "Lady Norton, I hope everyone is enjoying themselves this morning."

"Yes, thank you." Cora retook her seat, her gaze darting between the man and Prudence.

"I came to ask a favor of Lady Prudence," he said. "Norton has given me a drawing room to use as my own, for business matters and correspondence while I'm here. Will you join me?"

"She'll need a chaperone!" Lady Templeton's voice sounded like a cock's crow on a silent morning—sudden and much too loud.

"Of course," Bailey said.

But how would Prudence strangle answers from the man if one of her friends sat pesky in a corner? She looked to Cora for help. Any help.

Cora shook her head, then rolled her eyes and said, "Oh let us not worry about such matters. The room you are using is just down the hall. Norton asked my permission first. And if you keep the door open, we can all stay quite cozy as we are without a bit of impropriety."

Bless Cora straight to heaven.

"Excellent idea." Bailey strode across the room, grasped Prudence's wrist, and hauled her toward the door. Apparently, gentlemanly sentences did not extend to actions. He'd speak nicely, then haul her about.

She didn't fight it. She saved her energy for later battles and merely waved at Cora and the others as he swept her from the room.

Very few of his very large steps brought them to a small parlor Prudence had not yet visited. He left the door open as he dragged her toward a small writing desk near the windows across the room.

He released her only to pull a chair out from under the table. Then he plopped her into it and scooted it forward so hard she lurched backward, gripping tight to the arms to stay steady.

"Here." He waved a hand over the top of the desk. "What do you think?"

She blinked at the large ledger open before her, at the smaller notebooks piled beside it. "What is it I'm having thoughts on?" She turned to look behind her.

He paced back and forth, his hair falling over his forehead. "My books. For my papers. My notes. My calendar and schedule. Everything. I am attempting to buy out Kingtson and... other investors to be sole owner of one of our printshops, but I clearly cannot manage on my own." He growled, ruffled clawed fingers through his hair, stopped and faced her, though he would not hold her gaze. "I clearly need help. You'll help me?"

Oh. Oh no. The buzzing he'd settled into her skin when she'd sat in his lap... it dug deeper now, right into her heart, and that organ glowed, grew too large for her ribs to possibly contain. She swallowed, turned back to the paper. Better looking there than at him and his ruined hair and his face filled with doubt. And hope. Where was the grumpy beast from London? If only he'd return, she could resist him.

Blast it all.

"It took me three days to have all this delivered from London. Should I have asked your permission before bringing it all here?"

She shook her head, unable to speak, working through the lump in her throat to do so because if she did not speak, he would continue doing so, and she could not withstand those raindrops of his any longer. They melted her entirely. She'd be a puddle on the floor soon.

"No, no," she managed to say. "I'm happy to help. Delighted. This is just what I adore."

He strode to stand beside her, the warmth of his body like a fire-warmed bath, smelling of a bright summer morning—grass and sunshine. "You enjoy fixing the mistakes of clueless nodcocks?"

"I enjoy ordering chaos."

"Ah." He disappeared while she flipped to the front of the ledger, and when he returned, he dragged a chair with him. Once he'd placed it right beside her, he flung himself into it, propped an elbow on the table, and smiled at her. "Bloody good way of putting it. More complimentary to myself. Barely. But I'll take it."

She wanted to kiss him. More than she wanted to order the chaos he'd plunked before her like the most delectable of treats. But he wanted her brain, not her lips, and she could not think of a logical reason to do as she wished—climb from her chair to his and devour him with as much gusto as she'd set about organizing his life. More, even.

Odd, that.

Instead, she turned the pages slowly, taking in every number, every entry, acutely aware that he watched her, not the pages of his ledger.

"You must stop looking at me like that."

"Am I looking at you?"

She looked at him, her head tilted, the smallest furrow between her brows.

"I suppose I was. What should I look at instead?"

She pointed to a page. Ink spilled across in every direction, random numbers and names, dates and times. "What is this?"

He leaned over, straightened back up. "My schedule for May of this year."

"No." If so... the *horrors*.

"Yes. See?" He pointed at the scrawl of dots and lines. "That's the monthly meeting Kingston and I have with our investors."

She leaned so close to the book her nose almost touched. "At a coffeehouse?"

"We have few investors—your brother, Noble, sometimes a soldier fellow called Duncan—and we prefer comfort to formality."

She turned. Their knees almost touched, and the almost-touch scorched her through skirts and shift and stockings, but she ignored it. "Why do you not write such things in neat, ordered lines across the page? And in order by date? If this is an important item for your month, why is it cramped into a corner?"

He shrugged. "I dump everything in my brain down onto the page when I remember to. More often than not I'm distracted before I've written it all down."

"You need a secretary, Mr. Bailey."

"You'd be perfect for the job."

He wanted her. As his secretary. She wanted to delight in that. Somehow couldn't. Much.

"Thank you," she said. "It's not often a woman is praised or desired for her mind." Had that been his reason for courting her?

"My mother helped run our printshop. In Boston. Kept the books.

Bloody good at it, too. Was a great boon after she passed, having her notes all in perfect order. Not that it helped. I still ran the damn thing under."

She pulled another of his notebooks on top of the open ledger and flipped through it. "Is that why you've gone into the printing business? Because of your parents?"

"I..." He tapped the top of the table, each tap a drum beat in the silence stretched between them. "Yes. There's a shop. On Fleet Street." He stretched back in his chair and a grin stretched itself across his face. He seemed to see all the way to Fleet Street from Norton Hall. "It looks just like the one my parents owned. It's the first one I bought with Kingston and your brother. And it will be the first I run on my own. I'll rename it. So, there's a Bailey's Prints in London. To keep the memory of my parents alive. The door's just the shade of blue my mother loved most."

He'd woven his hands together across his abdomen, and he'd popped the front two chair legs off the floor so he balanced. She could not look away from the lean, stretched out length of him.

"You miss her," she said, pausing in the middle of turning a page.

He slipped a hand into his breast pocket, pulled out the miniature notebook with the stubby pencil stuffed between its pages, and tossed it onto the table. "Yes. My pa, too. Good people. They brought joy with them wherever they went."

"My parents, too. They loved each other terribly, and you could see it. I think... I think their love made everyone love more. Or want to love more. Were your parents in love?"

He chuckled. "My ma's the biggest reason my pa stayed in the States. He couldn't give up his heart, and she had a home there."

Her hands stilled on the notebooks, her vision blurring on the present, sharpening on the past, on golden days at her parents' side— the laughter, the full-heartedness. She swallowed a lump in her throat and said, "You know what it feels like, then."

"I do."

The present moment came careening back, sharp as a knife's edge. "Do you... are you waiting to marry for that? For love?"

"I don't know why I'm waiting. No one's felt right yet. I've not even really given it a th—" He let the front chair legs fall, and he snapped his mouth shut.

She jumped to her feet. "I knew it!"

"You tricky bit of baggage." He chuckled, pushing his palms into the table to stand. "You should let me finish my sentence."

She made for the door. He stalked after her. And before she could sail through it, he reached over her head, caught the door's corner, and slammed it shut. He pressed his body against it, blocking her entirely.

"You should let me finish my sentence, Lady P."

"I don't need to hear it."

"Until recently. I've not considered marriage much *until recently*."

She crossed her arms over her chest. "If that were true, you'd not have left me alone for three days after kissing me."

The corner of his lips tilted up. "Missed me, did you?"

"Let me pass."

"I don't think so. You're not done with my books."

She glanced at the cluttered desk behind her. The books were a temptation. He was a villain most likely, but that didn't mean she had to leave his life in chaos. She returned to the desk in what she hoped came across as dignified silence.

He opened the door, then returned to his seat. "I truly need your help."

"Clearly." She ignored him and opened each book, an easy plan formulating. "Now you must listen clearly to me, Mr. Bailey, or you'll be in another mess before the month is out."

"Yes, my lady."

She'd also ignore the tease in his tone. "This small one that fits in your pocket. It's where you dump your thoughts, everything in your head. Write it down immediately there. You must get into a habit, Mr. Bailey."

"Yes, my lady."

"And you must transfer the contents of this small notebook into the larger schedule which, I assume, remains in your office." She finally looked at him, found him entirely engrossed, frowning a bit, as if he worked to memorize her every word. "As soon as you enter your office, transfer it all. Put them in order by date, please. And in neat rows across the page. Do you understand?"

"Another habit?"

"Precisely. Every time you enter your office. Rows by date. And hire a secretary." She looked out the window. "I could see one hired for you. Or ask Andromeda to speak with Kingston about it. Those three things should straighten you out. But I'm afraid no one but yourself can help you when you're out and about. Oh!" She tapped on the miniature notebook, picked it up, and flipped it around backward, upside down. "Use the backside for writing down each day's important meetings and any pressing, timely matters you shouldn't forget. One side to dump your brain into and the other to serve as a reminder."

"Brilliant. Though I doubt I can live up to such a perfect system." His eyes were as open and blue as the summer skies outside the window. Not a hint of impish trickery in the corners of his kissable lips, though she could not help but wonder if that's what his compliments were—manipulations. Nothing he did made sense. Because...

Because a man could not truly want her. Plain, boring Prudence. He'd kissed her, brought her his books, asked her advice, called her brilliant... all of it added up to make her feel wanted.

Trickery or...?

"Prove it to me, Mr. Bailey," she said, folding her hands together on top of the books.

"Prove I'm going to muck up your system?"

"No. Prove you are courting me for me."

Even behind the knot of his cravat, she could see his Adam's apple bob. A swallow of indecision, hesitancy. She'd not truly wished to be right.

The paper beneath her palms was cool as she flattened her hands against it and pushed to standing. But the air around her warm as she made for the door.

A light tug stilled her, and she turned to find Mr. Bailey just behind her, a head and a half taller than her, something unreadable in his eyes. He pinched her skirts between thumb and forefinger. That pinch became a fist as he crumpled her skirts in his hand to pull her closer.

She swayed into the heat of his body as he bent his tall form around her, his gaze flicking to her lips.

He lowered. He stopped. Inches from her. "I can't kiss you again. Already kissed you too many times. Your brother's Guide says—"

"Curse the Guide. Toss it into the lake. Fling it into a bonfire. Kiss me or I'll know, Mr. Bailey. Kiss me or—"

"I-I-I can't."

She wrapped her hand around the one still clutched in her skirts, and one finger at a time, she unballed his fist until he had nothing to cling to and his hand dropped heavy to his side.

"I know, Mr. Bailey." She left him but stopped in the door frame, spoke without looking back at him. "I've always known." The kisses from three days ago tricks to acquire... something. And now that he had it, or thought he did, no need for kisses. Not any longer.

There existed few reasons a man would court her, and love or something like it was not one.

Chapter Eleven

Ben's eyes snapped open. Ledgers? *Ledgers?* Usually, he felt no hurry to wake from a dream of a lovely lady's naked limbs wrapped around his waist, of her body unclothed and spread before him. But this lady's body had been spread naked across a pile of ledgers with straight, even rows inked on them. And this lady's face had worn Lady Prudence's signature doubting expression—lips curled to one side, a single brow raised, sharp eyes digging holes into that which she doubted. And her hair, unbound and wrapped round Ben's hand had been the silkiest dark-blonde he'd ever felt. Ropes to bind a man, body and soul.

And... hell...

He closed his eyes and grabbed his cock and imagined ledgers. With Lady Prudence naked atop them. Because apparently his sleeping self knew a truth—well-organized schedules aroused him.

He grunted, his body growing harder as he pumped. Lady Prudence aroused him, not the ledgers. But they rather added to everything that made her up. He wanted to disarrange her schedule as she'd disarranged his fantasies, wanted to make her prim little mouth scream his name and put off being on time for more time with him.

He stroked harder, faster.

Yesterday, he'd wanted to do just this—throw her across the table, throw her skirts above her hips, and throw good sense to the wind. Press her into the open books he'd spread out for her, his open and chaotic life, and have his way with her just as she'd had her way with his system. Lack of one. He'd have kissed her breathless, made her moan, then flipped her so her small arse draped across the desk edge. Then she'd wrinkle the ledger pages in her fists as he thrust into her.

"Fuck," he hissed as he bucked into his hand. He wanted to fuck her. Just like that, on top of the ledgers he couldn't keep straight for the life of him.

As he came, so too did a realization. He'd never had such a mundane fantasy about a woman. Nor such an arousing one.

He groaned and rolled over, shoving his face into the pillow as he cleaned himself with the sheet. Apologies to the maids.

Ledgers and Lady Prudence. What in hell was happening to him? He leapt out of bed and crossed the room to view himself in the looking glass. Had he cut away his good sense with his beard?

He should return to London. If he stayed here, he'd have to keep pretending with Lady Prudence. She already suspected, especially after yesterday. She'd asked him to prove his sincerity. He'd been unable to.

He'd wanted to, though. Toss her down across that desk and—

That's why he should leave.

He *would* leave. He had her suggestions for his schedule. He'd hire a secretary. Now he could be done with her.

Because if he stayed, he might dive happily past the boundaries of gentlemanly behavior with that woman. And if there was one thing Ben Bailey didn't do, it was compromising a woman without intention to marry her. And he couldn't marry her. Not only did he not... want... to... Hell! Each word as difficult to call into existence as summoning a fairy. In his mind, they seemed like stage props, flimsy, poorly painted, and glaringly false in the gaudy light of the gas lamps lining a stage.

He could see the spare beams of wood used to prop those words up, but... they were true. They had to be because if they were paper lies, he'd muddled his way into a deep-as-the-Thames pile of horse shit.

He was lying to her.

No. He'd been lying to her. Now...

Hell.

He'd leave tomorrow.

The looking glass became a window, black as night, nothing but a void beyond it. He'd followed her about for so long now, he felt a bit... lost. Even when he'd been lurking reluctantly around the edges of her gaggle of suitors, he'd been watching her. She'd become his purpose. In a way. Similar to his printshop. And leaving felt like giving up.

He shook his head. Not giving up! Success. He'd completed this task, after all. Time to move on.

From observing her and from, had to admit it, lusting after her.

When had this attraction started? He'd been "courting" her for over a year, but only during the London Season. If he winnowed it down to just that timeframe, only a handful of months. Had it started three days ago in the portrait gallery? No. He'd been ready for it to go further then, glad of it.

To the night in the garden, watching Lord and Lady Norton tear at one another like desperate lovers. Had given him ideas. Not immediately. No. But her scent as she'd watched behind him had twisted together with the idea of midnight garden trysts in his dull brain until it had become him and her tearing at one another beneath the stars. How many times had he suffered through that dream since then? Too many to count, each one making him wake harder in the morning, forcing him to take his cock in hand to find relief.

Until the garden had been replaced with blasted ledgers. Of all damn things.

Sigh.

He needed to write to his grandfather. He'd not sent an epistle since he'd arrived. The old man would worry. Ben donned a clean pair of breeches, sat at the writing desk in the corner, dipped a pen in the inkwell, and tried to use his most legible hand to compose the letter.

Grandfather,

Have I told you about Lady P? Practical P? Pretty P, too, if I'm being honest. I only started courting her because her brother asked me to. I suppose the trouble is that she's an odd sort of woman. Doesn't want to marry. Doesn't seem to think I mean it. Of course, I didn't mean it. I don't mean it. I'm here for the brother's sake. And for mine. We have a deal—an exchange.

But last year when all those fools abandoned Pleasant P because of her sister's scandal, I felt a bit protective. Too protective, likely. And when this other fellow by the name of Norton showed up to show his support for her, too, I wanted to ram my fist into his face. What the devil does that mean? I hear my mama's voice in my head telling me what it means. One day you haven't a clue, and the next you know. *But that can't be it. But a few days ago, when she said she liked my beard, didn't mind my ink stains... I remembered how Mama used to say that. Punctual P also likes me like* this. *You should see me, Grandfather. All kitted out like a gentleman. You'd love it. I don't hate it. Not when she... anyway.*

I'm lost without a compass. No idea where I am or where to go. Not asking for help. Merely thought you'd find it diverting.

Your grandson,

Ben

He read it through, shook his head. Unorganized as usual. He'd not send it. Would give Grandpapa ideas to cling to, to beat Ben about the head with. So, Ben shoved the paper to the side and pulled up another. He dipped his pen in the inkwell and set it to paper. Much shorter, this one, much more to the point. Much safer, too.

Then he rang for his valet. He had work to do.

———※———

Prudence's eyes snapped open. Beard? And *hair?* Long as it had been and escaping a queue. But Ben Bailey the same as he was now in every other way—nicely dressed in fitted clothes and making amusing quips instead of glaring. What an odd dream to wake to. And what an odd feeling it had roused in her body. The same feeling, in fact, as he'd roused in her before—hot and restless. The sheets felt like chains on her legs, and she kicked at them. The sun slanting through the window and peeking in at her between the bed curtains felt like molten fire. Unsupportable. She rolled away from the heat, but it came with her, located as it seemed to be at the very core of her body.

And he'd not even had to touch her to make her that way. He'd merely had to appear in her early morning dream, bearded and, impossible to deny, beautiful. Also impossible to deny—she'd been right. He bore no interest in her. She'd asked him to prove himself yesterday. He'd declined to do so. Confirmation, that. Whatever she'd meant to him, she no longer meant it.

She groaned, shoved her face into her pillow, and flailed her legs. Why could she not remove the scoundrel from her mind? He did not truly care for her, yet he'd been in her dream, kissing her, touching her in places she knew men touched women, proving to her what he refused to prove yesterday. That he wanted her.

She'd never been touched where Dream Mr. Bailey had touched her before, had never felt that place between her legs so... alive and aching as it was now.

Needy. The only word for it. She slipped her hand between the bed and her body and rubbed there, and oh—the ache did not go away. It increased. She bit her lip, but that little bite of pain did nothing to release the need, to cover it. And the image of Mr. Bailey would not dissipate as all dreams should. It stayed—beard, queue, tight-fitting buckskins, a midnight garden, and Prudence pressed against a tree as Cora had been.

Mr. Bailey growled into her ear. Lovely words about ledgers and being his secretary, and oh they should not make her want to replace her own hand with his, but they *did*. She flopped over onto her back and arched into her own hand, needing something harder, weightier than her hand at her middle, growling because she did not have it. The arousal Mr. Bailey had blazed into her body would not dissipate but would not burn hotter either, and frustration growled in her throat.

She imagined him pressing his knee between her legs, pinning her hands above her head against the rough bark of the tree, and the fires inside her leapt higher.

"Ben," she groaned, her fingers focusing on a particularly buzzing bit of herself. Was that what the ladies had talked about? The little pearl some men could not find? Had no idea what to do with it, but that could—oh yes, she saw what it could do. As she pressed her thumb into it, a squeak popped out from between her lips. She slammed her eyes more tightly closed, imagined Ben hiking her skirts above her hips, finding that particular spot with his fingers.

And imagining his hand there, big and gloveless, ink-stained and rough... it tore a scream from her, rippled sensation like she'd never felt across her skin, turned her bones to liquid. As her body melted heavy into the mattress, and her hand fell heavy to her side to tangle in the sweaty blankets there, she managed to whisper, "Ben." And in the fantasy she'd weaved behind closed eyes, the dream Ben grinned.

She sat bolt upright, eyes going wide.

What... had she... heavens. *Heavens*.

She flew out of the bed and tore into her trunk. Dressed. She must dress for the day and put herself to rights. What time was it? She glanced at the sky. Oh no. She'd slept too late. The ladies might already be gathered on the lawn.

See what this unhealthy preoccupation with Mr. Bailey had gained her—a disorganized schedule, an inability to keep to times. Mr. Bailey's lack of punctuality was catching.

She called for her maid and was soon dressed and coiffed well enough, and she found Cora and the others assembled on the lawn. At least they'd kept to her schedule.

Unlike Prudence. Yet she managed a smile as she greeted them. "Terribly sorry for being late. I overslept."

They stared at her as if she'd just said she'd had to pluck a chick for the cook, but then they shrugged and turned back to what they'd been doing before she'd bounced in with too much gaiety in her voice.

Mrs. Garrison notched an arrow to her bow and took aim as the sun cooked them all. A bead of sweat ran down Prudence's brow, and she stripped her gloves off, light lace though they were, and tossed them to the grass.

"It's sweltering," she groaned. Or perhaps that was the remnants of the heat Dream Mr. Bailey had gifted her while abed.

Cora snorted. "You were hot before you arrived. Cheeks red as berries. What kept you abed this morning? Are you ill?"

"N-no. Merely taking advantage of the slower country pace."

Lady Templeton snorted. "You've set a bruising pace for us, Prudence. Every hour a new activity. But you yourself late. Someone feel her forehead."

The back of Lady Macintosh's hand slapped against the top of Prudence's head, and she beat it away.

"I'm perfectly well." But my, her cheeks were hot.

"You're perfectly good at organizing," Lady Macintosh said, abandoning her pursuit of Prudence's forehead. "This house party has been a splendid idea. It is nice to speak as we please and when we please. I think this house party will be a success in the future as well, when we invite others."

"If we can keep Lord Norton from inviting unexpected guests." Mrs. Garrison notched another arrow. The first had hit the bullseye, and she stuck her tongue out the corner of her mouth. "I'm going to split that one." She didn't, but the arrow *thunked* into place right next to the first in the middle of the bullseye. "Rats."

Lady Macintosh slipped an arrow from a sheath and eyed it. "Speaking of arrows and speaking freely... what *size* do you all prefer?"

"Size?" Cora shook her head.

Lady Macintosh held the arrow upright and wrapped her hand around it, scooted her hand closer to the tip. "Smaller or"—she moved her hand closer to the bottom—"larger?"

"Girth is more important, my dear," Lady Templeton said. "That's my stance."

Lady Macintosh repositioned her hand on the arrow. "This is just about the size of Lord Macintosh."

"Aroused or not?" Lady Templeton asked.

"Not."

Lady Templeton whistled. "He's an inch or more on Lord Templeton. But Fitz does know what to do with what he's got."

Cora shook her head still. "I'm entirely muddled."

"Gherkins," Prudence whispered. "Shafts, members."

"Oh! Yes, of course. I tend toward the more metaphorical in my poetry. Size does not matter unless we're speaking of the heart, the soul."

Lady Macintosh sighed and picked up a bow. "And that is why we adore your poetry. When will you treat us next?"

"Tomorrow, I think. But I was wondering if we might do something different from the usual. I'm working on something new, and it calls for open skies. Sunlight. Not shadows and darkness."

"Interesting." Mrs. Garrison hummed as she lowered into a wicker seat. "I approve. What shall it be, then?"

"I'd like to recite something out on the lake," Cora said. "We can take the rowboats out."

Rowboats and lakes. Difficult to control.

"I'm not sure I approve." Prudence studied the high walls of the house as if she could see the lake on the other side of it. "Everyone will be able to see us out there in the boats. They'll wonder what we're doing. And what if there is bad weather or one of us topple in or—"

"It will be fine," Cora said. "Norton took me out in a boat just yesterday while everyone was resting in the afternoon. Perfectly safe."

"Did he now?" Lady Templeton leaned closer to Cora, studied her face with both eyebrows raised. "Enjoying his company better than before?"

Cora waved away the lady's question. "He asked. I saw no reason to tell him no."

"And now you wish to recite poems in rowboats?"

"Rowboats have a certain romantic quality," Cora said.

"An unpredictable quality," Prudence grumbled.

"Are all rowboats romantic," Mrs. Garrison asked, "or just one particular rowboat ride with one particular husband?"

Cora grabbed a bow and arrow, marched to the stand before the target set up across the grass. She notched, aimed, let the arrow fly, and missed the target entirely. Clearly Prudence had spent too much time worrying about Mr. Bailey over the last few days. She'd come here to help her friend, and her friend remained unhappy.

"Lady Prudence?" a voice called from nearby, a man's voice.

She looked over her shoulder. The butler approached, a square of paper held lightly between his pristine gloves.

"Yes?" she asked.

"This is for you." He held out the paper.

She took it, and he left, and she felt the weight of four gazes heavy on her. She dared not look up. She recognized the scrawl across the front. From the letters almost a fortnight ago. From the ledgers yesterday.

"It's from Mr. Bailey."

"What could he have to write you about?" Cora asked, standing beside her and peering over her shoulder at the square of white burning in Prudence's fingers. "He can seek you out with ease."

"I've no idea." She slipped the note into her pocket.

"You're not going to read it?" Lady Templeton now stood on her other side.

"Later. When I'm alone."

"Unfair," Lady Macintosh said from behind her left shoulder. "What is it you two were up to yesterday?"

Prudence sighed, a rather dreamy sounding thing. "Organizing."

"The way you say that"—Lady Macintosh shook her head—"as if you enjoyed it."

"I did," Prudence snapped. "I do enjoy it, and Mr. Bailey recognized that, sought out my help."

"Ah." Lady Templeton chuckled. "You're beginning to like him. Whether he's courting you or not, he's certainly succeeding."

Cora wrapped her hand around Prudence's upper arm. "I know you were feeling more comfortable with him, but... is Lady Templeton correct? Do you hold a *tendre* for him?"

"I... No. I... well... perhaps but..." She growled, pulled her arm from her friend's grip, and headed for the gardens. When her friends' voices were nothing but lilting melodies on the wind, she sought out the shade of a tree in bloom and leaned against its trunk.

She rubbed her thumb once over her name in stark black ink and messy lines before taking a deep inhalation and opening the letter. No more than a note, really, short, but shattering.

Lady Prudence,

I am leaving tomorrow afternoon. As I came here with the express purpose of seeing you, I thought I should tell you first. Business draws me away. I've

much to do today to prepare for my departure and do not know if I shall see you at dinner. I shall implement your suggestions and, perhaps, see you in London.
   BB

Sunlight slanting through the branches above threw wiry shadows across the paper, across his farewell. Sunlight or shadow. Which was he? Which his intentions? She knew that now. He may appear a sunbeam dressed to advantage, but he belonged to the shadows, possessed his own reasons for pursuing her. And something in the last week had changed that, changed everything.

He no longer felt compelled to pursue her.

Yet she... curse it all, she rather wished he still did. Mr. Bailey was a rugged scoundrel and not a charming gentleman with a pure heart. But another part of her, as new as Mr. Bailey's short hair, viewed him with a different understanding.

He missed his parents.

He asked women for help.

He made her laugh.

Heaven help her, she might have begun to like the man a little more than she'd ever thought possible. She'd not allocated time for falling in love, but Mr. Bailey had never seemed to care for schedules, and he'd scrambled the ledger of her heart into utter chaos.

Chapter Twelve

Bloody storms. Ben hated them. And there raged one on the far edges of the sky. On every edge of the sky, it seemed, threatening the end of the road he had planned to travel down in mere minutes as well as half of Norton's estate, the lawn, the garden, the lake. Threatening the calm inside, too.

He tugged at this cravat. Too tight. Too bloody tight. Especially now he'd tangled it.

"Hell." He spat the word. Where was Lady Prudence? She could set the linen right again. He remembered that well, the flirtation of her fingers against his skin as she'd tidied his neckcloth his first day here. The spark of her touch, the...

Or his valet could. Yes, the valet could tidy the damn cravat. The right man for the job. Not Lady P.

"Norton!" he cried out, stomping down the stairs. "Norton!"

"In here. Stop yelling!" Norton yelled.

Ben followed the voice to Norton's study. He sat at his desk, his back to a large window, and beyond the window gray clouds rolling in.

"Where are the ladies, Norton?"

Norton looked up from a pile of papers, shrugged. "I try to leave them alone as much as can be. It's what they want."

"Yes, but have you noticed the sky? These particular ladies could very well be holding rods to the heavens, inviting lightning. Where are they?"

Norton looked over his shoulder. "Oh. I doubt they're tempting lightning, Bailey. Surely, they're cozed up in the library."

Ben stomped toward the door.

"But Cora did say something about the lake today."

Midstride through the doorway, Ben snapped back toward the viscount. "The lake?"

Norton had dropped his attention back to the papers, and he spoke without looking up. "Hm. Yes. She wanted to take out several boats at once. But surely, they've not gone out now." He glanced over his shoulder again.

"Yes, surely." Ben left Norton and found the library quickly enough. The door handle gave way easily beneath his hand. "Where the hell...?" He stormed down the hall, tried the parlor where the ladies often gathered, whispering behind closed doors. Not closed today. Also empty. He stepped out into the garden beyond the double doors, and the day greeted him with the distinct sound of thunder rumbling a warning across the gray sky.

"Hell." Surely, they had not gone out to the lake. But the storm had risen so suddenly. Nowhere in sight one moment, gathering with dark speed the next. They could have set off in sunshine only to find themselves trapped in a storm later.

Just as he had been.

A shiver crept down his spine, and he took an involuntary step back toward the house. Maybe only half a step, and from instinct only, because he soon forced his body to move in the other direction, toward the lake, toward danger, and toward Prudence.

The sky seemed to darken as he ran, the previously thick clouds, differentiated by curved, overlapping shadows coalescing into a large sheet of gray, promising rain. Torrents of it. On the horizon he ran toward, lightning flashed—a single bolt, magnificent, bright, and brutal. His legs pumped faster, and he crested a small hill, saw the lake, saw the three boats gathered at its middle. A woman with black hair—

Lady Norton—stood alone in one, her arms outstretched as if beckoning someone on the shore. The four other women occupied the remaining two boats.

The winds whipped harder, chopping across water that had been smooth as glass the day before.

He skidded to a stop just at the water's edge, the toes of his boots kicking up the roughly lapping water there.

He cupped his hands around his mouth. "Prudence!"

Five heads swung toward him.

"Prudence, return to shore right now or—"

Thunder rolled loud and long, and Lady Norton flinched, wobbled.

"Hell." Ben tore off his boots. "No one move!" he yelled, flinging the last boot to the dirt behind him and diving in. The water was warmer than a winter ocean, and he knew enough to know the difference. He almost stopped swimming to search his pockets. What would he lose this time? Nothing as dear as before, no mother's ring, no father's work. He kept swimming. Whatever he lost, worth it.

Each stroke and kick pushed him closer to the boats. Bloody big lake. Why had they gone out so far? What needed hiding so badly? A bit of education? He popped up his head to check the distance, found the boats, and corrected his angle just a bit, swam faster, dragged the water harder, his lungs burning. But if she fell, Prudence's skirts would weigh heavy as an anvil, would tangle her limbs, and marry her to the lake floor.

He swam faster.

And rammed his hand into something hard. The boat. One of them. Gasping for air and ignoring the ringing in his knuckles, he popped above the surface, treading water. Searching, counting. The three older ladies, Lady Norton... where...? There, peering at him with wide, blinking eyes from the farthest boat—Prudence.

"What are you doing?" she asked.

Mrs. Garrison glared. "Get out of the water, Mr. Bailey. Can't you see the storm?"

He looked to Lady Norton. "I saw you fall in. I was... coming to..."

"Save me?" Lady Norton provided. "As you see I did not fall."

He did see. And wanted to sink to the bottom of the lake. Stay there.

Thunder rumbled closer, and the women swung around to face it.

"Get swimming, boy," Mrs. Garrison barked. She sat up straight and pointed for the dock and the boathouse. "Ships for harbor, ladies."

They began to row, and Ben took slower strokes toward the boathouse than he had toward the boats earlier. He remained below the surface of the lake as much as possible, bobbing to the surface to let the rowboats pull beneath the darkness of the arched boathouse overhang and slot themselves between the narrow docks. He swam in behind them once the women had crawled out of them, and he could not pull himself dripping, sopping wet, up onto the dock fast enough. The ladies secured the boats, and he pulled sopping linen off his skin.

"It's about to rain," Lady Templeton said. "Should we stay here until—"

"No." Cora marched toward the door at the back of the boathouse. "I'm going to run to the house." She bolted into the gray-skied afternoon.

The ladies took off after her, and the boathouse door slammed closed behind them.

But Prudence remained at his side. She helped peel him out of his jacket and toss it to the dock as he yanked at his cravat, unwound it, freed his throat for breathing.

She mumbled all the while her hands flitted about his person. "What were you thinking? Silly man. To throw yourself into a lake with a storm coming." She *tsked*. "You know better. I'm certain you do. You're trembling. Why haven't you left yet? I thought you'd be on your way back to London by now."

The sky flashed yellow.

He flinched, closing his eyes. "I don't travel during storms."

Thunder roared beyond the arched brick portal to the water beyond.

"But you swim during them?" She placed her fists on her hips.

The sky opened up, and a sheet of rain fell to earth like a guillotine blade, then a whip of wild wind blew it sideways, beneath the arch, soaking them instantly. Soaking *her*. He was already quite waterlogged.

He grabbed her arm and dragged her farther into the boathouse. She came willingly, and when they reached the deep shadows at the back, she gasped, wiping water from her face, pushing plastered tendrils of hair out of her eyes.

"We will have to wait until it passes." She shrugged out of her spencer. Tried to. Glued to her skin, it would not budge, and without thought, he stood before her, pulling the collar of the garment away from her collar bone.

She froze, and he slowly peeled one sleeve off her arm, revealing a damp puff of a sleeve at her shoulder, spotted dark from where the rain had soaked through the spencer. The other. He must free it, focus on freeing it, or do something he shouldn't.

A boom of thunder shook the roof.

He froze and swallowed. "Damn fool thing going out on the lake."

"It was sunny." Her voice a shiver.

"Could have been killed."

"We were fine. Why did you swim after us?"

"I should toss you over my knee." He slipped her sleeve well off her shoulder.

"You will do no such thing. Are you scared of storms?"

"And teach you how to better behave." The wet material clung to her elbow.

"You're not listening to me." She jerked the spencer out of his hand and whirled away from him.

Thunder boomed, and the archway glowed yellow for a blinding moment. The boats rocked on choppy water in their narrow ports.

And before the chaos ended, he held her in his arms.

As the next bolt of lightning split the sky, he kissed her.

Hard at first, his hands claiming the back of her head, tangling with her wet locks, holding her close, holding her so she could not leave. She breathed into the kiss, filling him with life. Her breath warm, warming him.

An unexpected chill trembled through the air. The storm had brought with it a biting wind.

"You're shivering." She spoke against his lips. "Mr. Bailey, you're shivering. Sit." She tugged at him, and his legs gave way. His arse met something, a bench or box. Who the hell knew?

Another boom of thunder crashed down onto the roof.

Tossed him overboard, dropped him heavy as a stone into the Atlantic. He clawed, he reached, he ached for the surface, for air, and when he popped above the freezing surface and into the buzzing air, he held on to the only solid bit of anything he could find. A board, splintered and tossed about like himself.

No. Not a board this time.

Prudence, clinging to him as he'd clung all those years ago. Her arms were chains of comfort around him, her lips moving swiftly and softly at his ear, whispering, "Ben, Ben, where have you gone? You're safe. We're safe, Ben." Her hands smoothed through his hair, brushed up and down his spine. "You're too cold." She left him.

He grabbed for her but caught only air.

She returned so quickly, though, with something warm she wrapped around his shoulders before climbing atop his lap and resting her little head on his shoulder. The sound she made next to his heart echoed the shushing of the ocean on a calm day, and soon the Atlantic drained away, and the storm outside quieted to nothing but steady, hard rain. And when she kissed the tip of his chin, then wrapped her arms around his neck to kiss him gently on the lips, he returned fully, called back to himself by Prudence, persistent and perfect.

One moment you had no idea.

The next moment you knew.

Irrevocably.

"Your heart is no longer racing. That is good." She patted his chest, laid her cheek against it.

Moving for the first time of his own accord in God only knew how many minutes, he grasped the edges of the blanket she'd wrapped round him and gathered her into it, rested his cheek on the top of her head. Highly irregular for a man to hold a woman he wasn't wed to like this, alone. But how could he care with Prudence cradled in his arms, the weight of her body relieving his panic as nothing else could? If she would let him, he'd hold her forever.

"I'm feeling quite foolish," he grumbled.

"You were scared. But I hear *you* in your voice once more. Quite good. Do you have a fear of storms?"

He swallowed, closed his eyes. "I fell overboard during a storm when I crossed the Atlantic. Thought I was going to die. Was able to find something to hold on to, a board tossed over with me. And I rode the waves until it all ended, and the sailors fished me out." Terrified the entire time. Convinced that, until the water calmed and the sun shone through the clouds, he'd not enjoy a next breath.

"Didn't they try to save you sooner? The others on the ship?"

"Why would they? More pressing matters to tend to."

"What about those you traveled with?"

"I was alone. I had nothing but a few clothes in a trunk aboard the ship. I'd lost everything else in Boston trying to keep the shop in business. Had a few things in my pockets when I fell overboard, but I lost those, too. Nothing valuable to anyone but me."

"But very valuable to you, I'd wager. And yet today, you jumped in to save me. When I did not need saving."

"I thought you did. Feared you did." Had been willing to lose more so he didn't lose her.

"I'm perfectly well." She straightened away from his chest, but he did not let her pull out of his lap. "See? Not even a scratch."

"Why were you out there?" He stroked his fingertips up and down her neck, hoping she might settle herself against his chest once more.

She did not, but she did not leave, either. "Cora. She wished to go out. Truthfully"—her gaze fluttered away from his, settled onto her lap —"I saw the dark edges of the sky. I wondered if there might be unhappy weather. But... Cora seemed so bright about going... boating. I even revised my schedule to make it happen."

"That is serious. You alerted everyone promptly, I hope."

She swatted his chest, swallowed hard, dared to meet his gaze once more. "It's my fault she's miserable, and I'll do anything to make it better for her."

"That old tune? I thought you'd recovered from such misplaced guilt."

"Not misplaced." Quiet words, their almost silent nature giving way to the truth of their weight. So damn heavy.

He held the blanket round them with one hand and used the other to tilt her chin up. "Tell me? When did *you* fall into the ocean?" Would she understand his question, his true meaning?

She gave a rough huff of a laugh. "Yes, it felt like that. Tossed overboard, sinking, floating in darkness. Terrified." She leaned her forehead against his chest, and her breath warmed the sodden linen separating his skin from her lips. "The day my parents died I wouldn't let them leave. They were traveling to Clearford Castle for something or other. But I kept pestering my mother. I wanted her to bring a particular bonnet back to London for me. Then a shawl I'd left in the country. Then a ribbon. Then stockings. The list grew every time they set foot out the door. They were a good half an hour off schedule by the time I was done."

"Practical Prudence concerned with such frippery?"

She nodded, the tiniest thing. "I thought I needed it. Lottie had every man in London salivating. A diamond. And Andromeda promised to be the same in her own quieter way. I would be hoisted upon the marriage mart next, but I knew I would not take. I needed every bit of frippery as you call it at my disposal. Silliness. I was only seventeen, and my mother was not entirely set on my coming out at eighteen. She didn't think me quite ready. I was not. I know now."

He stroked her hair, let her lapse into silence as long as she pleased while the rain roared a song against the boathouse roof.

"If they had passed through that particular intersection half an hour sooner, as they should have done, the mail coach would not have slammed into them."

"No, Prudence—"

"Yes, Mr. Bailey." She straightened, squared her shoulders, then stood. "Schedules must be maintained or... or we all fall overboard. And the water is dark. And it is cold. And there is no bottom. Cora is floating right now, and I'll not let her drown. Do you understand?"

He stood, letting the blanket fall to the bench he'd been sitting on, understanding rising with him. "Yes, Prudence."

"Lady Prudence, Mr. Bailey." She wrapped her arms around her body, hugging herself tight.

He lifted her chin, found her eyes, more green than blue in the gray light. "Time to call me Ben, love." He kissed her.

He kissed her because she was trembling, and he could warm her.

He kissed her because she was alive, and he must celebrate that.

He kissed her because she hurt, and he could soothe her.

He kissed her.

And he didn't stop.

Chapter Thirteen

Her back hit the wall, but she did not feel the rumble of the blow through her body. Every ounce of her attention had been diverted to her lips. His lips. That meeting place between them which had become hot and wet and urgent.

A growl of thunder ripped the air around them. Or had the growl come from his throat as he licked a droplet of water from her neck? His tongue on her—like lightning through her body. The sky glowed yellow as her eyelids fluttered closed on a moan, and he parted her legs with a knee. A rough lift that pinned her better than before as his hands caught up her wrists and snapped them together against the wall above her head. He pressed his thigh—hard with muscle— against her very center, and as she had done in her dreams, she rolled her hips to meet that thrust, heard the rumble of desire in her own throat.

Dangerous, this. Entirely nonsensical. This man did not want her.

But he did. No more denying it.

Now, fogged in the memories of past pains, he sought her for comfort. She needed comfort, too, had never guessed *this* could offer it. His lips everywhere, his hold rough, his fingers seeking ways past the barrier of her damp bodice.

"Have you been hiding all this while?" His words hot against her ear. "Simply so I can find you?"

What did that mean? Her brain could not wrap round the question, not with him touching and kissing, not with the world shaking their small, dark shelter.

He kissed her temple. "Hiding your smile and your laugh, your courage and your well-organized mind." He kissed the tip of her nose. "Hiding, too, how much you like kissing. I've found you now. Apologies it took so long. You were right before me, after all. But what shall I do with you? Now that I've seen. Now that I know." He kissed her lips then, and she opened for him, savoring the invasion of his tongue into her mouth, pulling down her hands, reaching for him, finding his wet waistcoat. She balled her fists into it and pulled him closer, pulling the meat of his thigh tighter against her center. Pure pleasure made her gasp.

And the gasp made him snap. His hand that had pinned hers above her head moved down, ripping the shoulder of her gown down her arm, freeing her breast, and his hips rolled against her belly.

So many new sensations. The air on her nipple, then his hand there, squeezing, teasing. Then his lips and tongue, tasting until she tangled both her hands in his hair and held on because her legs had started the long process of simply giving up the day he'd arrive at Norton Hall, and now they finally, entirely, had. Only his leg thrust between her legs, his hands on her, and her hands in his hair kept her upright.

His entire body, too, molding itself to hers as her wet skirts had molded to her legs. As if no muslin or silk separated them. Only her body falling into his and his body, large and hard, keeping her safe.

A boom of thunder.

It unleashed her. Finding her strength in a flash of lightning, she surged up on tiptoe and bruised his lips with her own, tore at his bottom lip with wanting teeth, and ripped one hand from his hair to touch him everywhere she could reach. The strong column of his neck, the broad planes of his linen-plastered shoulders, the crisp hair evident between the white V of his undone shirt. Down his torso she explored, across the sharp ridges of his abdomen to the heavy line of wool at his waist. To the bulge there, long and hard. The storm had banished all thought, all doubt, so she palmed it, wanting to take its measure, and his hips bucked, pinning her hard against the wall once more.

Ah. The gherkin. No, no. She could no longer use that phrase. Needed something less silly now.

"Lady P," he choked out. "Not. There."

"Does it hurt? I was under the impression it felt rather nice when—"

"Yes. Feels bloody perfect." His voice like gravel. "Those lessons. About intimacy. With the matrons. Thank God for them. Do as you please."

She flattened her palm over him, then squeezed.

"Hell," he choked out. "I'm yours." The last two words barely audible as his head fell back on his neck. Still, he held her one hand against the wall, his strong fingers a manacle for her wrist. But the biting pain of bone and brick brought pleasure. Pleasure too where his other hand caressed her breast, teased her nipple.

Did she give it back in equal measure? She rubbed her palm up and down his member. Shaft? That was the wrong word, certainly. Much thicker than an arrow shaft. And quite larger than the sizes the ladies had demonstrated on that object the day before. She moved her hand up and down as his thumb caressed back and forth over her nipple, as his hand squeezed gently.

She moaned, tried to focus. Difficult with the room rocking about them, the boats banging against the hard edges of the docks. The *shush* of rain, the growl of thunder, the slosh of water—every sound narrowing the world, blurring it until everything but they two ceased to exist.

"What... what do you call it?" she managed to say.

"Call what?" He sounded as if he answered from another universe, as if speaking had never been more difficult.

"Your"—she squeezed—"*this?*"

"Cock." The single word guttural.

"Ah. Fascinating." And perfect. For this man had much to crow about. A chuckle died in her throat as his hands at her wrist and on her breast tightened, squeezed, demanded her attention, and she shook away the fog to look into his bright eyes.

"Say it," he demanded. Then his lips curved into a sultry grin. "I'd like to hear you say it."

No need to ask what. She licked her lips, preparing them. As if she had not said the word already a thousand times. But... different this time. With him. Here. Her hand just where it was. His hand, too.

She closed her eyes. "Cock." She squeezed his at the same time she spoke, and before she could open her eyes, he crashed his mouth into hers, consuming her with a kiss, stealing her every breath and thought.

The world that had been disappearing just moments ago? Gone entirely now, replaced with the world he made in her body, the buzzing need originating at her breast where he teased her nipple and striking south to gather between her legs. Beneath her hand his cock twitched and hardened even more, and beneath her lips, he moaned her name, his hand tangled in her hair clenching tight.

"God damn," he hissed, never breaking the kiss. "God damn, I'm going to—" He jerked, his hips rolling up into her hand as she squeezed his length as well as she could with the wool of his breeches in the way. He jerked again, his hips rolling again, his every muscle harder than stone, and when that stone turned limp, he released her hand, bracketed her head with his forearms against the wall at her back and rested his forehead against hers.

As they breathed together, her hands moving up to trace the outline of his prickly jaw, the thunder grew distant, disappeared entirely, and the violent sloshing of the boats in their docks stopped, too. Peace descended.

Then so did Mr. Bailey.

Ben.

He dropped to his knees before her and pinned her once more to the wall, this time with a strong, immovable hand at her hip. The grin he slipped her as he tilted his head back to catch her eye rocked the boathouse, shook the very foundations of the earth. Wicked and promising. Wild and determined. His hand shackled round her ankle as it had around her wrist earlier, smoothed its way upward over the silk of her stockings, across the naked skin of her thigh. Then back down. His fingers made an electric storm of her body, and when he lifted the hem of her skirts to pin them against her hip, she shivered, bucked, *needed*. With damn muslin gathered at her hip, he pinned her there, too, then with one deliberate and devilish wink, he ducked his head beneath the heavy, wet slant of her skirts.

And placed a kiss just above the curls at her very center.

She swallowed hard, her head falling against the wall, her palms flattening against it, bereft of anything else to do.

His kiss lingered for longer than she would have thought possible, but then his lips lifted from that lowest stretch of belly, and his breath tickled her lower. Much lower. Where her fingers had played while dreaming of him. The books had taught her what to expect next.

And he did not disappoint, his tongue dragging across her mound. Some noise she'd never made before squeaked from between her lips, and her nails dug into the wood at her back.

Madness.

"Not madness," he chuckled. "Don't overthink it now, Lady P."

She'd spoken aloud, and she did so now, though her lips barely moved. "S'what a rake would say."

Another chuckle. Then another lick, a suck, and then his big warm hands at her center, too, finding that pearl of pleasure which seemed to wind her high and tight.

She should think. She should... what? Flee? She should say no instead of moaning his name.

But none of those had been scheduled. So why not shatter beneath his touch?

"Stop thinking." Had any voice ever sounded so dark and delicious?

Nothing for it but to obey. To stifle all thought as he rubbed a thumb just so and then—she gasped his name—slipped a finger inside her.

"Ben." She trembled, her legs fading once more.

"So lovely and wet."

They both were. Nothing like soaked linen over tight muscle, apparently, to make a lady moan. She brushed her skirts out of the way as well as she could to clutch at his shoulders, to dig fingernails there and bruise him as her wrists surely were. To mark him as she gasped again, as he slipped another finger inside and kissed her, moved that thumb just so very right.

No guilt here or worry. No ticking clock or straight lines or ledgers. Only a man and a woman, the glory of skin touched and the promise of heavy breaths as her pleasure built as the storm had, rolling across her. Unavoidable, powerful, illuminating.

She broke like the storm, too. With a cry that shook the skies. She curved around him, collapsing, and he gathered her, sitting, placing her in his lap and holding her tight as her trembling rage of a body gentled into strummed silence.

As she laid her head on his shoulder, she mumbled, "How do I always end up here? Your lap. Odd."

He kissed the top of her head. "It's the perfect Prudence Perch."

She snorted. But did not get up.

What now?

Didn't want to consider that. Not yet. Later.

Now, she'd—

The wall behind them shook, and they startled upright, his arms around her becoming chains, impossible to break. The wall shook again. No, not a wall. A door.

"Unlock the door," Norton demanded. "Now."

"Bloody hell." Ben tilted up her chin. "Quiet."

"He knows we're in here."

"Yes, but—"

She wiggled out of his hold, stood, and called out, "Just a moment, my lord. The door is, um, stuck."

Stuck behind the weight of a glaring man's big body. Bailey looked as if he would not move, arms crossed over his chest, legs stretched out straight in front of him. "Sod off, Norton!"

A muffled gasp.

"Language, Mr. Bailey," Prudence said.

He jumped to his feet and towered over her. "Like your language earlier, Lady P? I do like the way your lips shape the word co—"

"Lady Prudence, I assume everything is perfectly proper behind this door?" Lord Norton demanded.

Not at all, actually. Every bit of proper had drained into the lake quite some time ago.

"Y-yes," she managed to answer anyway.

Mr. Bailey snorted, his gaze dropping to her shoulder, to her—

"Curse it all!" She yanked the torn sleeve of the gown back up her shoulder, fit her naked breast back behind the barrier of shift and stays and gown. She was a mess. Entirely and utterly, and—"Oh! Mr. Bailey, you've ruined me." She hissed the words, keeping her voice low.

"Not yet." He smirked. "But—"

She rushed around him and flung open the door, letting Norton stomp inside as she fled into the clean sunlight, her feet silent on the soft, wet grass. "I'm returning to the house now it has stopped raining." She waited for no answer, only ran all the way up the lawn and into the house, never stopping until she was safe behind her bedchamber door.

Her heart felt heavy and light as a dry leaf all at once. It could drop like a stone to the bottom of the lake or fly off into the heavens, leaving her behind. She pressed both hands against her chest and slowed her breathing. Hearts had schedules, too, beating in a steady rhythm, predictable and safe.

But hers would not fall into predictability, routine. Not now when she could close her eyes and feel *him* everywhere.

She may have, in kissing Mr. Benjamin Bailey, unintentionally riled a bear.

Kissing? Ha. Ravishment, more like.

And a bear? Ha. A pagan god who would set the world on fire to get what he wanted.

And, contrary to all she'd thought true, Mr. Benjamin Bailey, Ben, wanted her.

Chapter Fourteen

Norton held the fireplace poker as if he meant to ram it through Ben's gullet. The former vicar looked wild, not at all his tame, quiet self. His knuckles on the handle shone bone white, and the slap of the poker's steel across his palm every three seconds or so echoed in the study where they'd met after Ben had dried himself off and found new clothes.

"You will do the gentlemanly thing, Mr. Bailey." Each word unmoving and hard like a damn boulder in the middle of the road. No getting around them.

"You're making assumptions, Norton." Correct ones, but Ben would rather dive off a cliff than disparage Prudence's name and reputation.

"You were locked in a boathouse with her. Alone. For quite some time. And when I arrived, I heard..." He blushed, looked away, the poker taking up a home in his palm.

"You heard nothing, and I'll call you out if you say otherwise."

"You'd fight me?"

"I'd put a bullet right between your eyes."

Norton turned with a sigh and relinquished the poker to its rightful place fireside. "What are your intentions toward Lady Prudence?"

"Same as they have been." Not true. But again, some information did not need to be public. Especially since his intentions were now exactly what everyone had always thought them to be. Except, of course, Prudence's brother. Ben shifted from foot to foot. That would be an unfortunate tangle to unravel. But he'd do it. "What are your intentions toward your wife?"

Norton's eyes turned to marbles. "Your situation has nothing to do with my marriage. You're evading—"

"And so are you. Her. You've spent perhaps two days with her since I've been here. Who knows how many nights, or—"

"This is not about me, damn you!" Norton roared. He took three rage-fueled steps forward, stopping before Ben with fisted hands and a ticking jaw.

"It is about you." Ben nudged Norton out of the way and took a chair near the fireplace, settling one ankle over the other knee and relaxing into the cushions. "Because I intend to keep *my* wife pleased. And her happiness, apparently, depends on the happiness of *your* wife."

"You're not even married."

"Yet. Now, I'm not the man to keep Lady Norton happy, but you"— Ben let his gaze trail up and down Norton's frame—"supposedly are."

Norton snorted and stomped toward the windows. When he got there, he raked both hands through his hair before letting his arms drop heavy at his sides. "She's not happy? Lady Prudence said that?"

Ben remained silent. No reason to rub salt in the wound.

"I've been busy," Norton said. "It takes more time than I ever thought to be a viscount, to run an estate." He turned and leaned against the window frame as he studied Ben. "You'll understand one day."

"Hopefully not for a damn long time. But even then, I'll not ignore my wife."

"You don't know. You—"

"I know what I want, Norton, and no matter how my name changes, my heart won't. I know you were married under difficult circumstances, but you must at least *try*."

"Like you have tried to keep Lady Prudence pristine."

"I *will* strangle you, Norton. Remember that." Ben leaned forward, clasped his hands together. "What is it you want from Lady Norton? A body to bear you an heir? A companion? A friend? An enemy?"

"I don't know what I want." Norton scrubbed his palms down his face. "I don't know. I was a vicar because I had to be. No other options. And then I was a viscount because others died. And then I got married because I must."

"And in all of that you never knew desire?" Ben stood, stalked toward the other man. "None of it drove you? Boiled purpose in your blood?"

Norton met Ben's gaze with empty eyes and a slack jaw, with stooped shoulders and a curved spine. "Can't say it has." A pause. Then a snap in his body, spine straightening, shoulders pushing back until he stood taller. "Except for once."

"Then cling to that. Because a man with no purpose or desire can't begin to know how to make a woman happy."

"And how would you know, Bailey?"

Ben smirked, slapped Norton in the shoulder. "If I told you, I'd have to call you out and sometimes, in some lights, I like you too well to do that."

A knock on the turn, brief and precise before the door flew open.

And Lady Templeton stormed in. She stomped right up to him, a marshal gleam in her eye. "What have you done to Lady Prudence? And do not feed me lies Mr. Bailey. I recognize that glassy look in her eye. She's been good for nothing since returning from the boathouse. Cheeks red as can be. Only one thing puts that sort of flush there." She poked Ben's shoulder. "What are your intentions?"

Ben sighed. "Am I never to escape that infernal question? You need not browbeat me, Lady Templeton. Norton has been doing a fine job."

"Have I?" Norton asked. "I rather thought you were the one brow-beating me."

Ben shrugged. "When a fellow needs it—"

"You need it." Lady Templeton poked Ben's shoulder once more. "What did you do to her?"

Ben grinned. "We-ell..."

Lady Templeton waved her hands between them. "No, no. I do not need the details. But answer me this: What do you intend to do about it? Once a man puts such a dreamy gaze into a lady's eyes, he must make good on it or break her heart. And I'll not have that. None of us will. And you should know better than to make an enemy of us." That *us* rang like a church bell through the room, pealing with heavy finality. She did not mean the *ton*. She meant the ladies who had assembled at Norton Hall this week. A very select group of women who had taken it upon themselves to protect the Duke of Clearford's sister. And any other young lady such as Lady Norton who fell under their wide wings.

Ben softened his expression, and he held his palms up to show he meant no harm. The exact opposite, in fact. "I appreciate you, Lady Templeton. I appreciate what you have been doing with Lady Prudence and Lady Norton and however many others you have included in your little... select group or club or whatever you call it."

"What are you talking about?" Norton asked. "What club?"

But the words were like a fly buzzing about Ben's ear, and he waved them away. "I have nothing but good intentions toward Lady Prudence." He'd certainly never intended to hurt her. And now he wanted... he wanted... "I desire nothing but Lady Prudence's happiness. To be the cause of it."

At some point during his speech, Lady Templeton's face had gone slack, her mouth dropping slightly open, her eyes going more than slightly round. She took one small step away from him, her hand clutching in her skirt. She snorted, a tiny noise, and looked away from him. How had he annoyed her?

"Is every gentleman in London to know about our books, then?" She gave another little snort. "It used to be a simple enough concept to keep quiet. If one reads naughty books and discusses them, one keeps such activities *secret*." She threw her hands in the air, waved them about wildly. "With all these young ones falling in love, they think they can tattle and prattle as much as they wish."

"Books?" Norton said. Ben said it, too. In fact, they said it at the exact same time, and then also together: "What books?"

Lady Templeton froze, then like an iceberg turning on the water, she shifted with miniscule movements to look at them over her shoulder. Slowly, the rest of her body followed so she faced them entirely, clasping her hands before her. "I thought you knew. What exactly... do you know? About our... what did you call it? Group? Club?"

"I was under the impression," Ben said, "that you and the other older matrons of the *ton* were educating young motherless girls on what it means to be a married woman."

"That's right," Lady Templeton said, but the words came out higher than her usual voice and forced, as if the words had stuck in her throat. "Yes, quite right. An educational endeavor." Her voice came out more naturally that time as she lifted her chin and sailed for the door. "Have a lovely afternoon, Mr. Bailey, Lord Norton. We'll see you at dinner, I suppose."

Norton got to the door before her, put his body directly in her path. "What books?"

Ben pinched the bridge of his nose, Norton's question wavering into the past. Books, books, books. And *scandal*. And Prudence's sister, Lady Charlotte. And Lord Noble's insistence that a particular book discovered on Lady Charlotte's person in Hyde Park actually belonged to him. But had it? Had they tricked everyone?

Ben started to laugh. Between great guffaws, he managed to say, "Lady Charlotte's scandal. It *was* her. The whole time." He bent double, resting shaking forearms on trembling knees. "And everyone b-believed it." Oh God, he was going to laugh himself right into a fetal position on the rug.

Lord Norton's voice tried to cut through his hilarity. "Do you mean the book discovered in Hyde Park last Season belonged to Lady Charlotte, and not to her husband, as was claimed?"

Still Ben laughed. How could he not? *That* was the secret they'd been hiding? He'd thought himself so clever, figuring it out without Prudence discovering a thing. And he'd been all wrong. He laughed harder.

What a bloody magnificent group of women.

"Do *all* of you," Norton asked, his voice low and hard, "assembled here this week read these books?"

Lady Templeton sighed, a choppy thing, as if cut in half by a kitchen knife. "Yes, in fact, we do. And I seem to be the one who has given away the secret this time." Another sigh, longer this time, before she grumbled, "I'm just going to go jump in the lake now." She reached for the door handle again.

Ben stopped her, reaching out to brush her arm. "No, no. It's fine. No more lakes. At least not today."

"Would you jump in to save me?" She scowled, her dark brows striking toward one another.

"Likely, and I'm still not recovered from the first unnecessary attempt." Still his belly shook with mirth.

She continued glaring, and he tried to stop laughing. Impossible.

"Then she knows *everything*?" Norton asked. The quality of doom in his voice killed Ben's laughter, so he could finally pull in a deep breath and stand up straight. Norton seemed to sink into the ground, though. "She knows everything I do not. God. She must be laughing at me." He shook his head slowly. "What stories she must have told you." He spit each poisoned word.

"What are you rambling on about?" Lady Templeton demanded.

"Cora!" Norton cried. "*Cora* who knows, *knows* absolutely everything about how a man and a woman... about ways to take pleasure... because she's read every damn book on the subject! And me. Ha." That single bark of laughter, bitter and black. "God, you all must be laughing at me."

"Do calm yourself, Lord Norton," Lady Templeton said. "I'm afraid I do not understand anything you are saying. The only one laughing here is your friend Mr. Bailey. And frankly his behavior, annoying as I find it, is more becoming at this moment than yours."

Norton stormed into the hallway behind him. Ben and Lady Templeton followed.

"Where are you going?" Lady Templeton called after him.

"London." Norton marched up the stairs. "Mother Circe's Nunnery. For an education to match my wife's." His words remained, echoing after he disappeared.

"Hell," Ben hissed.

"A brothel?" Lady Templeton exchanged a worried look with Ben. "An exclusive one, but *still*."

"Where's Lady Norton?" He grasped the newel post and tapped his foot. "Maybe she can talk her husband out of this nonsense."

"She and Prudence went for a walk. It was on Prudence's schedule, but the others and I did not wish to go. They should have been back half an hour ago for tea."

"Also on the schedule?"

Lady Templeton nodded. "She's never late."

"Of course not."

"But I think they wanted some time to speak alone. About young girl things, you know."

"I haven't the foggiest, Lady Templeton, but I do know that Lady Norton needs to be here. Now."

"Because her husband seems to have gone quite mad."

"I'll go after him, and you go after them."

They parted ways, and Ben bounded up the stairs after Lord Norton, found the man's bedchamber door wide open. The viscount had thrown open a trunk and was tossing various items of clothing inside.

"What the hell are you doing?" Ben rested his palms on either side of the door frame and watched the restless viscount bounce about the room.

"I already told you."

"I thought our earlier conversation, before Lady Templeton's revelation, had helped you discover what it is you want. And I thought, a supposition gleaned from your reactions and mannerisms, that the one thing you realized you wanted was your wife. Did I misjudge the situation? Or do you possess so little steel in your spine that a little detail about the type of books your wife enjoys reading can send you running like a coward?"

Norton swung on Ben, a shirt balled in his fist. "Cora is the first and only woman I have lain with. Seven and twenty years alive, and a virgin. How do you like that, Bailey?"

Ben's eyes popped open wide.

Norton growled.

"Sorry." Why were mouth muscles so difficult to control? He ran his hands down his face to pull down the corners of his lips. Not funny. Couldn't laugh. "I think it's a bit more than I wish to know about you, to be honest." There, he'd said that with a straight face.

"Do you know how many times we have slept together?"

"Again"—Ben propped a shoulder against the frame and settled in —"too much information."

"Once. First, I was waiting for her to be comfortable with me. And then when she indicated she might be ready, she began her courses. And then"—Norton flung a greatcoat over his shoulders and stuffed his arms inside—"it was... tepid at best. I didn't wish to scare the girl." He froze, his gaze targeting his boots. "I wanted her so badly. Was sure I would terrify her with my need." A harsh, brittle bark of laughter. "I bored her instead. This is all my fault."

"Not necessarily. Takes two, and all that." Sounded damning though. Ben might run off to a brothel, too if he thought he'd bored Prudence senseless during their interlude. Not a chance, though. Lady Templeton said he'd put a glassy look in her eye. No matter her reading preferences, he'd pleased her. He tucked a lock of hair behind his ear and straightened the sleeve of his coat, all with a little, impossible-to-control grin.

Norton scowled at him.

No time for preening, then. Ben cleared his throat as Norton threw more items of clothing into the trunk and slammed it closed. He yelled for his valet.

Ben rubbed his ear. "There are more productive means of calling the servants."

Norton yanked the bellpull so hard it fell from the ceiling. He cursed, then stormed from the room.

"Similarly unhelpful," Ben said with a wince, eyeing the now useless bellpull before following Norton downstairs.

Norton bellowed for his butler. "I'm going out. Have the trunk in my room delivered to London as soon as possible." He disappeared outdoors and toward the stable.

Ben trailed after him at a more sedate pace. Nothing he could do to stop the man other than physically restraining him. Or going after him. But that would mean leaving Prudence. Soon, a galloping horse appeared—Norton atop, greatcoat flapping in the wind—*whooshed* across Ben's vision, and disappeared down the drive.

"No hat." Ben scratched his neck. The storm had fully passed, and the sky spread bright blue above him, tinted yellow in the warm glow of the hot sun. "His face is going to be bright red before he reaches London. Hell. What a muddle." And how unhappy would Lady Norton be when she returned home to find her husband gone, having run off to a London brothel? And then what would Prudence think?

Prudence. He understood her better now. Not only the books, which were a kind of education if you considered it that way. And why not? But what they'd shared in the boathouse. He knew where to touch her to make her cry out. And he knew what made her heart cry, too. A heavy responsibility to know so much about a person. One that could rearrange a world, dislodge a man's purpose, and send it spinning into space.

Chapter Fifteen

"Men are most confusing."

Prudence could do naught but shake her head. Every bit of her agreed with Cora.

"And they are much better in fiction, don't you think?"

Again, Cora spoke words of wisdom, but...

"Perhaps," Prudence ventured, "men of flesh and blood possess some benefits over those of paper and ink."

"Oh? How so?"

The sun threw happy rays across Cora's face as they trudged back toward Norton Hall. It had sunk lower than Prudence liked as they'd walked. Her schedule a catastrophe now. But then, she'd not had ravishment by Mr. Bailey on her list of items to accomplish that day, and she... could not regret it.

"A man of ink and paper, for instance," Prudence said, "cannot keep one warm." Or jump into a lake to save one. When one did not need saving in the least. The thought mattered more than the reality, though.

"Not in the conventional sense, perhaps, but when I am abed at night with a book in hand and the blankets heavy over my legs, my imagination is quite warmed by the men I read about."

"Yes, but…" Wouldn't it be better with such a man beneath the covers with you? Couldn't say that. Had never really thought it until…

Mr. Benjamin Bailey had ravaged her. Most thoroughly. An unplanned event that quite rearranged her schedules from henceforward. Now it seemed every hour called for ravishment.

"But?" Cora elbowed Prudence's ribs.

"Don't you enjoy Lord Norton's attentions at night?"

Cora whipped her gaze to the grass beneath their boots, her cheeks flushing.

Prudence chuckled. "Answer enough."

"It is so very different from what I imagined. He's so very careful with me, so… accommodating."

Ben had been none of those things.

Ben? Not Mr. Bailey?

Apparently so.

Prudence wrung her bruised wrist with the other hand. Her gloves and the cuff of her spencer hid the marks Ben's passion had left her with. She enjoyed knowing they were there. Tender to the touch, yes, but the mere thought of them brought back memories she wanted to relive over and over again.

She swallowed, fanned her cheeks. "My, it's hot today."

"It's as if he does not wish to hurt me."

"Norton?"

"Yes. Who else but Norton?"

Prudence cleared her throat. "Do you wish you had not married him?"

"No. It's not that. It is merely that I wish he'd treat me as he did the night in the garden when we were caught."

No tenderness that night. Only mindless passion.

"Are you going to tell me about the boathouse?" Cora asked.

"What about the boathouse?"

"You were caught there a terribly long time. And Lady Templeton and the others are of the mind that something… *happened*."

Prudence shook her head. "Men are most confusing."

"So we've established. How, in particular, has Mr. Bailey confused you?"

"He didn't want me. I know he didn't. But now... it seems he does."

Cora rolled her eyes. "Of course he wanted you. He came here, all changed. And why wouldn't he want you?"

"Hm. Still, it's rather odd."

"You doubt him even now?"

She didn't want to. After that morning, her body begged her not to. Her heart begged, too.

"I don't. Yet, I can't imagine why he would want me."

Cora snorted. "Why wouldn't he? You're pretty and clever and do not tolerate fools."

"That sounds like Lottie."

"And you're kind and loving and protective of those you care for."

"That sounds like Andromeda."

Cora swept in front of Prudence and took her hands, shook them, squeezed them. "No, it's *you*. You are all those good things."

"Thank you." Prudence squeezed her friend's hands in return and locked their arms together. "We should return to the house. We're terribly late."

"Are you going to marry Mr. Bailey?" Cora asked as they set their steps more quickly toward Norton Hall.

"Marry him? He's not proposed."

"But if he does? You will say..."

Yes. No. Well... "I think I'm scared to answer that."

Cora laid her head on Prudence's shoulder. "Men are also most terrifying."

"No." She did not fear Ben. "What if I let myself hope?" Let herself love. "And then I was right all along, that he did not want me but wanted a dowry or a... a... something else. Whatever else he thinks he gets from marrying me."

"He gets you. And if that's not enough, I suggest we set Mrs. Garrison on him with a bow and arrow."

Prudence laughed as the hall came into view. Her steps quickened. Seeking out Ben was not on any schedule she'd contrived. But her schedule had given way to chaos during the storm.

"Look," Cora said, pointing toward the front of the house, "there's Mr. Bailey now. And... how odd... the ladies as well. All of them."

Ben and the others marched toward them through the grass, and as the two parties grew closer, Prudence walked faster, the grim set of Ben's jaw enough to make her heart race.

"Something's happened," Prudence whispered.

They were almost running when they met the others, and Ben's hands swallowed Prudence's shoulders as his gaze flew to Cora.

"Lady Norton," he said, "there's been a bit of a change in circumstances."

"What do you mean?" Cora asked, breathless.

Lady Templeton stepped forward. "It's my fault, I'm afraid. I thought he knew, thought Mr. Bailey knew."

"Never assume," Mrs. Garrison snapped.

"Assume what?" Cora looked, grim-eyed, toward the hall.

"I know about the books," Ben said, his gaze finding Prudence, softening. "And so does Norton."

The world went still. Even the birds seemed to have silenced their song.

Prudence shrugged out of his hold, her gaze flying to Lady Templeton. "You told them?"

"Why?" Cora demanded.

"It was a mistake." Lady Templeton pulled herself up tall, refusing to be cowed even in such an hour. "I blame you young ones, gadding about, falling in love—"

"I'm not falling in love," Prudence protested.

"Not even a little?" Ben asked. She waved him away, but he caught her hand and held it tight. "Norton has left."

"Left?" Cora's voice came out as a squawk. "To go where?"

More silence.

"Where?" she demanded.

"London," Ben said. "We only tell you now to prepare you. He left in a hurry. And with a bit of a fuss. You may want to prepare a story to tell the servants."

"And we didn't want you to make a fuss in front of everyone inside," Lady Macintosh said. "It wouldn't be dignified, and in a case such as this, it's imperative to retain your dignity."

Cora's face paled. "Where in London has my husband gone?"

"I wouldn't tell her that," Ben mumbled.

"Tell her." Prudence ripped her hand away from his.

"Mother Circe's Nunnery," Lady Templeton said, her gaze going far into the distance over Cora's shoulder. "In the West End."

Cora lifted her face to the sky with closed eyes and straightened her shoulders. Then, as if she were a ghost, she glided forward toward the house.

They walked behind her, gathered close enough to whisper and still hear.

"What will she do?" Lady Templeton asked.

"She should tell everyone Norton received a letter concerning some difficulty in London," Mrs. Garrison said.

Ben snorted. "What difficulty?"

Lady Macintosh snorted right back. "Anything. That's not for servants to know."

"And who do you think you are, Mr. Bailey?" Mrs. Garrison asked.

Ben blinked. "You seem to know my name well enough."

"But we are not familiar enough with one another to allow *teasing*. And this is no time."

"My grandfather says bleak times are the best times for teasing."

"You used to be a growly, monosyllabic sort of man." Lady Macintosh *tsked*. "What happened?"

Ben shrugged. "Must have been the beard. Quite itchy. Entirely pickles one's temperament."

"And who is this impertinent man, your grandfather?" Lady Templeton demanded.

Still, Cora floated before them, a wraith under the dimming sky.

"Baron Brightly," Ben mumbled.

The three older women stopped, stared at him, then stared at one another. They seemed to speak all at once.

"Did we know that?"

"A baron."

"We should have known that."

"Yes, but the way he used to *look*."

"And speaks."

"Never even crossed my mind to consider..."

"And he's the baron's heir," Prudence said.

Now they all looked at her.

Ben groaned. "Did you really have to do that, Lady P?"

Prudence nodded.

"Benjamin Bailey," Lady Templeton said.

"Baron Brightly," Mrs. Garrison mumbled.

"Heavens." Lady Macintosh's lips twitched.

"Don't laugh," he warned.

Lady Macintosh tempered her twitching lip. "Never. Unlike your dear baron of a grandfather, I know now is no time for teasing."

They entered the house and watched Cora ascend the stairs, melt into the shadows at the top without a single word.

"The girl always did have a flair for the dramatic," Lady Templeton said.

"My friends." Cora reappeared, standing like a queen at the top of the steps. "I thank you for your support, but I am afraid I must call an end to this house party." She held up a hand to stop any disagreement. "I will instruct the staff to help you with preparations for leaving." Then she turned and left once more.

They stood in the entryway, staring upward for several moments at the spot where she'd been, as if they all waited for her to return. She did not, and the ladies, grumbling and whispering amongst themselves, followed Cora upstairs.

Leaving Prudence alone. With Ben. But she could not turn toward him. She seemed stuck, her gaze riveted to that spot where her friend—pale and tall—had stood, had sent her away without a tear.

A brush on her arm, up and down. His fingertips. "Prudence, are you unwell?"

"I do not think Cora will speak with me."

"She appears to need a moment alone. But I am not asking about her. How are you, Lady P?"

"I... I am... shocked, I suppose. You, ahem, *know* then?"

His fingers landed just above her elbow, traced circles there, the touch as light and gentle as a whisper. "Yes."

"And you think..."

"No, actually. Haven't had time to think about it, what with Norton stomping off like a child denied his favorite toy."

She winced. "He was very angry, then? At Cora?"

"Hm. Maybe angrier at himself."

"Will he... you think... tell others? About us? About the books?"

He stepped in front of her, forcing her to look into his face. She found the same gentleness there that she found in his touch. "I don't think so, no. What purpose would that serve?"

"And you? You'll tell—"

"No, I most decidedly will not."

Did she trust him?

He ran his knuckles down the curve of her face. "I will not. I swear."

Yes, she did.

"Is that a smile, Lady P? Finally?"

"Not at all." She tangled her hand in his, knowing she shouldn't, incapable of stopping when the comfort he offered warmed better than a fire. She lifted his hand to her lips and kissed his knuckles. Another unlikely, inadvisable action. A kiss so quick, it seemed her lips barely grazed the rough hair on the back of his large, strong hand.

"Prudence." Her name, a sound as warm as his comfort, a heat that promised to be scorching if tended right.

She dropped his hands and made for the stairs. "I must, I suppose, prepare to leave. And so must you, Mr. Bailey."

"Ben," he called from down below.

"Ben," she whispered, sinking into the same shadows that had swallowed Cora.

She wanted to stay with him, to let him tease her into gladness. But she could not take such a blessing. Not yet. Not with her friend brought so low.

Something woke Prudence before the sun rose. The smallest squeak, or the softest shush of two objects brushing together. The sound, whatever it was, echoed a small, raw feeling through her. What? She turned on her side in the bed and peered out the sliver between the closed curtains at the window.

Loneliness?

Perhaps.

Her friends had left yesterday, and today she would leave, too. But she had no right to feel this way. Only Cora, abandoned and silent. She'd not even come down for dinner, and not even the ladies' teasing of Ben over fish and wine had been able to liven the mood. Not even the kisses he'd put on the tip of her nose, the top of her head, had filled in the hollow space inside her. Because of Cora.

No use sleeping. She felt wide awake, jittery even. Ben had insisted on traveling with her, accompanying her back to her brother's door as a protector. She'd be confined with him all day in a traveling coach. Not entirely inappropriate. Her maid would travel with them. Still...

She jumped out of bed and splashed water from the basin on her face. It did not calm her. Perhaps she should speak with him alone before they left. She had this terrible itch all across her skin that seemed to think... seemed to suggest...

Once they got to London, she'd never see him again.

Silliness. Everything he did and said showed he wanted her. He'd not proposed marriage yet, but... surely that was not far behind, and—

Her hands flew up to her mouth on a gasp. She wanted to marry him. She'd never wanted to marry anyone. Never once felt tempted. But now... oh what a temptation Ben Bailey proved to be. She could imagine it, actually imagine seeing his scruffy face every day, hearing his teasing tones every morning, aching for his rough touch every night. The face, the tones, the touch... of a friend. A friend her heart could curl up against and start to purr.

She flung her wrapper over her shoulders and made for the door. He'd be asleep, but she needed to talk to him, to know if he felt the same. Right this instant. No better time on the schedule for certainty than now.

At the door, she paused. Beneath her foot, the floor felt different, uneven, smooth in one place, worn in another. A pale square peeked out from under her toes, and she knelt to retrieve it. She went to the window to inspect it, found her name scrawled in Cora's hand across one side. A note. She unfolded it and read.

"Oh *no*. Oh no, oh no, oh no!" She ran. All the way to Ben's room and banged on the door. "Ben! Ben!"

Fumbling and curses from inside, then the door flew open. Ben stood in the moonlight, his startled eyes wide. He reached for her, grasped her shoulders. "Prudence? What is wrong? What's happened?"

"This!" She waved the note before his face.

He snatched it and strode to the window, dragging her along with him. "Hell," he said after he read it. "She's gone to London?"

Prudence nodded. Words? What were words? They'd all quite flown away. Because Ben stood in the moonlight naked from the waist up, his breeches slung low on narrow hips, every inch of skin on show. Her mouth went dry. So much skin, so much muscle. She reached out, poked the slab of muscle that he likely called chest. Everyone else called it that, but if his did not look like other chests, could it use the same moniker? She poked it again. Then laid her hand flat against it.

"Prudence." His voice gravelly.

"Hm?" She trailed her hand downward, over the hard ridges of his abdomen.

"I don't think you should touch me right now, love."

"Oh?"

"Yes." His hand cupped the back of her neck, and his thumb rubbed gentle lines into the skin at her nape. "Not only because it seems your friend has run away to a brothel, but because you woke me from a particularly scandalous dream in which you wore even less than you're wearing now. Me as well." He leaned close until his lips brushed against her ear. "Nothing, love. We were wearing nothing. And we're so close to wearing nothing now, I find it difficult to focus on priorities."

"Which are?" Her hand stopped at the band of his breeches, her gaze riveted on the large bulge straining there.

"Difficult to remember, but... hell." He crashed his lips to hers and stole her breath, gave her a hard, needy kiss in return. Tongue and teeth and lips and warm breath until she clung to him, fingers finding nothing but skin to hold on to, the back of his neck to wrap around, the hair there to tug.

"Hell," he cursed again and set her from him. "Priorities." He marched her to the empty fireside. "Stay there." Then he marched all the way to the other side of the room, grabbing his shirt as he did and throwing it over his head. "And I'll stay here. Now." He crossed his arms over his chest. "Are we to do something about this?"

This. Yes, *this*. Cora.

"She's gone to London alone," Prudence said. "How could she? It's much too dangerous. On horseback? Alone!"

"She'll make good time."

"That is not the point, Mr. Bailey."

"You're right. The point is that she intends to march right up to the front door of a well-known brothel and demand they relinquish her husband."

"Fool notion," Prudence bit out.

"She's a married woman."

"Still! It is not done."

"And you're overly concerned about what is done and what is not?" She took several steps closer to him. "You have no idea how much I do to keep everything a secret. Cora can enjoy her evenings, and the ladies can enjoy their books because I oil the clockwork. No one sees me, but—"

"I see you." He demolished the distance between them, gathering her into his arms.

"You are supposed to stay over there."

"I promise not to ravish you." He nudged her temple with the tip of his nose. "What do you wish to do about Lady Norton?"

"Go after her." She rested her fists and her cheek against his chest as his arms tightened round her. "Stop her from making a mistake."

"Her life is not yours to organize."

She stiffened, pushed away. "I must leave."

He looked out the window, at the moon spilling through the glass. "Now? No."

"Yes. It's the only way to possibly catch her."

"No."

"I will." She tugged out of his arms.

He pulled her back, crashed her against him. "I'll stop you."

Laughing, she narrowed her eyes. "You may try, Mr. Bailey. You may *try*." She ducked then, quick as she could, out of the circle of his embrace, and darted for the door.

"Hell." He lunged for her, missed. "At least wait for morning." She slipped back into the hallway, and he followed. "Wait for sunlight, Prudence. Your brother will dissect me if I let you travel at night."

"It will be too late, then. I go now." She returned to her room and threw open the wardrobe, found a serviceable carriage gown of pale blue and her stays. "Help me."

Surprisingly, he played lady's maid without a single objection, his strong fingers tightening the stays and securing the gown as she held her hair back. "I thought I'd undress you before I ever had a chance to dress you, but here we are." He sighed. "I'm not complaining. Entirely. Now wait here. I'll be right back."

"I'm not waiting." She sat to pull on boots.

"Not forever, Lady P. Less than a quarter hour. I can't ride about the English countryside in breeches only."

"I'm not asking you to come with me."

He gathered her into his arms once more. Why was it so easy to let him do so?

"Why else did you come to me, then?" He dropped a kiss on her forehead. "No, if you insist on going, then I'm coming with you. And"—he tilted her chin up—"if you leave before I return, I will catch up with you, do you understand?"

The heat in his eye promised far more benefits than consequences of upsetting him.

"What will you do?" Her voice breathy.

"Throw you over my knee," he hissed near her ear, "and make sure you never endanger yourself again. Mainly by keeping you in my bed and under my body at all hours of the day and night." His teeth tugged on her earlobe, and she almost melted into the floorboards. Only determination kept her upright. What had Ben called it? Priorities. Yes, those. Cora.

He left, and she plaited her hair and set it in a simple coiffure at her nape. She pinned her hat on and shoved a full coin bag down into her stays between her breasts. Then she donned her spencer and waited.

She intended to hie off into the night alone with a single man of questionable reputation. She intended to risk her own reputation to save her friend's. Quite the to-do list. And it had never been more pressing to get it all done on time.

Chapter Sixteen

Ben wouldn't enjoy Hell, but he'd understand what got him there. Enjoying a bumpy ride to London with a woman who clearly did not share his joy. And under such worrying circumstances, too. The gig he and Prudence had commandeered from Norton Hall was well sprung, but narrow, and the wheels over the bumpy roads often bounced Prudence into his arm, his leg, his hip.

Finally, after a bump which sent her flying and landing with her hand atop his unmentionable bits, and with a scowl that scrunched her face, she hooked her arm through his and secured her body to the conveyance with his weight. By melting her body hard against his own.

Delightful.

All but her scowl. And her wounded heart.

That the only reason Ben couldn't fully relax, couldn't fully appreciate the improper closeness of a man traveling down a public road with the woman who would be his future. He hoped. He must speak with Clearford soon. Today or tomorrow. He'd told Prudence he'd not tell a soul about the books, the library. He'd meant it, and that included her brother, too. He'd *have* to lie to Clearford, then, tell the man he'd discovered nothing or give him a watered-down version of the truth. But would the duke believe him? There existed several points against Ben's veracity.

First, Ben had been lying already, and Clearford knew it, knew him capable of it.

Second, Ben would ask for Prudence's hand in marriage, and the duke would know—a husband must keep his wife's secrets.

Finally, the lie he planned to tell Clearford—that Prudence had been taking marriage lessons from older women—might not be convincing enough. After all, if Prudence had been learning how to be married, how come she'd not been playing nice with the swarm of suitors her brother had collected about her?

Damn.

And if he did succeed in convincing Clearford, would the man agree to let Ben wed Prudence when he knew how he'd begun courting her? Would he insist Ben tell her the truth first? He probably should anyway, but...

It didn't matter. It *didn't*. And he couldn't tell her, not when she was still so skittish around him, melting under his touch when the blaze between them burned hot (or when she risked popping out of a traveling conveyance) and freezing at other times, questioning his motives.

As she should.

But it didn't matter now. Those motives long irrelevant. More relevant were her reasons for trusting him but not trusting him.

Perhaps if he knew *why*.

He licked his lips, squeezed her arm to his side, and held the reins lightly in his hands. Kept his tone just as light. "Prudence, why do you doubt me?"

She startled, looked up at him, looked back at the road. It seemed as if she might pull away, so he tightened his arm to his side, pinning her there.

"Is it because of how gruff I can be? How unrefined? How—"

"No. That's not it at all. I..." A pause in which he held his breath. She seemed to hold hers, too, but then she made a humming sound and said, choosing each word carefully, "I suppose it's not that I doubt you, but I doubt... myself."

"You're going to have to explain that one. *Will* you explain it?"

Because he could tell—what he asked her to talk about was important, a deep-down kind of thing, like falling in an ocean and losing your mother's ring. A thing you fear to put into words because you had already judged yourself so harshly you did not dare let others know.

Her hands on his arm tightened, and they traveled in silence. She wouldn't tell him, and now he wanted to know more than ever. But he couldn't ask her again, not if it took that much effort for her to find the words.

But then she leaned her head against his arm. "I know I am not so... great."

Relief tingled along his skin. Thank God, she'd decided to speak. But what foolishness fell from her lips. "You are not *great* Prudence, you are magnificent. Spectacular."

She laughed. "Thank you. I should not have used the word *great*. It is a paltry word, but then... I am a paltry thing, too."

He opened his mouth, slammed it shut. He'd been about to tell her how wrong she was. But that would have been a betrayal as great as the one he already visited upon her. Should she ever find out. Who was he to tell her the contents of her heart? So he waited, listened.

"Did you ever have any siblings?" she asked.

"No, never. Just me."

"Then you cannot know. How easy it is to be lost in the crowd. Every child has their... role. Samuel the heir, the duke, a man with power and good looks. Lottie the beauty, fierce, too. People admire her even when they do not necessarily like her. Andromeda the kind one, soft and gentle. Then the twins—identical, novel, fascinating. You can see how it's easy for plain Prudence to disappear."

He could not. Perhaps once, but... he couldn't even remember that blind fool of a man. He wanted to bark at her about her brilliance, lecture her for hours on the singular delight she'd proved to be. But he gave her silence so she could continue.

She settled her hand atop his on the reins and wove her fingers between his. "When I am in a room, men look right through me. Mostly it is a boon. I have not wished to be seen. What's the use, after all, in wishing for something you cannot have. My invisibility has allowed me to do as I please. Mostly. So when you... saw me and then you... wanted me... I could not fathom it. It had never happened before. After all, every suitor I've ever had has been browbeaten by my brother into courting me. Men dance with me, bring me flowers, because Samuel demands it. Not because they want to."

A knot formed in his stomach. He might retch. He gripped the reins till his knuckles shone through his skin. He must hold them tight or let them tremble.

She bent her fingers, stoking the insides of his where they over-lapped. "When you were pursuing me, I knew you only did so because of Samuel. He'd asked you to. You'd stayed true during Lottie's scandal because you are friends with him, not because you have any attraction for me. The only explanation, really, for your loyalty. You've been a good friend to my family."

But not nearly a good enough friend to her. That became clearer by the moment.

She turned her head and placed a soft kiss on his shoulder. "Thank you. I apologize for doubting you. But you see why, don't you? When you followed me to Norton Hall, when you kissed me, when you paid me attention and said nice things to me, all I could think was that you did so because of Samuel. But"—she hung her head, hiding her face from him—"now I begin to suspect it's because of *me*."

"It is you, Prudence." The words roared out of him, unstoppable, untamable, fueled by fear as much as by the truth. He stopped the gig, pulling it over to the side of the road and letting the reins fall loose across his thighs. He lifted her chin, forced her to see the truth in his eyes. "I don't think of your brother at all when I do this." He kissed her, trying to show her. He would show her. In every way, every day. He wanted her, and Samuel be damned.

Though her brother had put her in Ben's line of sight.

Now he knew for sure. She could never know that particular truth. It would shatter her.

He kissed her once more, biting her bottom lip and cupping the nape of her neck. She curled her hands on his chest and let him do as he pleased, do as she pleased, too, nipping at his lips and tentatively exploring his mouth with her hesitant tongue. She deepened the kiss as she grew brave, stoking his desire in a way certainly not suitable for the side of a public road so close to London.

"Damn," he whispered, pulling out of the kiss. "Damn." For so many reasons. He rested his forehead against hers, closed his eyes. "Do you believe me?"

"Yes." The word a pleased sigh.

"Good. Now I'm afraid we must continue. On the road. Not with... that."

She laughed and handed him the reins, then clung tight to his arm once more. She faced the end of the road with a brighter face than before. He'd given her that joy, that boldness. And if she knew the truth, why he'd really begun to court her, he would be the reason she lost that joy, too.

The road grew more distinct as they reached the outer limits of London, the buildings more crowded, and the difficulty of navigating the road pushed his worry to the edges of his mind.

"Do you know where we're going?" Prudence asked, clinging to his arm, cheek nestled soft against it.

The streets and pavements grew more crowded around them. Right now, they were no more than a country couple in a gig, of no importance to those bustling about their daily business. But if anyone recognized them...

"I do know where we're going," Ben said, slowing the gig behind a cart.

"That means you've been there?"

He shifted, the gig seat digging into his arse more than it had been a moment before.

"Most men of London make their way there at one point or another."

She patted his arm. "Naturally. I'm quite aware of ravenous masculine appetites."

"Naturally."

"Are the women there happy? Hm. I suppose you can only answer for the women you've met there, and not all of them, but are they? Those you've met?" She tipped her chin up and rested it on his biceps, her large eyes—more blue than green today—blinking up at him. So calm and curious.

He scratched a hand through his hair. "I hope so. It is likely a better experience than most in their profession. Still not what most if any of these women would have chosen for themselves. When a fellow thinks about it too much, it rather makes the entire thing unpalatable. That's why, when I say most men make their way there at *one point* or another, I put heavy emphasis on the *one*. For me, at least. Just the once."

"But your appetites appear healthy enough."

He laughed, but he wanted to kiss her instead. "Around you they are, Lady P. But I do not wish to lie with ladies who do not wish to lie with me."

"Ah. Logical. But of course, ladies desire you." She popped upright, releasing his arm with a pretty scowl. "You're... you're *you*."

He scratched his jaw. "And until recently *me* could hardly be considered desirable. Ladies have no fondness for beards or baggy clothes or untrimmed hair. That's not to say I've been a monk. There are those who find oddities desirable. For a time or two. Then the novelty wears off and they prefer someone more—"

"Look!" Prudence bounced and pointed to the side of the street. "Is that—"

"Lady Norton. Yes. What do you wish me to do?"

"Follow her slowly. If we confront her now, she'll bolt and likely lose us. She can move more quickly in this crush on a horse than we can in this gig."

"Very well. But with the nunnery so close... we do not have much time. I hope you have a plan to get her away from the door."

"No. Not as yet. I'm working on it, though."

He maneuvered the gig between two carts, keeping an eye on the slowly moving Lady Norton. The walls of the nunnery rose before them, and Lady Norton, dressed all in black, swayed her horse toward them as if toward her death. Prudence bounced beside him, her gaze riveted on Lady Norton, then swinging side to side over the street and its occupants before planting once more on her friend.

"Stay calm, Lady P," Ben mumbled.

"I am," she snapped. Then, "I'm not. Stop the gig."

"Pardon?"

"Cora has stopped. She's dismounting. I must go or I'll be late."

"Late to do what?"

"Stop, stop, please, Ben."

He slowed the gig, unable to do anything but obey her. As soon as it rolled almost to a stop, she launched herself out, landing low in a tangle of skirts, her bonnet having slipped over her face. She shoved it back, fisted her skirts to haul them higher than her ankles, and ran.

He lost sight of her as he rounded the corner into an alley next to the brothel. Quiet there, and dark. He jumped down and ran after Prudence, leaving the horse nickering behind him. Then—the black-veiled figure of a woman scorned. And just behind her, the very top of the bonnet that had tapped against his shoulder and ear all morning. He sliced between two men walking side by side, ignoring their belligerent cries and pushing his legs faster.

Lady Norton climbed the steps to a door he'd entered through before. Innocuous, like every other door around it on this seemingly harmless street. This brothel positioned where it was for a reason. A nice enough neighborhood for the nice gentlemen who visited, near enough to Mayfair to offer convenience for that set. Which meant if Lady Norton caused a scene, those who cared could see. Those who mattered would whisper. And married or not, Lady Norton would find her reputation tattered. She did not care. She moved like a ghost, floating toward her doom. Until her body yanked backward and out of view behind a carriage.

Ben darted around the side of a horse but still could not find her. Nor Prudence. Where were they? Ah—there! Finally. The sight of Prudence set his roiling gut at ease, though panic lit her features. She held Lady Norton's wrist, and that lady struggled against her hold.

Prudence's lips flew, mobile and determined, though Ben could not hear what she said until he reached her side.

Neither woman noticed him stopping beside them, puffing for breath and using his body as much as possible to hide them from those passing by on the street.

"There are other ways," Prudence hissed.

Lady Norton tugged.

Prudence held tighter. "Do you care nothing for society? For friendship? There are those who could still remain at your side, but those who could not. Fell Norton some other way. Do not take yourself down with him. I could not bear it. To lose you."

"Let's move this conversation into the alley, ladies," Ben said, voice low. "This is no place for arguments." Men approached from every side. Any moment now one of them would come their way, set his steps toward the door at their back, recognize one or both of the ladies standing there—a viscountess and a duke's sister.

"Yes," Prudence said. "Speak with me in private just one moment, away from the hurry of the street, away from"—her gaze darted toward the building—"danger. Please, Cora."

"If it's revenge you want, Lady Norton—"

"Do not call me that," the viscountess snapped.

Ben swallowed. "If it's revenge you wish, my lady, the best way to take it is to live a most excellent life. Confrontation, ruination, that helps no one. Hurts only you. You seem a clever woman. Surely, you're intelligent enough to think past your anger."

The viscountess blinked, then her entire body deflated, the arm that Prudence held losing its tension and her chin sinking to her chest. He took advantage, wrapping an arm around each woman's shoulder and guiding them toward the alley where he'd left the gig.

"Keep your heads low." He stuck his head up, whistled.

"What are you doing?" Prudence hissed.

"Keep. Your. Head. Down." A man caught his eye, and he winked. Once the man looked away, he said, "I'm playing the part. A happy man escorting two of the nunnery's ladies out for a good time."

Two identical feminine gasps of outrage.

"Such a sight is normal on this street. It's best to appear as normal as possible. We don't want to stand out, do we?"

No objections to that, and he picked up his pace. Not too fast. Not fast enough to bring more attention to them. Once in the shadows of the alley, he helped Lady Norton up into the gig. She sat there, limp and sullen, while Prudence paced behind them, chewing on her thumbnail.

"We are safer here," Ben said, "but we cannot remain here long."

Prudence stopped beside him and held her palms up to Lady Norton. "You understand why you cannot go in there, Cora?"

Cora nodded, her face pale and shining in the dim light.

"What were you thinking?" Prudence crept closer to her friend, head slowly shaking.

"I... I was so angry. I could think only of my papa. Of his women. And how my mama knows. She *knows*, Prudence, about every woman, and she simply ignores it. I... I do not think I can ignore it."

"Don't." Prudence climbed up to sit beside Lady Norton, took her hands, and squeezed them.

Ben walked toward the end of the alley that spilled out onto the busy street beyond, giving them what privacy he could while still keeping them within the radius of his protection. Still, though, he could hear Prudence's words, soft and low and brimming with compassion.

"Don't ignore it, Cora. But do not hurt yourself in the process. Go home. Wait for him to return and speak to him. Ask for a separation if you please. I know many husbands and wives live separate lives. And if you do so you will have such... *freedom*."

Was that what Prudence wanted? Freedom? The sort obtained through the obscurity of spinsterhood? He tapped a foot. The men walking by... did they have wives *and* mistresses? Did they leave shattered hearts wherever they went? Did they leave ladies pale and trembling in alleys? He searched each face, hoping to see Norton. So he could slam a fist into the man's eye.

"I don't want to go home," Lady Norton said behind him. "I... I don't know where home is."

"Perhaps," Prudence said, "Your parents—"

"No."

"Back to the country, then? To Norton Hall?"

"No." A bit of spirit back in that word. "Can I stay with you?"

"Do you wish to see Norton gutted?" Prudence asked. "Because if you stay with me, we must tell my brother why, and since he supported Norton on several fronts, he will feel, I'm afraid, betrayed by the man. He will likely"—she cleared her throat—"go after him."

"Good." So, Lady Norton liked knives, too, particularly those stuck in her husband's gullet. She was more stab-happy than the duke. Wouldn't do. Ben whipped around and joined the women.

"I've a suggestion. Let us take an evening to think about what to do next. I know a place we can go. Not too far from here. It will be safe. No gossips, no brothers, no foolish husbands, or even more foolish parents. No one either of you knows."

"And where is that?" Prudence tilted her head.

"A little house on the edge of London belonging to one Baron Brightly."

Prudence's eyes glowed bright enough to illuminate the alley, and the corner of her lips twitched. "Your grandfather."

Ben unfolded the footman's seat at the back of the gig. "One of you climb on the back, then, and off we go."

Cora settled herself without a word. Her face ashen and rigid, then hidden as she lowered her head and pulled the brim of her bonnet over her face. Ben unfolded the hood to better hide them, then carefully left the alley and pulled into the bustle of the street. He set course for Bright House, what his grandfather called his home, and for safety.

Chapter Seventeen

Ben stopped the gig in front of Bright House. The sun sank low behind it, making it shine as its name suggested. It sat on the north boundary of London and enjoyed the open skies of the country. The curved eaves over the front windows always reminded Ben of happy smiles or the sweep of bird wings in a watercolor. Every window glowed with welcoming candlelight, and the door flew open.

His grandfather lumbered out with a furrowed white brow and long, swinging arms. "Who's this, then?" He stopped before the gig and hooked his hands on his hips to study the conveyance and its passengers.

Ben hopped down and rounded the gig. "Just your only grandson."

He and Ben were of a height and similar build, and his grandfather had not lost his strength in old age, though his formerly yellow hair was white now. His blue eyes were sharp as ever.

He rubbed those curious eyes, then looked at Ben again. "No, you're not. I have but two grandsons, and none of them look like you."

"Come now, Grandfather. A shave of a beard and a haircut is not enough to make me entirely unrecognizable."

His grandfather's brows, always his most expressive feature, shot up to his hairline as he hinged forward at the waist and peered at Ben's chin. His hand shot out, and he snagged Ben's jaw between tight fingers.

"Ow! Let go."

He swatted Ben's hands away as he turned Ben's head from side to side. "The beard... yes. Why, I've not seen that jawline in years. Pity. Forgot you had a good one." He laughed, loud and long, and patted Ben's cheek. "Good to see you, my boy. And who are they, then?" He nodded at the gig, the ladies sitting in it. "Oh, never mind, Ben. You never do introductions right." He swept forward as Ben helped first Lady Norton and then Prudence to the ground. "I am Baron Brightly, and you two are quite lovely. Please give me the honor of your names so I may know what angels are called."

Ben snorted.

Prudence laughed.

Lady Norton peered up at the house, more statue than woman.

"This is," Ben said, coming to stand between the women and gesturing to the viscountess, "Viscountess Norton and this is my"—he gestured to Prudence, realized his blunder—"well, that is, this is Lady Prudence."

"*Your* Lady Prudence?" His grandfather chuckled, tapping his lips and turning his attention toward Prudence. "Well, well, Ben's Lady Prudence, it is a pleasure to make your acquaintance."

"I'm not *his* Lady Prudence." She glanced at Ben, then lifted her chin as she faced his grandfather.

"Quite right," his grandfather said. "If I were you, I wouldn't be his either. One never knows when he might grow all the hair back."

"True, and then I'd be stuck with him. And all that hair."

"You like the hair," Ben grumbled.

His grandfather tilted his head, studied them both. "Are you entirely certain you don't want to be his Lady Prudence? I wouldn't mind having another young person about now and then."

"I'm not entirely sure he wants me." Prudence sighed, and though she likely meant it as a tease, her words worried him. Still, she did not know? Would he ever convince her, then?

Ben tugged at his cravat. "Are we going to stand out here all day?"

"My grandson is a fool. But if you will not be his Lady Prudence, perhaps you will be mine? Tea?" Ben's grandfather offered a winged arm to Lady Norton. When she took it, he patted it. "You'll be mine, too, then, yes?"

She did not answer, only marched into the house at his side.

"I do love a side of silent dramatics," his grandfather said. "You are all just in time for dinner. Or rather, just in time for me to tell Cook to make more of whatever she'd planned."

"I do love being punctual." Prudence took Ben's proffered arm and followed him inside the house.

Stepping across the threshold filled Ben's lungs, made him feel light. How long had it been? Too long. "You'll be quite stern with me then, Lady P. I've been late in returning home these days."

She patted his hand. "You've been busy. But you'll improve."

Hell, but he wanted to kiss the top of her head, to change the trajectory of their stroll toward the stairs, up them, and through the door of his bedchamber.

But he followed his grandfather to a parlor and settled Prudence into his favorite overstuffed wingback by an open window. She'd like the air. She'd like to watch the pink light of the dying day. And he'd like to watch her enjoying it.

Cora separated herself from his grandfather and made a slow circle about the room.

"So then," his grandfather said, "what has brought this interesting little party to my doorstep?"

"Refuge." Ben propped an arm on the top of Prudence's chair. "Lady Norton needs a bed this night, and time to determine what move to make next."

"Oh dear." His grandfather sank into the matching chair across from Prudence, hooked his foot beneath a beaten ottoman and pulled it close enough to prop his feet atop it. As he sank into the chair's cushioning, he steepled his hands atop his belly. "Nothing too serious, I hope?"

Lady Norton stopped before a landscape painting, her spine stiff beneath all that black. "If we are inconveniencing you, my lord, we will—"

"No, no!" his grandfather boomed. "Not at all. Have a bed. Have all of them. I won't ask questions." He cupped a hand around his mouth and sat up, leaned across the space between him and Prudence, and whispered, "Her husband?" He closed his eyes and stuck his tongue out.

"Grandfather!" Ben barked. "Even I know that's rude."

His grandfather shrugged.

Prudence rolled her lips between her teeth, then ducked her head. The gentle shake of her shoulders told him she attempted to suppress laughter. When she sat up straight, she had managed it, and she folded her hands neatly in her lap atop wrinkled skirts. "No. Not that. We are not in mourning. He has not..." She made the same gesture as his grandfather, eyes and tongue and all, a brief flash of a mad moment. "But he might wish he was after Lady Norton figures out how to proceed."

Ben's grandfather settled back into his chair. "Ah, well, men are fools. Myself excluded, naturally. Ben?" His eyes narrowed, and Ben had to plant his feet to the floor to keep from retreating. "Why the sudden change, my boy? The clothes and all?"

Ben scratched the back of his neck. "No reason. Is that a new clock?"

"No changing the subject." His grandfather wagged a finger at him before settling his gaze on Prudence. "Is that what he calls you, my dear, other than my Lady Prudence of course? Are you his *No reason?*"

Prudence's mouth dropped open, and her eyes rolled around, no doubt seeking an answer the room would not serve up.

"Now is not the time, Grandfather," Ben grumbled.

"And why not?" the old man asked. "After all, the worst times are—"

"The best times for teases," Prudence said. "I agree." She grinned, and that curve of lips felt like a physical blow, one which could drop him to his knees. He already wanted that—to kneel before her and pledge himself. But now she shared a sly look with his grandfather, and Ben's heart felt damn well... complete.

He'd do anything for her, his life wet clay in her lithe hands, an empty broadsheet for her to press crowded with ink.

"I need to be alone." Cora stood, suddenly, within their little circle, having crept toward them on silent feet without even a rustle of skirts.

I would like to retire for the evening. Is that possible? I do not wish to be a burden, but—"

"Not a burden, dear woman, not at all." His grandfather creaked to his feet. "I'll have dinner sent up for you. Will that please you?"

"Yes, very much indeed," Cora said, lips as thin as her voice.

His grandfather patted her shoulder and ambled toward the door, bellowing, "Bexton! Mrs. Bexton?" He threw the door open and bellowed the name down the hall once more.

"I'm right here, you old loon," a bodiless voice said from the hall-way. "What do you want?"

"That's Mrs. Bexton, his housekeeper," Ben explained. "It must be the worst of times for her every hour of the day for he teases her constantly. Don't know why she hasn't left yet."

Only his grandfather was visible in the doorframe, and he'd hooked his thumbs in the waist of his pants and grinned like a madman. "Need rooms prepared for three guests. And dinner for three more as well. One portion to be sent to the pink room." He glanced back toward the parlor, toward Lady Norton. "No, ah, scratch that. To the green room. With all the dark trimmings. Will likely suit our guest's mood best."

"Guests? Three of them?" Mrs. Bexton cried. "On such short notice?"

"Should I tell them you can't manage it?"

"Grandfather," Ben warned. "Be nice."

"Oh!" A woman shuffled into the frame of the doorway, bumping his grandfather out of the way. She possessed steel-gray hair under a pristine white cap and a hooked nose. Her eyes shone bright and welcoming. "Mr. Bailey. Such a treat, and you've brought friends. Of course we can have rooms prepared. For such a charming lad, anything." She turned sharply and disappeared once more.

Ben's grandfather yelled after her, "I'm charming, too!"

"See," Ben said, "she recognized me instantly. I'm not too changed. Prudence... Lady Prudence knew me right away. In fact, she prefers me the other way."

"Do you now?" His grandfather sat back in his chair with a groan. "Interesting."

"I-I wouldn't say that."

"What?" Ben nearly bent his body in half to lean over the chair and stare her in the face.

"I-I like you"—her cheeks flushed the prettiest, brightest pink—"however you are, but I like how... how confident you seem now you've tried a new look. I suppose you were confident before, but then it seemed like defiance. Desperate. Oh, don't growl at me."

"I'm not growling."

"Were too," his grandfather said.

Prudence's fingers twitched in her lap as if she wished to do something with them. He could think of several things she could do, but she kept them tamed and still. So much like her—a calm that hid the potential for *anything*.

"But now," she said, "you appear ready to conquer the world."

Ben straightened slowly, scratching his chin. Funny she should say such a thing when, by choosing her, he'd be courting defeat. No more printshop, no more retribution. No more atonement for legacies lost.

Mrs. Bexton shuffled through the door. "The rooms are being readied, my lord."

"May I go up now?" Lady Norton asked. "Is it too much of a bother?"

"No, not at all. Right this way." Mrs. Bexton waited by the door.

Prudence bounced from her chair and followed Lady Norton to the hallway. "I will come with you."

Lady Norton nodded, and they disappeared behind Mrs. Bexton.

Ben dropped into Prudence's abandoned chair and met his grandfather's gaze. They remained there for some seconds. A standoff Ben would win. He certainly would not speak first. He crossed his arms over his chest and leaned into the back of the chair, made himself comfortable, showed he could not be broken.

"So then," his grandfather said sooner than Ben expected him to, "you're in love."

That he had not expected. He did his best to hide his shock, then decided no use hiding anything. "Mother always said one second you have no idea and the next..."

"You know. Yes. A sentiment I have always shared."

His mother and grandfather had met but once, before Ben's birth when his father and mother had traveled to England for a month. That trip had been enough, apparently, to convince his grandfather to approve the marriage. An unheard-of victory for love. A baron letting his heir move across the sea, knowing he might never return. They'd promised to return some day, though. And never had the chance to.

"Who is she? Her family?"

"Her brother is the Duke of Clearford."

"A duke's sister." His grandfather whistled. "Does the man know you work?"

"He knows I own several printshops. He owns one of them with me." Unfortunately. "The shop I told you about. The one that reminds me of Boston."

His grandfather's expressive brows made a united front above his sharp eyes. "I thought you meant to buy out the co-owners? I recommend against uniting family and business matters."

"I would prefer not to as well." He had no choice.

"You're not marrying the chit to get the shop at a steal, are you?"

"No. I consider that an insult." Shouldn't really. Not after all he'd done. "I'm not sure the duke will sell to me after I ask for Prudence's hand."

His grandfather settled deeper into his chair. "Do not worry, Ben. You do not have to work. You are my heir, and you—"

"I do. I do need to work. I failed Mother and Father once, and I won't do it again."

"Bah." His grandfather pushed to his feet and crossed the room, threw open a cupboard and grabbed a full decanter and tumbler. The glass clinked together, and he snapped them to the table, unstopped the bottle, and poured himself a generous amount of what Ben knew to be quality whisky.

"Are you going to offer me any?" Ben asked, stretching his legs out in front of him and clasping his hands together behind his head.

"No. Grow a brain and perhaps." He snorted.

"Are you calling me a fool?"

He grandfather returned to his chair and took a swig of his drink before answering, "I am. Because you are a fool. What happened in Boston is that you were a *child*, a fifteen-year-old boy with no business running one. You were grieving and alone. Yet you survived. You made the decision to come to me."

"Because I'd run the printshop into the ground."

"Because you had the courage to do what it took to survive. You made that journey alone."

"And fell overboard. Lost Mother's ring, Father's last paper, and—"

"And *survived* something most would not. Then you conquered Mrs. Bexton's heart here in London and made friends with a duke's heir of all people and went into business running a print empire."

"Helping run it. Mainly I stay in the back and manage the machines."

"Something that partner of yours knew little about before you. Bah." His grandfather shook his head. "Wake up, boy. You're no failure." He sipped from his glass once more, then studied the amber liquid as he swirled it round and round. "You remind me of your father. There are not many men who would throw over a title and a life of ease to live in an entirely different country with the woman he loves. Your father did, though, and you're your father's son. I see it in every line of your face." He sighed and took another sip. "Have you told *your* Lady Prudence about all this?"

"Not entirely." And he couldn't. Not entirely.

His grandfather took a longer sip this time, then met Ben's gaze. "You should. When a fellow's in love with a woman, he should tell her everything until every cowardly corner of his heart is laid bare before her. She'll shine light there, you'll see." He tipped his glass toward Ben. "One way or another, she'll bring a light and show you every place that needs dusting." He inhaled deeply. "But also every bit that's good and pure and worth her time."

"How'd you know? That I... that I lo—"

"You arrived on these shores with a scraggly bit of scruff you called a beard. Looked like baby bird feathers glued to your cheeks by a tottering two-year-old." His grandfather lifted the glass to the candle-light, tipped it this way and that. "You refused to shave it, no matter how I teased. I think you thought it a part of who you were in Boston. Couldn't let it go. It filled in, scraggly patches fading away. Still, you kept it. But for her... you shaved it all away. You mean to step into a new life with her." He smiled at the glinting candle-lit glass. "Yes, and I hope you become the man you're meant to be at her side."

His grandfather stood, downed the rest of the whisky, and made for the door. "I'm going to check on dinner. Famished, I am." He stopped in the doorframe and regarded Ben over his shoulder. "Whether it's a fashionable coat, a printshop, or a woman, what we want most changes as we do. Don't stick tight to one prize and neglect another."

When his grandfather disappeared into the hallway, Ben rolled his eyes. He didn't need his grandfather's maxims.

"And Ben."

"Gah!"

Only his grandfather's head peeked at him from the side of the doorframe, grinning. "If you're too much a coward to embrace changing, some other man will embrace *her*. She is not yet, as she was quick to point out, *your* Lady Prudence." He slapped the frame twice, then disappeared once more.

"Not... my... Hell." His grandfather's warning buzzed in his arms and legs, making a muddle of his mind. They had returned to London.

And to the suitors. The Season was coming to an end, but still there was plenty of opportunity for some other man to woo Prudence away from him.

And if Ben didn't take what he wanted, some other man would. Of course they would. Prudence was everything any man—if he possessed a brain—could want. Clever and kind, pretty and passionate. That day looking over his notes and ledgers and schedules, she'd made him feel capable, as if with her he could accomplish anything. He wanted to help her feel the same. He didn't want her to ask *why* when a man found her attractive. If he had it in his power to change that, he would. Now. And by any means necessary.

His grandfather, as usual, had the right of it. Men changed. What they wanted melted away to be replaced by new desires. Ben still wanted to honor his parents, honor their love and their strength. But if he couldn't have that and Prudence, well...

Ben Bailey would never compromise a woman he didn't intend to have. But he intended to have Prudence. Even if it meant giving up everything else.

Chapter Eighteen

Prudence sat in the big comfortable bed and stared at the wall. On the other side of the wall, her friend brooded. Alone and hurting. Cora would not let Prudence in. She'd knocked, she'd asked, and she'd been sent away.

"Just do not run away while I'm sleeping," Prudence had begged, ear and palms pressed against the locked door.

Cora's muffled response came after a long pause. "I will not. I promise."

That exchange an hour ago, and an hour after she'd left the dining table, hoping that by skipping an after-dinner drink with Ben and his grandfather, she might offer Cora comfort.

Cora did not want comfort, but... somehow... Prudence did. So odd. Nothing horrid had happened to her. She'd saved Cora from ruining herself in front of a brothel. She'd met Ben's terribly lovely grandfather, and soon, perhaps tomorrow, she would return home, finish the Season, and... and what?

The future seemed a void. Now that Lord Norton knew about Cora and the books... could they continue? The house party they'd experimented with during the last week, would that survive? And if not, what then? What would give her life purpose? What would fill up her hours?

And just as confusing—Mr. Benjamin Bailey. His intentions... she'd questioned them from the beginning. She'd flung those questions out the window now. Torn those suspicions to shreds when he'd harnessed a horse to the gig and secreted her away from Norton Hall in pursuit of Cora in the dim hours of the early morning. He would not do all that if he did not want her.

She gathered the blanket up to her chin as she leaned against the headboard, pulling her knees to her chest, clutching to her certainty along with the folds of cloth. So difficult to trust a man like him could want a woman like her. Like trying to believe in fairy stories when you're old enough to understand they are not true. Never have been. Illusions.

No. She closed her eyes and burrowed her face in the blanket. She would not let doubt defeat her. His every action spoke of want, of desire and longing. For her. If she could not believe him, well, that impugned his honor. She'd be branding him a liar. The fault remained with her. She flung herself out of bed and wandered to the mirror, forced herself to view her reflection there. Not as beautiful as Lottie. Not as sweet as Annie. Not as interesting as the twins. No, no. She shook her head. *Don't look for what is not there. Look for what is there, for what Ben sees. What Cora sees.* She pressed her eyes closed so tightly fireworks danced across the black field of her eyelids. Then she opened them. And looked again.

Her long hair waved down her back, reaching almost to her rear. It caught the wavering candlelight and looked a bit like fire-warmed bronze. She liked it—the color and how it fell in soft waves. Her lips shaped an unexpected smile. She liked how that looked, too, a bit... impish, a bit defiant, too. She'd never have used those words to describe herself, but perhaps women who organized naughty libraries *should* be described in such terms.

She met her own gaze in the looking glass. Saw the doubt swimming there in eyes that could not seem to decide on a color. Blue or green? Doubting or confident? Her eyes could not make a decision;

they would always be both, depending on the circumstances of lighting, what gown she wore...

Perhaps she would always be both, too. Doubting. And confident. Not confident yet, but perhaps soon. She'd work on it. She closed her eyes and made a mental to-do list, putting herself as item number one. Not Cora or her recitations, not the library. Just Prudence. Just... loving herself.

A knock on the door stole her breath and flung her eyes wide open. Soft as it had been, her heart still raced. She would always remember the knock that had roused her from sleep so many years ago now, the innocent sound a harbinger of her parents' deaths, her great aunt's pale, round face so filled with sorrow Prudence had known in an instant—the world forever changed.

Had something happened? To Cora? Or to Ben?

"Prudence?" She knew that muffled voice. Another soft knock.

She opened the door, and Ben tumbled inside her chamber, closing —and locking—the door behind him. No look of doom about him, no paleness. Only high color and his big body moving fast, only purpose and determination.

"What are you—"

He kissed her. Hands cupping her cheeks and hips surging into her. He took big, swallowing steps, marching her backward as he parted her lips with his tongue and ravished her.

A man. Kissing her. In her bedchamber. At night. The most intimate of moments. Should be at the very top of her list.

He bit her bottom lip, tugged it, clawed his hands up her back, gathering her shift in a knot against her skin. Her body jolted into a life it had only begun to know, a life of wanting.

What list? What doubt?

Only Ben and his hands, Ben and his lips, Ben and his low growl just next to her ear. She moved without much thought, following his lead, going where impulse led her—his soft hair, his rough jaw, his broad shoulders, his hard abdomen. So easy to explore with only that thin layer of linen between his skin and hers.

They kissed and kissed until she could do nothing but cling to him, nothing but lean against him, her arms wrapped around his neck, letting him hold her and kiss her and what felt like... love her. They kissed until growling madness became soft surety. Him going nowhere. Her hanging on. Their hearts happy to beat in a steady rhythm next to one another. They kissed until she realized how hard he was against her belly, how needy she felt between her legs. And they kissed until she stopped it with a sigh and spoke into the V of his shirt, open at the neck, revealing a dark slice of skin dusted with hair.

"Why are you here?"

"I thought that clear." His voice hoarse as if he'd spent the last half an hour screaming. When she did not answer, he tipped her chin up, forcing her to meet his gaze. "You're not questioning me again, are you? I've had quite enough of that, Lady P."

She shook her head. She... was not questioning his desire for her. "Did you come to talk? Or kiss? Or... something else entirely?"

"Oh, sweets, something else entirely." He lifted her hand to his lips, kissed her knuckles, burning her up with a naughty, gaze-locking grin the entire time. He flipped her hand, kissed her palm, her wrist—he froze. He scowled. "Prudence, what is this?" His fingertips lightly outlined a bruise there.

"From the boathouse, I suppose. When you"—she cleared her throat—"shackled my hands to the wall."

He cursed. "I hurt you." He loosened his hold on her so her hand lay open on top of his palm. The bruise, glowing and accusatory. "I hurt you." His voice softer, damning.

She flipped her hand, wove their fingers together, and fit her palm inside his bigger one. "No. I mean, yes. But"—she shivered—"I do not seem to mind. I... I like it when you are not so gentle. I like it when you tease, too. Though gentle is lovely, too." Her cheeks so hot that they'd surely burn to ash. "The words you find to say to me... they make me feel as if I could fly."

He squeezed her hand, kissed her temple. "I will give you every nice word you could ever need, and a rough tumble when you wish it. Still, I will not hurt you."

"It's curious, but..." How to say this without seeming addled? "When I see the bruise, I know it was no dream—what we did in the boathouse. When I brush against it, and it pains me, I know there was a moment in time when a man wanted me so much he... he lost control a little bit. I like knowing it was not a dream. I like knowing... I can make you lose control."

He crushed her to him, stroked his fingers up and down her back. "You should not need a bruise to know you're wanted, Prudence." He dropped to his knee before her, hands slipping away from her body and into his pocket. "You asked me why I came here." His hand reappeared quickly and along with it, a ribbon. He held it up to her. "I used to carry bits of ribbon about before I cut my hair. To pull it back and out of my way. I still do, actually, though I don't need them anymore. I suppose it has become a habit. But it's good I have it now. I had planned to give you nothing but my word, myself, tonight."

"Ben, what are you doing?"

"Isn't it obvious?" He tied the ribbon round her wrist, covering the bruise. "I want to marry you. The night I fell overboard, I lost the last bits of my mother and father. Her ring, the last pamphlet he ever printed with his own hand. I'd always kept them in my pockets, you see."

She hit her knees before him, curling her hands against his chest. "Your poor pockets are so burdened. Cigars, rings, newspapers, and ribbons. No wonder you need such baggy trousers."

"Can we focus, Prudence?"

"I am focused. On the problem of your pockets."

He cupped her neck and took her mouth in a quick kiss, retraining her attention, and when he released her lips, she looked up at him with serious eyes.

"Losing the ring, the paper... it was more than that, wasn't it?" she said.

He caressed her neck with his thumb, up and down in a rhythm which helped him speak. "I lost those tokens of my parents that night. But, perhaps, if I tie this ribbon tight enough, I will not lose you." He fondled the ribbon on her wrist. "And every time you feel it there, know a man wants you. Know *I* want you." His gaze lifted from the ribbon, focused on her. "I want you to be my wife. And before you ask why, let me educate you." He took a breath and wet his lips, then held her with a look that traveled so deep within her she would never be able to dig it out.

"I see myself better when I am with you. My mind calms and focuses and the tangled, never-ending list of things I must do, and times I must do them by, simply straighten themselves out. They give way, entirely to one thing. One person. You. It is not why I began courting you. It happened slowly. A little bit in the garden that night. A little bit while walking the London streets. A little hidden behind a pack of dog arses and splayed across a chaise. A lot, I must confess, in front of my horrid attempts at organization. I have an uncontrollable fantasy now of spreading you naked across my ledgers and notebooks, but only after you tidy them first. Watching your mind work quickly to put things to rights..." He huffed a laugh. "A little bit of foreplay I never anticipated needing so badly."

She laughed, too, because something like joy but brighter—the brightest thing she'd ever felt—bubbled up inside her, and it must get out. As laughter. As the uncontrollable curve of her widening smile.

He reached for her hand and pulled her to her feet. "Prudence?"

"Hm?" She could barely even make that sound around the width of her grin.

"Will you marry me?"

Somehow, she managed to tame her lips into a straight line, raise a brow. "I thought you would ask me to be your secretary."

"That, too. If you wish. And only if I can take you on top of my desk, across the ledgers, when I wish."

"When I wish, too?"

He kissed her again, toppling her backward onto the bed. He lifted his lips from her only enough to ask with a growl, "Is that a yes?"

"Yes." She clutched him more tightly. "Yes, yes, yes."

He laughed as he kissed her, and nothing had sounded sweeter, tasted sweeter, than happiness on his lips.

"I want one more thing from you," he said, scattering kisses along her jaw, her neck.

"Anything."

"You. Tonight. Right now. I know we should wait, but I feel like I've been watching you forever, watching you and being fascinated at every turn, and I keep thinking if I peel back one more layer, I might see all of you." He pinched her shift, tugged it, pulling the thin muslin tight against her breasts outlining her nipples, hard and tingling. His eyes devoured the sight, fogged over with heavy lust. "There are still layers."

A well-known voice inside she knew, one she needed to silence, spoke up, "What if you peel back the final layer and are... underwhelmed by what you discover?" Why must it be so very hard to look at herself differently? Had she made such a habit of it, of never even looking in the mirror so she did not have to be disappointed, that she could not now change?

"Impossible. Prudence, look at me." His hand firm at her chin, shoved it center, and she found his eyes, serious and dark just above her, demanding everything. "Impossible. Because I love you."

I love you. She had never thought to hear a man say those words to her. But she did not have time to relish them. He continued on at a rapid speed, astounding her with each word he dropped into the soft, heated space between them.

"I love every part of you I have come to know so far. I love Practical Prudence, and Prim Prudence. Who is very close to Proper Prudence. But not quite. And sometimes you are Prickly Prudence. I love her, too. And while you are all the others, you are always Pretty Prudence as well." He wrapped his hand in her hair and smoothed his thumb along the strands of it. "I like this bit of you." He lifted her hair to his lips and kissed it. And then he kissed her cheekbone. "I like this, too. And I particularly love these." He kissed her lip and cupped her breast.

"Which of those?" she asked, breathless and breaking their kiss.

"Both. Of course." He tilted his head, studying her. "Do you know who, surprisingly, I adore?"

She shook her head.

"Punctual Prudence. Can't help it. She drives me wild. No laughing, Lady P. I assure you that it surprised me, too. But... do you know one thing I have never thought of you as?"

She shook her head again.

"Timid. Timid Prudence is not a Prudence I have ever seen. It does not even start with a P."

"There are a great many words that do not start with a P. And some bad ones that do."

"You're ruining a perfectly good argument, Picky Prudence."

"Apologies. Do continue."

"My favorite Prudence is the passionate one. Passionate about helping others, passionate about making sure the world runs like a well-oiled clock, passionate when I touch her, and passionate when she touches me. Then, the passion is quite infectious." He stroked the side of her face, his smile disappearing but from his lips only. In his eyes, it still glowed. "I love you, Prudence, and I can't have you doubting that. What shall I do to convince you?"

She wanted, more than she ever had before, to let go of the doubt which had always bound her round as tightly as her stays. She wanted it more than anything.

So, what if she just... did?

What if it was a choice one must make over and over again—to discard doubt and believe in one's self? Well then, she would make that choice right now, and she would continue to make it every time doubt arose. Because *the* words trembled on her lips, and she tossed her doubts to the wind and found the courage to say them.

"I love you, too, Benjamin Bailey. I love the bearded beast and the refined man. I love your teasing, and I love your fears. I mean, I wish to soothe your fears. I love that you trust me enough to share them with me. I will hold you every time a storm blows across the skies, distract you in whatever way I know how. I love how much you love your grandfather. And I love how you helped Cora with so few questions. I do not love that you are such good friends with my brother, but I suppose someone must be, and you have a heart kind enough to do it. It does rather make me question your taste, though."

"Let us call it a mutually beneficial business arrangement and not a friendship, then."

She laughed and nudged his nose with her own, closed her eyes. "I love that you have purpose, the desire to achieve everything you wish, even if you do not have the patience for the small things. I even love *that*. Is that not strange? I hate chaos of any sort, and you are the epitome of it." She brushed a strand of hair out of his eye and tucked it behind his ear. "But I do so love *you*." And here was another choice to be made. She could let him stay as the world wheeled by from night to morning, or she could ask him to leave. He would not dismiss her preference. But choosing to let him stay felt like choosing to throw away her doubt. It must be done. She wanted it done more than anything.

No, she wanted *him* more than any. So, she cupped his cheeks with her hands. "Stay tonight, Ben." And then she kissed him. Again and again and again, she kissed him.

Chapter Nineteen

W ith each kiss Prudence's certainty grew, each doubt crushed beneath the searing hunger of his touch.

Until she could remain still and quiet and small no longer.

She broke the kiss and pushed away from him, scooting toward the headboard.

He glanced up at her, a lock of hair falling over one eye, the other glinting from beneath lowered lids. "Want me to chase you, love?"

She grasped the tie at her bodice and tugged. "I want to find out if you really do like what you find beneath my... layers." The small bow holding her final scrap of clothing in place gave way easily beneath her fingers. The bodice sagged open, and one shoulder of the shift fell down her arm, revealing one breast, cold in the night air. She shivered.

The glint in his eye flashed, and she shivered again. Not from the cold, but from the way he worked up the bed toward her, slow and methodical, every ounce of his focus vibrating on her revealed body. He didn't need words for her to know—he liked the bit of her beneath all the layers quite well indeed.

His hand crept up her belly, between her breasts, and smoothed over her collarbone toward her shoulder. He hooked his thumb beneath the half of her shift still covering her other breast and took it with him, uncovering her inch by shiveringly delicious inch. She wriggled her arms out and wrapped them tight around his back. The muscles bunched beneath her touch. Backs? Muscular? She'd never considered it. Now she'd likely never stop considering it. *His.* The solid feel of him, a man to protect her heart. His easy movements rippling beneath his warm skin, a man to dance with her in pleasure.

When his breath warmed her breast, she hissed and arched, and when he rolled his tongue around her nipple, her hands became claws, her nails sinking into his back. Into the linen covering his back. She fisted it, tugged it, groaned when it would not budge, her brain clouded by the sensations he worked through her with his kisses. While his mouth tended one breast, his hand tended the other, and her body felt weightless, perfect.

Still his shirt would not budge. She released it and pressed her palms to his chest, shoved with a grunt. And with a laugh he popped off her, coming to his knees, straddling her, and yanking the shirt off above his head.

"You next," he said, his voice dark, his eyes darker. He clutched her shift at the neckline and tore, muscles bulging. The muslin gave way, and a rip screamed across the room.

Then she lay open and naked before him, and he looked like a starving man come to feast. He didn't touch her, though. He lifted one side of the destroyed shift and rubbed it between thumb and forefinger.

"Such very fine material. So very delicate. The very best for a duke's sister. Tore like paper. Shall I buy you stouter ones once we're wed?"

"Yes. You must have a challenge, after all. Can't make things too easy for you."

"You think you've been easy for me?" He fell forward onto his hands, which hit the mattress on either side of her head, caging her in as he dipped his head. The tips of their noses touched.

"Quite. I seem to give into you at every turn."

"You run from me. From yourself. No more, Lady P."

"No more." She twined her hands around her neck and pulled him down for another kiss.

His cock dug into her belly, a foreign sensation, but everything about this, new and different and wonderful.

He licked the spot between her breasts she'd never even thought about before. That, wonderful, too, and she raked her fingernails down his back to tell him so.

"What do you like, my well-read lady?" he asked, nipping down her belly to her navel.

"Whatever *you* do." She found his biceps, hard and well-formed working the presses, like knots beneath her palms, steadfast and strong. "Whatever *you* do, I like. As long as it's *you*."

He looked up at her, his head slightly shaking, the scruff on her chin, scraping her belly. That shake seemed to say he could not fathom it. But the gleam which took over his expression next said he did not care to dive into the fathoms of knowing. He planned to relish the reality.

He dove between her legs and pleasured her as he had in the boathouse. Each lick and suck more potent now that her skin had been revealed entirely to the air. No more barriers between them. Not a single one, and that drove her pleasure higher, deeper, harder.

But the man she loved moved slowly, so slow, as if they had the time to love every inch of skin and every inch of soul beneath that. He kissed up and down her arms, lingering in hollows. He worshiped her throat and behind her ears, and he made his way down her legs, returning after every exploration to her core, where she needed him most.

She did not stay idle during all this. She set out to discover what she liked best about him. Surely, she had a favorite bit, though with him large and strong and poised above her, her mind tended toward— everything. She adored everything about him in equal measure.

The wide chest which held his heart. The broad shoulders which carried those who needed his help. The trim waist and ridged abdomen he hid behind clothes too big for him. The thick legs which had kicked hard to reach her through the storm. The tongue he slipped inside her sex, making her moan. Those clever fingers teasing her nipples, and... oh yes, that too—his cock. She'd not truly touched it yet. In the boathouse, a barrier of wool had remained in place.

That same barrier remained.

Her hands flew to the buttons of his fall, flicking and tugging.

"Yes," he groaned, his hands joining hers, making short work of their shared goal. When the buttons all slipped loose, he wriggled out of the breeches, tossed them aside, and settled over her once more.

She did not hesitate to touch him, wrapping her hand about his length and reveling in the unexpected that astonished her from every direction. From above, Ben's hiss, his every muscle turning on at once. In her hand, the leap of his cock at her touch. In her own body, the surge of power. She could turn this man to velvet stone with a touch. That touch itself unexpected. Softer, hotter. She knew what to do with her hand just so. Up and down as he bracketed her head with his forearms dropped down to gift her with a wet kiss.

After several slides up and down his length, learning him, what rhythm and speed he liked, he jerked away from the kiss and unwrapped her hand, placed it flat on his chest as he reached between their bodies, and slipped two fingers inside her.

Their eyes met.

"Now," she said, biting her lip and loving how he looked at her as if he could not look away. She needed him now. Her every limb tingled, and that same perfection she'd experienced in the boathouse hovered just out of reach. She wanted it. She wanted him. All of him, all this. She knew the danger. Knew the outcome. A swollen belly and a new little human in nine months. But they were betrothed. No reason not to welcome such an event.

"You're sure?" he panted, positioning the tip of his shaft between her legs, teasing her with it in soft strokes of her sex.

"Yes, Ben. Yes."

He found her opening with his fingers first, and then he inched inside her carefully. She flinched and wrapped her arms around him more tightly. She felt so very full, and he'd barely begun his task. Her sisters had warned her about this, that it might feel... difficult at first. But they'd reassured her that the right man would take his time, would care for her pleasure as well as his.

"Prudence? Are you well?" His voice graveled near her ear. "I will not go further if it pains you."

Ben, the right man. No doubt there.

She dug her nails into his back and rolled her hips up, meeting his, inching him more deeply inside her. "I am well. As long as you are here with me, I am well."

He kissed her, the kind of kiss that made a woman forget everything else, and in the memory-demolishing pleasure of his lips, he thrust again, joining her fully.

She gasped.

And he kissed an apology into her lips.

It was fine, though. No real pain. Just an unexpected fullness, a tightness which eased with each passing moment, with each kiss and soothing word that dropped, as well, from his lips. Because he kept her mouth so well occupied, she tried to tell him with her body how wonderful she felt, rolling her hips against his and smoothing her arms up and down his body as far as they would reach. The more she moved her hips against him, the more he moved, as well, until his kisses slowed and he lifted slightly, panting, and gazing down into her eyes.

"I love your eyes," he said, slowly retreating from her body. "And I love your lips." He thrust back home. "I love your hair, too." He retreated and returned again, moving his hand to grasp her hair, making a fist around the tangle of it spread across the bed. "But your eyes, Prudence. There is always something happening behind them." In and out, harder and faster. "And I want to know what it is." Harder, faster.

Her body began to move with him, learning the rhythm, loving it, needing to meet each of his thrusts with one of her own. His words as much as his body moved her right up to the edge of decimating pleasure. And when he slipped a hand between their bodies and rubbed circles against that most aching bit of her, she fell entirely off that edge. Arms flung wide, she arched off the bed. He kissed her into silence, his hips losing the smooth rhythm from before to pump into her with a fervency beyond control. Each thrust doubled the pleasure already rippling through her, and though every muscle seemed impossible to move now, she opened her eyes. She found him watching. Again, as if he could not look away.

When he came with one final, hard thrust, he never blinked. She'd always felt he saw her across a ballroom when no one else ever did. Had always been able to pick her out of a crowd when no one else seemed willing to. And now he saw deeper, too, and she let him see, and when he collapsed against her, she welcomed the weight, hugged him hard, the only directive her arms seemed capable of following.

He gathered her close, and they scooted to the top of the bed. Without breaking touch, they climbed beneath the covers.

"I should leave," he yawned.

"Stay just a moment." She burrowed into his chest.

"I'll stay forever if you let me."

She fell asleep satisfied. Not just in body, but in the knowledge that forever looked so different, so much better than it had a month ago.

Chapter Twenty

Ben woke with empty arms and knew instinctively they should not be empty. His eyes flew open, searching.

Finding. There she stood at the looking glass, tugging her stays up over... his shirt.

"Prudence," he said, voice heavy with sleep. "Wrong article of clothing, love. That's mine, I do believe."

She caught his gaze in the mirror's reflection and scowled. The shirt hung loose on her arms and fell to her knees. "Yes, and you ruined my shift last night, so this will have to do. I assume you have extra shirts here. Or you can borrow from your grandfather. I do not and cannot."

"Excellent point." He pushed to sitting and leaned against the headboard, bending one arm behind his head. "Need help?"

"Dressing?"

"Or undressing."

"No, thank you."

He put a hand over his heart. "You wound."

"It is not that I do not want to, but there is no time. The sun is already promising to rise. You must dress and leave quickly. And I must see about Cora."

He sighed. "Naturally you would put your schedule ahead of your desires. And you are quite right in this instance. I shall attempt to follow your lead."

He threw the blankets back and swung his feet to the floor, stood and stretched nice and long, positioned just so his naked body would appear reflected behind her and to the side. Her gaze snagged just where he wanted it to, and her cheeks burned red. He put his hands on his hips and looked about the room. "Now, where did I put those breeches? Ah, there."

He rescued the pants from their wrinkled pile on the floor and returned his attention to his future wife.

He'd never seen Prudence stare at anything with so much heat. Except, perhaps, a perfectly organized schedule. Good to know *he* ranked that high. She shook her head, blinked several times, and managed to wrench her gaze away from his image in the looking glass.

"Tighten my stays, please?" she asked.

He did, dropping his breeches and dropping a kiss to the back of her neck, letting his fingers linger everywhere he touched. She remained still as a statue, holding her breath, as if she feared to move. When he stepped away from her and said, "all done," a full-body shudder brought her to life, and she snapped out an arm to grab the gown she'd draped across the back of a nearby chair. She stepped into it and gave him her back once more.

"Tie the tapes? Please?" Her voice a breathless whisper.

He did once more as she bid, but this time he kissed the back of her neck before and after each time, making sure she did not turn to stone once more. Her breath became heavy pants, and when he stroked a line down her neck and nipped at her earlobe, she moaned, letting her head fall to the opposite side to give him more space for exploration.

He turned her around. Eyes glazes, lips slightly parted, gown wrinkled from yesterday, hair plaited and streaming across one shoulder. The most beautiful sight of his entire life. He loved her with his entire soul, his rapidly beating heart, and his quickly hardening cock. He stood before her naked and vulnerable, all hers to do with as she pleased.

"Ben." His name a breath on those pretty pink lips.

"What is it you want, Pretty Prudence?"

"Trousers," she barked. Then she swallowed and spoke more moderately, "You should put trousers on."

"Should I? Does my nudity bother you? You, who've read so many *books*?"

"That's not it. It's only that I... I like your legs and... and your —*ahem*—backside. They appear... very strong. Like the rest of you. I find it... quite appealing."

"I see no problem, then."

"It's a distraction." She sat in the chair her gown had been draped across and picked up a pale strip of silk. Her stocking, and beside it a ribbon, pale blue and delicate. She lifted her skirts above her knee and readied the stocking.

"I like your legs and arse, too, love. Those stockings, as well." He knelt before her and took the stocking from her, held it open. "Here you go."

She dipped her toes in, and he slid the stocking up her leg, reached for the ribbon, and used it to fasten the stocking in place. Then he fastened the other, too, and ran his hand up and down her leg, looked up at her. "Pretty Prudence, I want nothing more than to bend you over the bed and thrust deep inside you." He quirked a grin. "But we must hurry and—"

"Do it." Each word a breathy plea.

"Pardon?" He found her other stocking and ribbon, and he dressed her other leg, kissing her knee just above the fabric.

"Curse the schedule. We have time for this. Please, Ben? Don't we have time for this?" Her hands were fists on her skirts. Her eyes were lust-hardened opals.

"For what?"

"I-I can't say."

"Can't or won't?" He pulled her to her feet, wrapping her braid around his hand. "If you want me to do something, you need only ask. But be specific." He tugged her hair, just a bit, arching her neck and opening it enough for him to kiss the curve of it.

"Bend me over," she moaned. "I want you inside me."

"Since I am brilliant at disarranging schedules, I'm happy to grant your request." He reached between her legs, dove his fingers into her curls and parted her sex. "You're ready for me."

She bit her lip. "So very much. *Please*, Ben."

He whirled her before she'd finished speaking that tiny word. Two large strides brought them to the side of the bed, and she fell against it eagerly, her breasts and belly sinking into the mattress and the lovely, rounded globes of her arse lifting into the air, pressing against his thighs, just below his hips.

He widened his stance as he dragged his fingernails up and down her spine. She shivered. He could make this woman shatter. He could make this woman feel loved. And if he could do that, he could do damn well anything.

The doubts she harbored about herself—all wrong. And if she ever found out why he'd first begun to court her... he couldn't think on that. Only keep it from her. Forever if he must. Because he'd rather die than see his Prudence toppled by doubt.

Last night he'd been soft, desperate to make sure he would not hurt her, desperate to know she wanted what he did. Now he knew. She would not be repulsed by his sudden need to have her hard and fast. Perhaps if he took her often enough, she would not need a ribbon to know how he felt about her.

That ribbon there, now, a dark slash against her skin. Lust tore through him. Her—his to take and his to protect. He slipped his fingers into her first to make sure she was ready, and when he found her wet, he somehow found control, too, control enough to stroke his hands up down her sides, over her arse. He wrapped her hair around his hand and pulled her back, bent over her, and whispered into her ear.

"You are wanted, Prudence. I want you. Now. Forever."

She bit her bottom lip and closed her eyes, as if she could not believe it. A moment of doubt before her eyes popped open, and she thrust her arse back and against him. "Show me."

He released her hair and grasped her hips and thrust deep inside her.

She gasped, a sound that turned into a moan. He should be gentle, go slow. Last night had been her first. But her doubt did not need tenderness. It needed passionate proof. He gave it to her, slow thrust after slow thrust, showing her how he felt.

He put the words on his lips, too. "I love you. I love you." Harder, faster, his own body rushing toward the edge, ready to leap off. He slipped a hand between her and the bed, found that little pearl hidden in her curls, and showed it love, too. When her body arched with a scream, she muffled in the mattress, he found his release too, taking one more hard plunge into her, shivering into ecstasy, and then falling on top of her, stroking the hair away from her face to place a kiss there.

He wanted to hold her as he had all night, but the navy sky lightened to gray, so he pulled from her and found his shirt. As she lay limp on the bed, he cleaned her thighs and between her legs. When he'd wiped away the evidence of their lovemaking, he pulled her to standing and turned her to face him.

"Steady, now love," he said. "Find your legs."

"What legs?" she breathed.

He chuckled and nuzzled her neck. "I must go now."

She sat heavy on the bed and watched him pull his breeches on. Then after one final kiss, he left her. His room was not far from hers, and he let himself in just as the gray sky took on a hint of orange.

"Good morning, Ben."

Ben yelped. "Hell." He clutched his heart, gasped for breath. "You scared the life out of me."

His grandfather sat on the edge of his bed, facing the door, arms crossed, glaring. "I assume you've been in Lady Prudence's room?"

"What are you doing here, Grandfather?" Ben strode to the wardrobe and found a shirt, yanked it over his head.

"I came to see if you wanted an early morning ride, but I see you have already enjoyed one."

"Don't be crass."

"Then don't act crass." His grandfather stood and crossed the room to the window, stood looking out so Ben could see only his profile in the gray gathering light of the coming morning. "And don't compromise a lady. I thought you knew better."

"Are you going to tell anyone?" Ben found a cravat and wound it loosely round his neck.

"No, of course not."

"Then she is not compromised." Ben finished the simple knot at his throat and reached for a waistcoat. "But I will if I have to. She is *my* Lady Prudence now, and I'll fight any man who says otherwise." Including her brother. Including his own nefarious past actions.

"You're going to do the right thing by her?"

"Do you even have to ask?" He would be insulted if he didn't know his grandfather used every word to protect Prudence.

"Have you asked? For her hand? You were much too unsure last night."

"Entirely sure now."

"Then I suppose I'll forgive you." His grandfather finally turned to view Ben, some of the anger drained from his countenance. "If she said yes."

"She did." Ben couldn't keep a smile from his lips.

"Don't be cocky about it. Why wouldn't she say yes when you have such a delightful family?"

Ben buttoned the waistcoat and stood next to his grandfather. "I've not done things as you would have liked me to. But I'll do things the right way from now on. If that's what she wants."

"Wise man. Would you like to ride out?"

Ben shook his head. "I believe the ladies will wish to leave early today, and even if they don't wish it, they should. I'll make sure they do. We cannot hide here forever. I must talk to Clearford."

"Too true." His grandfather wrapped him in a hug. "I'm happy for you. You'll have your printshop and a lovely wife in the same year."

The printshop. Yes. But only if Clearford bought his lies.

He released his grandfather and guided him toward the door.

"Do be a good boy from here on out, eh," his grandfather said. "I don't want to hear any unsavory rumors about my heir."

When he left, Ben flopped onto his bed. It did not smell like Prudence. A failing, that. So much to do, his mind a cluttered mess only capable of focusing on one thing: Prudence.

Perhaps on the way to her brother's house she'd help him compose a list of things to do. Exchange his tiny apartments for more expansive lodgings befitting his wife, procure a ring, procure a marriage license, have the banns read. Could he add to that list of items obtaining the dream he'd long worked for?

He didn't want to tell the duke a damn thing about Prudence or her friends, but if he didn't, he would have failed once more to honor his parents' memory.

Chapter Twenty-One

Cora's silence had begun to feel like a heavy buzzing in the air. All morning while they'd broken their fast, as they'd bundled up into the baron's roomy coach, as they'd trundled through London streets and toward Mayfair—Cora had said not a word. Prudence had long since given up encouraging the somber woman at her side into conversation.

Ben had proven a much more loquacious companion, but one whose every word burned heat into Prudence's cheeks. The ribbon he'd wound round her wrist last night remained hidden beneath her glove, but she felt it like the hot tracing of his fingertips across her sensitive skin.

The ribbon and Ben's words, the look in his eyes when he gazed on her, the way he sprawled on the other side of the coach—his mere posture an invitation to climb atop his lap—all colluded to make her mind and body a jumbled mass of longing. Better to remain silent entirely lest she do something mortifying. Like moan. Or proposition him.

And all with an audience.

Heavens. She'd agreed to marry this man. And nothing but joy shot through her at the prospect. She'd never have guessed she would know this, never have thought to feel so loved.

The streets outside the window grew wider, the trees larger, and the homes statelier.

"Almost home," Prudence said, catching Ben's eye.

Cora squeaked. Her mouth twitched. Then she opened it, and for the first time all day, Prudence heard her friend's voice. "I need to do a reading."

Prudence flashed another glance at Ben. Did he know about those? Or had Cora just spilled their remaining secret?

"Reading?" Ben asked. "Do you wish us to drop you at Hatchards?"

"A poetry reading." Cora turned to Prudence. "Will you organize it?"

"Of course. When?"

"Your sister's ball."

"But that's less than a fortnight away. We cannot—"

"We must." Cora's eyes should have been the glittery glass of a woman near tears, but they were clear, determined. "No matter how."

"There's always Hyde Park," Prudence said, "but—"

"You both lost me two turns ago." Ben sat up and leaned forward, bracing his arms on his knees, stretching the buckskin across his muscled thigh. "Please do catch me up."

No noticing muscled thighs! Not right now. Prudence focused on her friend instead.

Cora considered Ben, tucked a strand of hair behind her ear, and tilted her head. "Since you know everything, you may as well know this. I write erotic poetry. And recite said poetry aloud. And the women of London come in droves to listen. In dark rooms at midnight above and below crowded ballrooms."

Ben's gaze floated lazily from Cora to Prudence, and he whistled. "What don't the two of you do? Are you sure that's all? Do you recite poetry, too, Lady P? Perhaps you perform nude dances, or—"

"That is quite enough, Benjamin Bailey." Prudence sniffed, giving her best Lady Templeton impression. "There are no such dances, and my mind is not of a poetic turn."

He held up his hands, palms flat toward her. "Very well. But how do you organize an event no one's ever heard of? And in such public places? It's... well, hell, Prudence, it's radical. A scandal."

"I'm aware. That's why I'm careful. We all are. Or... we try our best to be." She explained the system to him—the gossip and abandoned rooms, the ribbons as marks, the candles in skirts and tinder boxes in pockets.

He grunted. "That's overly complicated."

"And how would you do it?" Cora looked out the window as the coach slowed. "We're almost there. I see Norton's townhouse." A pause, nothing but the clatter of the wheels beneath them. "My townhouse."

Ben shifted, as if the seat had grown unaccountably uncomfortable in the last few moments. "I would have a regular schedule. The first ball of every month or some such."

"That is a fine idea, Ben." Prudence blinked at him, mouth slightly agape. "And that *you*, of all people, came up with it..." She shook her head, shook the surprise from her eyes. "But we cannot know if the locations will prove salubrious."

"Hm." He scratched his jaw. His beard had begun to fill in his cheeks, and the sensitive insides of her arms, her thighs, the curve of her belly all held the red marks of his stubble. He grinned at her as if he knew the direction of her thoughts, and she tried, unsuccessfully, to control her blush. "Since you rely on gossip so much, a newspaper man might be of some use. One of my papers, *The Current*, special-izes in gossip, society news. I've certainly seen notes in its pages of who is redecorating what. I venture a guess I know before any of you do."

Debatable. He may have the papers right off the presses, but they had Isabella. Prudence's younger sister seemed to know everything about everyone in London and beyond.

His long, strong fingers, gloveless, continued scratching. "There has to be a safer way."

"The house party was about that," Prudence said. "An attempt to find a safer way. There have been too many close calls of late."

"We stop now."

Ben and Prudence turned toward Cora. She sat with her back to them, but her reflection told her secrets—a stone face and marble eyes.

"We must stop everything," Cora said, "the library especially, until we know what Norton intends to do or say about it all. He does not know about the poetry, though. And I've a new poem. My best yet. Composed entirely last evening." She swayed, listless as the coach stopped before the row of townhouses. "I will stop after this." Finally, she turned, but not to Prudence. "Mr. Bailey, if you discover a safer, more practical way of delivering the location of my reading to those who need to know, I'll be forever in your debt."

"No need for that, my lady." His voice fell with the soft gruffness of a kind heart, and if Prudence had not already loved the man, she would surely have fallen all the way off the cliff now.

"Yes." Cora opened the door, stepped onto the street, and looked up at them. "You would not want Prudence harmed in any way. Thank you for that. Perhaps you will prove a better husband than my own."

"But how did you know?" Prudence asked, half rising then falling back to the seat. "About Ben. And me?"

"Because it's rather like the stories I write. When the hero will do anything for the woman who holds his heart."

"I hope it does not end as poorly as your stories do," Prudence mumbled.

Cora managed a chuckle. "I am happy for you." But she dropped her gaze to the ground and closed the door. Through the window they saw her motion for the driver to continue on.

"Will she be well? Staying alone?" Ben moved across the coach to sit next to Prudence as it lurched into motion.

"I cannot say. I'll certainly check on her tomorrow. Perhaps I can convince her to stay at Clearford House for a time."

"Do you think Norton will return home? And more importantly, do you think she'll shove him down the stairs when he does?"

Prudence picked at her skirts. "Perhaps I should visit her sooner than tomorrow. Or stay with her tonight."

"Decide later, Lady P." He wrapped an arm around her shoulders and pulled her against his shoulder. "For now, close your eyes and rest until I return you safely home."

She did, the world fluttering into nothing behind her eyelids. His jacket, where she burrowed her nose, inhaling deeply, smelled faintly of cigars and much more strongly of Ben, that mix of paper and ink and male that made her feel safe, loved.

Perhaps she needed no reminder, no slim black ribbon around her wrist.

Nuzzling his chest, she said with a yawn, "Will you ask Samuel for my hand?"

"I will speak to him, yes."

"Do not let him bully you."

He squeezed her. "Perhaps I shall bully him."

She chuckled and let the sway of the coach relax her, let the so-close beating of his heart comfort her, and all too soon, they stopped. They exited together and entered the house, and Mr. Jacobs greeted them.

"Lady Prudence! We did not know you were to return today." His gaze focused on her arm. Where it entwined with Ben's arm. And her shoulder, where it braced against Ben's shoulder. The butler sniffed. "*Mr.* Bailey."

"Still object to my presence in this house?" Ben asked.

"Mr. Jacobs, you don't!" Prudence pulled away from Ben. "What could you object to?"

"Less now than before," the butler grumbled. "He looks less like a ruffian now. But still..."

"Lady Prudence approves of me now. And she approved of me then." He flashed a ruffian's grin, though he no longer possessed a ruffian's figure. "Right, Lady P?"

She narrowed her eyes. "I'll rescind my approval if I please."

"You won't." He took her hand and brought it to his lips, kissed her knuckles. "You won't let Mr. Jacobs color your opinion of me?"

"I think Mr. Jacob's opinion of you will change," she hissed, voice low, "once he knows you're heir to—"

He snapped his palm over her lips. "Ah, ah, ah, Lady P." He leaned close and whispered, "I'd like the old crank to learn to like me for myself."

"You do like making things difficult for yourself."

He nudged her toward the stairs. "I'll go speak with your brother. If he's home. Jacobs, is Clearford home?"

"Not for you," Jacobs said, slicing a hand between Prudence's body and Ben's.

Ben winked at Prudence, then ambled off down the hall toward Samuel's study.

Prudence found her bedchamber empty, and she pulled the bell to call for a bath. As she waited, she dared to pass by the looking glass, a surface she never quite allowed into her periphery. No use looking when she knew what she would see, knew there was a means of improving the reflection there.

But she boldly stood before it now, wearing a rumpled gown, lumpy because of the man's shirt serving as a shift beneath it. Her hair a mess, and her stockings sagging. But also... glowing and happy? A bit impish about the eyes and nose. Hair changing color in the light from honey to gold, the shadows that fell across a yellow gown.

She smiled.

And then she hopped, gasped, because an argument shook the ceiling and rumbled the walls. And she knew the voices shouting, too —her brother, her betrothed. She ran, flinging open the door, terrifying the maid just outside, and flying down the hall. She stumbled down the stairs and twisted her ankle. But still she continued, the voices roaring loader. When she reached the door of Samuel's study and wrapped her fingers around the handle, she could finally hear them clearly.

"Marry her?" Samuel roared. "You've been lying to her!"

Lying... to who? The words sizzling in the air hardly made sense. Prudence released the door handle as if it had become a burning coal, her body falling backward through thick, sludgy space until her back hit a wall.

"I thought you were willing to sacrifice your bachelor friends, Clearford. Desperate times, I believe you said." Ben's voice like she'd never heard it before, a low drawl devoid of the boredom she'd become acquainted with first and the teasing she'd come to know at last.

"It is merely that lies are not, perhaps, the best foundation for a happy marriage. Happy, Bailey. That's what I want for her, for them all. Happiness and safety."

Lies. That word again. *Lying,* too. Horrid in all its permutations. It seemed to pin her to the wall, sit like a boulder, heavy on her chest.

"And I'll give her that," Ben said, "You have no problem with a bastard for a brother-in-law. And Noble's an arse, but you welcomed him into your family quick enough. Why not me?"

Prudence pushed past the agony blooming in her chest and left the wall, found her hand once more on the door handle.

"It's not about you," Samuel said.

"Damn right, Clearford. Nor is it about you. Your rules and your demands. Your holding what I want to get what you want. It's about—"

She pulled the door open and stepped into the room in one fluid movement. "Who is it about, then, if it's not about you, Samuel?"

Both men faced her with slack jaws and panicked eyes. They seemed a study in opposites. Her brother polished but frayed at the edges, a hair or two twisting out of place above his ears, his shirtsleeves rolled up haphazardly past his elbows. Yet no one would notice the tiny tatters if they did not know to look. Ben looked, however, much as he had when she'd first met him—rumpled and scruffy and not at all refined. Yet the core of him remained steady, the emotion in his eyes unwavering. Neither man's appearance reflected the truth about him.

Neither had her reflection from just moments ago reflected the truth. Back to that shrapnel of a word again—*lies.*

"Prudence," Ben stepped toward her.

She held out a hand, palm flat, to stop him. And it did, more effectively than a bullet. "What did you mean? When you said my brother holds something you want and is using it to get what he wants?"

Samuel exhaled a strangled sigh and fell into a chair, his body going limp. "'Tis nothing of any import, Prudence."

Ben paced a step away from her, then paced back, his jaw ticking. A moment of looking into her eyes, and he said, "Very well. No hiding it now. Your brother owns shares in a printshop I want. And he won't sell them to me."

"What must you do to earn them?" She didn't want the answer. She *didn't.* Why had she asked that horrid question? Because it had floated to her lips on a familiar wave of self-doubt.

Ben swallowed but held her gaze. "Court you. He wanted me to discover what keeps you from marrying."

Ah. Yes, now everything made sense. Those anomalies she'd puzzled over so long finally clicked into clarity. Why had he followed her to the country? Why had he changed his appearance? Why had he kissed her, pursued her?

Because of Samuel. For a printshop.

She'd known it could not be for herself.

She'd been right.

And like the fortune teller who correctly predicts the end of the world, she wished she'd been wrong. All thought and feeling drained out of her with a held inhalation. Her mind, her chest, entirely empty, she turned and left the room.

A hand on her shoulder, warm and strong, stopped her. "Prudence, I'm sorry."

She rolled her shoulder, trying to dislodge Ben's hand. It would not move, so she let it lie there like a haircloth, a penance and reminder of her foolishness. "You told him about—"

"No. I told him nothing. Well... I told him you were friendly with a group of society matrons who spent their free hours teaching you about womanly things, being a wife and mother."

Must she thank him for that? Must she gift him her gratitude for hiding that which he'd sought to uncover through dubious means?

She ripped her shoulder from his grasp and finally turned to face him. With trembling fingers, she pushed the cuff of her gown up, ripped the glove off her hand. There, stark black against her skin—Ben's ribbon. She yanked one, loose end of it, and it fell free of her wrist.

"Prudence, stop." His voice gravelly, his hands lifting toward her, then dropping hard.

She held the ribbon out to him. "I would sincerely like to never see you again."

His jaw twitched. "No."

She dropped the ribbon on the floor. It fluttered in a wayward spiral to the marble below and lay like a discarded snakeskin, dark and limp.

"I hope you are happy with your printshop, Mr. Bailey." She looked toward the study doorway where her brother stood, shoulders stooped. "Because if happiness was your goal for me, Brother, you have failed. Spectacularly." She gave another laugh and made for the stairs. She still wore Ben's shirt beneath her gown. It burned her skin, acid and fire, and if she did not rip it off and cast it into the flames of the bedchamber grate soon, she'd melt, become a puddle of bone and blood in the hallway.

Heavy bootsteps behind her, and she didn't dare look back, no matter how fast and hard they came. "Prudence, wait up. Talk with me. I love—"

She whirled at the foot of the stairs, coming face-to-face with him. "Do not lie to me anymore."

"I'm not." Hard finality in those words. "I may have begun for your brother—"

"For yourself. Be honest."

"For myself. But I knew from the moment in the portrait gallery behind those damn dog arses that something had changed. I went to Norton Hall for your brother, for myself, but I stayed for you, Prudence. And I will hit my knees before you right here before Clearford, before damn Jacobs hovering in the doorway—don't slink away like you're not eavesdropping, Jacobs—to prove to you I love you."

Proof of love. Because she found it so hard to love herself, she'd needed that from him. Now she had proof of the opposite, and her heart could not see past its tears. They gathered in her eyes, too, and she pressed the heels of her hands into the sockets to keep them back. She should not need proof. Something in her was still broken because she did.

"Not even if you dropped to your knees before all London, Benjamin Bailey. Not even then." Because she loved him, and he'd not even wanted her. She'd been a means to an end, a task to tick off on a to-do list before tossing it into the fire.

She fled, her name on his tongue trailing after her, but not the slam of his boots. By the time she reached her chamber, the tears had come, and she made a puddle of herself beside the bed, leaning into the mattress, hiding her face in the blankets. Better darkness than facing the looking glass across the room.

A knock on her door. "Prudence?"

"Go away, Samuel! You... you horrid man!"

Silence into which Prudence poured her sobs.

Then, "Luv, I'm coming in."

"You stay out there, Samuel!" The words didn't come out right, too strangled and stark.

The door creaked open and snicked closed.

"Go away!" she demanded.

"I'm sorry."

She stormed to her feet, hands fists at her side. "And I have heard those words enough today! How can you even understand, you bone-headed nodcock?"

"Prudence!"

"Am I not polite enough for you, as Annie always is?"

"No, I—"

"And I certainly do not have Lottie's looks or the interest inherent in the twins."

"Prudence—"

"No. You will remain silent while I speak." Few steps took her to his side, and she poked his chest. A light poke, really, but he fell into the door behind him as if she'd dealt him a great blow. "You are supposed to be my brother. Not my... my madame!"

"What do you know about—"

"More than you can even guess, Brother dear. You want my secrets? You do not deserve them, you arse-end of a... a... hedgehog!"

He flinched.

"You say you want me happily married? But how can that ever be when the only men interested in me are more interested in *you*?"

"That's not true."

"I can't even attract a suitor on my own! They must be curated entirely of my brother's cronies." She inhaled, a deep, ragged sound like a sob. "Even *you* know how hopeless I am."

"What?" He shook his head. "Prudence, no—"

"You've made it quite clear you think me incapable of producing any emotion in a man. And... and I suppose you are only right. I am too pale and uninteresting, too plain, and too practical to catch a man's eye."

His hands curved around her shoulders, and he pushed her backward until her legs hit the bed. And because she could no longer hold herself up, she fell to the mattress, sitting slumped like a beech bent beneath a hard wind.

Samuel squatted before her and tried to catch her gaze. "I do not think you incapable of attracting a man. I merely think you are unwilling. And what has ever prompted me to think otherwise? It is why I set Bailey after you, to find out why you would accept no man's attentions."

"Those men do not want me. Why would they?" She picked at the gathered material of her skirts in her lap, pinching them into a wrinkled mess. Those last three words, a collection of syllables she'd felt deep inside her for so long as an unbreakable truth, no longer felt so comfortable on her tongue. Could the woman she'd seen in the looking glass so recently really been the lie, and these sour words the truth?

Samuel spun on his toes and sank to his rear as he leaned against the bed beside Prudence's legs. He let his head fall back, and his eyes closed. "Is this truly how you feel about yourself? And I have made you feel that way? Hell, Pru." He hid his face into his hands, groaned. "God, I'm sorry. So sorry. I never meant." He dropped his hands and caught her gaze, his eyes blazing with determination. "It's *not* true."

When she didn't look up at him, didn't respond, he elbowed her leg. "It's *not* true, Prudence. You're lovely. And clever. And you're funny, and when you were a little girl, you used to run around behind Mrs. Blalock, pretending to be the housekeeper, and no one organized my cravats like you did." He laughed. "And you were reading by the time you were five. Long books I had trouble with still. And you went off to the country with an unhappy husband and wife to support your friend. Most people would run from being put in such an awkward position, but not you. Prudence, you *are* worthy. So very worthy. Why do you think I give advice to the gentlemen on courtship and not to you? Because you and your sisters—you are *perfect*. And men are fools. And it's why I've fought so hard to see you all wed."

She snorted. "You just want us out of your hair." She brushed the tears off her cheek.

"Yes. No." He sighed. "I want you happy. I want you loved. And I'm terrified that with only me to care for you, to oversee your courtships and your marriages, I'll fail. I'll launch you into muddles like Norton and his wife find themselves in. I'd never forgive myself for that. Ben told me a bit about it. It's not good." He scratched at his hair. "I sent Ben after you because I trusted him to watch over you, to find out why you were not accepting any of your suitors without hurting you. He may look a beast, but he's surprisingly good-hearted. I would not have trusted you with anyone else. I see I was wrong. Nothing new about that, I'm afraid."

"You blackmailed him into courting me." What had Ben said? He'd gone to the country for Samuel but stayed for her? Yes... she'd felt that shift. He'd even tried to leave, hadn't he, the day of the storm. But what had happened in the boathouse—like the new clean world after a deluge. Had it truly been a new clean world for them, too?

"It is not my finest moment," Samuel admitted. "I was wrong to do so."

She snorted.

"You won't say, 'oh, no Samuel, you were not entirely wrong'?"

She snorted again.

"I deserve that. You're worthy of every good thing, Prudence, including love. And... if Ben says he loves you... he wouldn't lie. You must believe me on this. He may have begun courting you because of me, but he would not have said everything he said minutes ago if it weren't true. That's not the man he is. For what it's worth, out of all the men who've fallen in love with my sisters, I approve of Ben the most. Noble is a git. And Kingston comes with complications. But Lottie and Annie are happy with them. If you love Bailey as he says he loves you... I have high hopes for your happiness as well. At least this time, I can take partial credit for it."

She swung her leg sideways, hitting his arm. "You're insufferable. You told him to lie to me."

"I know." He inhaled deeply. "I'll apologize every day if I need to. I love you more than I can say. All of you. So much it's like a fear in my gut sometimes. I'm getting everything wrong. I know."

"You are. Most of it." She slid off the bed and held out a hand to him. "But you must leave us be to find our own way. You can't... you cannot continue to interfere."

He took her hand and let her pull him to his feet. "I begin to suspect you're right. But... it is my duty, as it would have been our parents' duties had they lived, to see you well-off." He did not release her hand as they faced each other, and she did not shake his grasp away, though irritation lanced through her. "But I promise to take what you say into consideration. I'll take what your sisters have to say into consideration. I'll... I hardly know, but I'll figure it out."

She squeezed his hand and swung him toward the door.

He paused just before exiting, his hands wrapped around the frame. "Will you forgive Bailey?"

"I don't want to talk about that right now. I need to be alone."

"Of course. I'll"—he looked about the room, lifted his arms, and dropped them to his sides—"go be a nodcock elsewhere."

Any other day she might have laughed at that. Today she could not, so she simply closed the door behind him and tried, in the buzzing loneliness of the room, to discover her next move, her next list of actions to itemize on a bit of clean paper.

But the large oval of a looking glass seemed to taunt her, draw her nearer, and when she peeked inside it, almost against her will, every fear boiling inside her sizzled into nothing.

The same woman stood there as before. Her eyes puffier, yes, and her cheeks mottled. But the same woman who'd let a man into her bed and loved it. The same woman who'd told that man her truth when he'd disappointed her. She'd told Samuel what he could do with his suitors as well, and perhaps influenced her sisters' futures for the better. Not even Lottie or Annie had thrown Samuel's faults in his face. But it had needed doing.

And if Prudence excelled in one way, it was getting things that needed doing done. She glowed with her *own* power. She'd been lied to, manipulated, but still she stood, strong and ready to do what needed doing.

Cora wanted a poetry reading, needed one to pour her grief out of her body and into the air. Prudence would provide one.

Because whether Ben loved her or not, Prudence was determined to love herself.

Chapter Twenty-Two

T he rain beat against the windows so hard Ben almost didn't hear the knock. The metallic clank of his hammer on the broken press had also swallowed up the announcement of a guest. The printshop was closed today, closed until he'd transformed the entire damn thing from London Life Prints to Bailey Prints, hanging sign and all.

But the knocking continued.

"Persistent pest," Ben mumbled, testing the lever that lowered the top half of the press onto the paper. Still stuck. Damn.

The knocking continued, muffled, clearly from the shop's front door at street level, but audible all the same, even from the lower back room where he worked in the bright afternoon light streaming through the windows.

But why answer the door? Painted blue like the one in Boston. Seeing it would only remind him that he no longer liked the color so much. Preferred, instead, the blue green of a keen lady's eyes.

How long had it been since he'd looked into them? Almost a week? Difficult to tell, every day and night running together.

He deserved this. He could have told her at any time, made a joke of it, planned with her to tease Clearford in some way, to drive the man mad. They'd driven him someplace else entirely, though. The duke had arrived at the printshop with his solicitor a few days after Ben had left Clearford's house. Had looked wearier than before, defeated. They'd exchanged no words other than those related to the sale of Clearford's shares.

And Ben didn't flinch a bit to know he'd received those shares through duplicity. Clearford remained in the dark still, and perhaps that was for the best. What would he do with the information, after all? And what harm did these women and their reading proclivities do anyone? Not Clearford's job to pass judgment.

Not Ben's job to lie through his teeth and expect reward in the love of a pretty Prudence.

The knocking on the door turned to banging loud enough to drown out the banging of Ben's hammer on the broken press, and then it stopped entirely.

"Finally." Ben tossed the hammer aside and brushed his hands on his pants, leaving a smear of ink behind. Perhaps he needed some oil. He rummaged around for it in the shadows.

And heard another knock. This one much closer, ringing out from the door at the end of the room that led into the alley behind the shop.

"Bloody hell." Ben stormed toward the door. Why couldn't all humanity leave a man to wallow in peace and quiet, to lose himself in the fixing of machines because the one machine he couldn't fix was his own damn heart? "Damn persistent"—he threw open the door —"Prudence?"

"Yes, I am. Why didn't you answer the door on one of the first one hundred or so knocks? My knuckles are raw."

He snatched her hand before she could move away, stripped off the glove and held it tight, rubbing his thumb over her knuckles. Were they too red? The skin torn and irritated? A bit perhaps. At least the thin barrier of the glove had offered some protection. He kissed them.

She yanked her hand away, retrieved her glove from the floor, and slipped it back on. "I did not come here for that, Mr. Bailey."

He crossed his arms over his chest to keep from reaching for her again. She smelled like rain and some sweet summer flower, and his fingers felt an itch he couldn't ignore, to touch her, to never let go.

"You're wet," he grumbled, stepping to the side. "Come in."

She did, looking everywhere but at him, the light of curiosity in her eyes brightening everything her gaze settled on. "I've been in the workshop behind *The Daily Current* before. This one is similar."

"Yes, mostly."

"The presses seem different. They're quite elaborate." She weaved between a row of presses, her hands clasped behind her back, a rain battered, beaded reticule swinging from her wrist. She craned her neck to look up at the golden eagle perched on the top of the press.

"My father believed in having the most sophisticated equipment. This design is from the States. Elaborate, yes. Gaudy, even. But quite advanced. What's used at *The Current* is older. Kingston likes it that way. Would you like to see the cylinder press?" He didn't wait for her answer but swept past her to lead the way. "I've hired a few men to learn to work it, fix it. And I won't get rid of the flatbed presses, though some using the cylinders have. If my father believed in keeping up with advances in the field, my mother believed in caring for your workers."

"This shop is for them, isn't it?"

He stopped and turned to find her still, several feet away from him. "Yes."

She swallowed, looked down, then back up. "I came today for two reasons. The first was to see what it was you loved if not me—"

"Prudence—"

She held up a hand. "I thought it a building. A collection of things. A means of making money. But it's not that at all. It's your parents." She strode toward him and cupped his cheek, her hand warm beneath her damp glove.

One moment you have no clue. The next you know.

He'd thought to experience the truth of that statement only once. But it seemed with Prudence, he'd realize how much he loved her over and over again, whether it be in the comfort of her palm or the brimming sadness behind her eyes.

What could he do to make it right? Because he couldn't give up. Couldn't give her up.

He closed his eyes and nestled his cheek deeper into her palm. "I loved them with everything I was. And I failed them. And when I saw this shop, I saw a way to make it right. It seemed like fate. The door, my mother's favorite color, the same color as the door to the printshop in Boston. The hanging sign, the same shape. I could not buy it on my own then, and when I finally could, your brother—"

Her hand dropped away from his cheek. He felt the loss of it in his bones, but he managed to stay upright and find his way toward the cylinder press. He dragged his fingers across the rounded top of it.

"What I did was not right, Prudence. I do not pretend it was. I knew even as I did it that I flirted with the line of good behavior and bad. Only I thought, and your brother thought too, that you are a woman who could not be hurt."

"You thought I did not have a heart." She spoke from right behind him.

"No. I thought you had put your heart elsewhere, that you would hide it away from men, for some reason. I did not think you would ever hand it to me. And I found myself giddy when you did."

"And your heart?" She stepped forward to stand next to him and ran her fingertips along the machine's edge as well. "Does it reside at the bottom of the Atlantic with your mother's ring and your father's final printed pamphlet?"

He swallowed. "No. It's wailing right now." She sniffed, clearly doubtful, but he continued, "From inside the ribbed cage of another's chest."

She shook her head and followed the outline of the machine until she stood on the other side of it, opposing him. "I came here for two other reasons. The first is to let you know the day after we returned to London, I began my monthly courses. I am done now, and clearly, I am not with child."

Well that seemed the final nail in the coffin of his hopes. Her mouth said *I am not with child,* but the meaning behind those words clear—no need for them to marry.

"And the second reason?" he asked.

She inhaled deeply, pushed her shoulders back. "I need your help. Cora, as you know, is intent on holding a poetry reading at Lottie's ball. But I am intent on finding safer ways of hosting such events. You saw the outcome of our attempts in the garden the night Cora was compromised. I'd been forced out of the house and could not find my way back in. I could not set the markers for the others to find the room." Beneath the press her toe began to tap, and she slung her chin toward her shoulder with a huff. "There must be a better way. There *is* a better way. With your help."

"Details, Lady P."

The pet name seemed to rush a pretty pink across her cheeks, and her eyelashes fluttered. But only for a mere moment before she shook such softness away. "I know you intend Bailey's Prints to publish political pamphlets, to be home to authors of intellectual note with new ideas. But I would ask you to print one more pamphlet of an entirely different sort."

"About?"

"Those things typically considered women's interests. What is in fashion, what is out of fashion, gossip about how certain ladies are decorating or redecorating their houses, who is out of Town and who is in, that sort of thing. Kingston has allowed my brother to write a column for one of his papers. And this pamphlet will be written by my sister Imogen. With the help of Isabella."

"The twins?" He scowled. "They can't."

"They can anonymously."

"How would what amounts to a gossip column help your situation?"

"You said you wish to help in any way you could. Was that a lie, too?"

"No. But I cannot help if I do not know the details."

"You can provide a press on which to print our little periodical. That is the only help we need. You need not know the rest. Disappointing, I know, for a man who likes to uncover others' secrets."

He wanted to upend the printing press, to send it smashing against the wall. He wanted to throw Prudence over his shoulder, take her up to his office, and throw her down on the small sofa there. He wanted to put his head between her legs and pleasure her until she tangled her hands in his hair and screamed his name. He wanted to thrust into her over and over again until she allowed him to wrap his black ribbon around her wrist once more.

Instead, he said, "If you suspect me of lies, Prudence, then why come to me for help? Don't you think I will just run off to your brother and tell him everything?"

Her chin dropped to her chest, and she rounded the side of the cylinder press and headed for the door. He followed, helpless not to. When she opened the door into the alley, she leaned against its frame, half in half out of the shop.

"I am enraged with you," she said, her voice steady, not a hint of her anger evident there. It flashed, though, in her eyes—furious lightning. "I'm enraged more, frankly, that I don't distrust you. I know somehow, deep in my gut that you will not tell my brother a thing. But"—she shrugged, gave a little laugh—"what have you really told him so far? Nothing much."

He risked moving closer until he stood only inches from her beneath the door frame. He bent his neck and inhaled deeply. God, how he'd missed the smell of her.

Her breath hitched. "No cravat," she muttered. And then her fingers were on the V of skin exposed by his open shirt. "You're a mess. Surely, it has been at least a week since you've shaved. Have you brushed your hair in that time?"

He shook his head slowly.

She *tsked*. "I want to hate you." Confusing words for what her hands were doing, curling around the neck of his open shirt. "But more than that *I want you*." She jerked him right up against her body and kissed him hard.

Between clashes of teeth and lips, he slid one hand around her waist to find its home. The other he propped against the door frame above her head as he rolled his hips into her.

"I'm a fool," she said, touching him everywhere.

"Never," he breathed against the skin of her neck. His tongue darted out and licked a line from collarbone to ear, tasting the sweat and rain on her skin.

She gave a little growl, clutched him to her more tightly, and spun him so his back pressed against the door frame, and she pressed against him. He bent his knee and parted her legs, hitched it up and into her body until she gave a delightful little gasp of pleasure, throwing her head back. They had barely begun, but...

"I cannot stop," he said. He picked her up, and she wrapped her legs around his waist, clinging with her arms around his neck. He slammed the alley door closed and marched with her back into the warehouse, brought her to the long, beaten-wood table at the far edge of the room, and set her down atop it. He placed his hands on the table on either side of her hips and gathered her skirts, rucked them up to her waist as she kissed him wildly.

She'd missed him, too.

He slipped a hand between her legs, found her wet there and not from the rain. That rain beat steadily still against the windows and on the roof, a melodic companion to their panting, chaotic breathing. She sank her teeth into the visible skin in the V of his shirt, and he stabbed his fingers into her hair, pulled her head back to reveal the curve of her throat, which he kissed and kissed and kissed.

Somewhere between fake courting her and kissing her, he'd fallen irrevocably, brutally in love. And he could not live without her now.

A few flicks undid his fall. He stepped between her spreading legs, and with one thrust sank deep inside her. She cried out, the scream a ripple of pleasure through the air. He thrust again and again, slow and steady, and her hands on his shoulders, his abdomen, easily dipping past the waist of his too-loose trousers, set him on fire. A pleasure to burn for her touch. Each caress drove him faster and harder. One of her hands clung to his neck, and he took her other and placed it just over the curls between her legs.

"Show me how you do it, Lady P. When you're alone in bed. Thinking of me."

She gave a little growl, clearly not liking his insinuations. But she did not shy away from touching herself, and her fingers began to work methodically. Of course. His punctilious Prudence. Her head fell back with a moan.

"That's it. That's it, love." The tension in his body twisted tighter.

"Prudence, listen. You're safe now, but if I do not pull out, you will not be."

Her eyes flashed. She understood him well enough. She grabbed the back of his head, holding his hair as hard as he held hers, holding him so close to her face that they were eye to eye, nose to nose. "Do not stop."

Her command much too much. A wildness unfurled inside him, and he pumped uncontrollably before releasing everything he ever was and ever would be. He claimed her as deep satisfaction roared through his body. And then he placed his hand over hers between her legs, and his lightest touch was enough to send pleasure shattering through her body. Her every muscle clenched as her back arched, her entire body a tense curl pushing away from him as her hips rolled against him, driving him more deeply home inside her. Then she flung herself forward to hang on to him, her muscles going limp and heavy.

He pulled from her and gathered her into his arms before sitting on the table and holding her in his lap as he had that day in the portrait gallery. He curved into her, nuzzling the side of her face as their breath mingled. The rain continued steady and hard above and around them, and the shadows of the shop seemed to thicken and hold them close as he held her closer.

Then she rustled, her hand slipping into the folds of her gown and reappearing holding a silver pocket watch. "It is time for me to leave. I am meeting my sisters on Bond Street. We need new gowns for the ball."

He let her slip from his lap, though every muscle in his body screamed at him not to. She smoothed her skirt and straightened her shoulders when she stood on her own two feet again, and then she made her way as promptly toward the door as if he had not just tupped her on a workbench in his printshop.

Once she'd flung the door open again, she turned to face him. Somehow, he had followed her from the bench across the shop and to the door. No thought needed. It would always be like this.

He dared to tuck a lock of hair behind her ear. "I'm afraid I've entirely mangled your coiffure."

She patted it, scowled. "I'll put on my bonnet. It's in the carriage."

"Make sure to buy something spectacular, Lady Prudence. Though whatever you buy, no matter how pretty, it won't hold a candle to you."

Her cheeks blazed bright. "Benjamin Bailey... Whatever am I going to do with you?"

"I have a few suggestions," he grumbled.

She lifted her hand and pushed back the cuff of her gown. She wore a pink ribbon there, tied loosely. She untied it. "Hold out your hand."

He did, and she tied the ribbon around his wrist, hesitating only a moment when her fingers brushed against the black ribbon tied there. She swallowed hard but finished the pretty little bow, then clasped her hands before her.

"I trust, Mr. Bailey, that when we deliver the pamphlet, you will print it as is?"

He bowed. "Of course, Lady Prudence."

"Yes. Well, then." She gave a tight smile, and her eyes lingered on his frame just a moment more than was polite, and then she turned and left.

Ben stood in the door frame as the rain soaked his head and chest. He could not rip his eyes away from the sight of a pink ribbon and a black tied round his wrist. She still loved him. That was the only possible meaning of the little bit of pink velvet. She still loved him but was strong enough to punish him a bit for his sins before forgiving him. Brilliant, beautiful Prudence.

How much would it take to convince her of her worth?

He'd dedicate the rest of his life to finding out.

Chapter Twenty-Three

Not all the pretty gowns in the world could distract Prudence. What in heaven's name had she done? Letting Ben ravish her in the back of his printshop had not been on her list of things to do. But as it ever was with ravishment, it had rather taken her by surprise.

At least it had not made her late to Marie's. The modiste did not abide tardiness, not even for a duke's sisters. One reason Prudence adored her. The other was the small, private parlor in the back where Marie escorted Prudence and her sisters every time they had a fitting. It felt more like a cozy talk at home than an excursion to get pricked with pins. Now the twins sat in matching chairs, flipping through fashion plates, and Lottie sat next to Prudence, sipping tea, having already finished her fitting. Andromeda had been dragged up onto a pedestal across the room where Marie, a tiny woman with steel-gray hair and straight pins held between her teeth, was undressing her.

Five women and none knew where she'd been this morning, what she'd *done*. Certainly, she'd not intended to do it.

He had warned her twice, told her *twice* that he would stop, had waited for her answer. And still she let it happen, had wanted it to happen. She had certainly not been with child this morning, but now?

She'd not know for some time. What she'd done felt like a promise, a commitment, and no matter what her body demanded, her heart could not yet give it.

Yet she'd tied her ribbon round his wrist. A gesture that seemed even more intimate than what they'd done on the worktable. She'd tied it on a few days ago only because, after even such a short period of time, she'd missed the feel of Ben's black ribbon there.

Marie bustled out a door, leaving the sisters alone.

"Prudence." Lottie leaned over and tapped Prudence's hand. "Are you well? You've been rather pale and silent since returning from the country."

"Of course she's been out of sorts," Isabella said. "What happened between Cora and Norton is quite shocking. I hear the viscount has taken up residence at Hotel Hestia."

"But I thought he had returned home!" Andromeda stood in her shift and stays only, waiting for Marie's return.

"Yes," Prudence said. "He turned up at their London residence not long after Cora arrived home. And he proceeded to make things worse. They argued heatedly, so Cora tells me. But she will not say exactly what he said, only that he promised not to say a word about the books."

"I don't blame her for keeping her silence," Lottie said. "Arguments are best kept between a husband and a wife."

"Someone should tell Norton"—Imogen peeped out from behind a fashion plate—"that *other things* are best kept between a husband and a wife as well."

"What do you mean?" Prudence held a cup of tea but could not bring herself to drink it. It sat lukewarm between her hands on her lap.

"I imagine Isabella can tell you." Imogen put her nose back behind the plate as everyone turned to look at Isabella.

"Well," Is said, lowering her voice, "I've heard the viscount is not only residing at the hotel. Rumor has it he has invited numerous women *of ill repute* into his rooms."

"No." Andromeda's blue-green eyes widened. "I never would have thought him that sort. Did you think he would be so public with his affairs, Prudence?"

Prudence rested the cup on the table and shook her head. "He always seemed so pleasant. A mild-mannered sort of man. Cora is devastated."

"I did not know," Lottie said, "that Cora liked him well enough to be devastated."

"She could be mourning her reputation," Andromeda said.

Prudence traced her finger around the rim of the full cup. "I think she had always hoped to avoid the sort of marriage her parents have."

Marie bustled back into the parlor, silencing all gossip. She lifted Andromeda's gown over her head and fastened it at the back, fussed with the skirts until they fell with utter perfection down Annie's frame. The gown was made of a sheer, bright yellow fabric. It brought out the roses in her cheeks and fit her to perfection.

When Marie had taken notes for final alterations, she waved for Prudence to take Annie's spot. Usually, when Prudence climbed atop the pedestal, she avoided looking right at herself. Today, she did not, studying her reflection as Marie helped her strip to her stays and shift. The reflection she'd seen upon returning to London had not faltered in the last week, though she'd feared it every day. And every day, she pushed fear down and made a choice—chose to love herself, no matter what men like Ben and her brother might do. She chose to see herself as worthy of love.

Marie patted her shoulder. "Wait just there, my dear." She disappeared once more.

"Lottie, Andromeda?" Prudence viewed them through the mirror's reflection.

"Hm?" they said together, looking up.

"I have two secrets I'd like to share with you. Is and Im, too."

"Oh?" They all said together, sitting straighter, leaning closer.

Prudence took a deep breath. "First, did you know I have often felt... lesser? Than all of you?"

Silence and wide, blinking eyes.

Then Imogen barked a laugh. "Surely you jest, Pru."

Prudence shook her head.

"But you cannot feel so," Lottie said. "Why would you?"

"Have we... made you feel that way?" Andromeda asked.

"No!" Prudence leapt from the pedestal and joined her sisters around the tea set. "Never. It is only a... a trick of my own mind, I think. And that some others, some men, have often made me feel so. I am quite... invisible at times. In society."

Isabella rolled her blue eyes. "*Society*. They all wish *they* were invisible so they could do as they pleased."

"You are above reproach, Pru." Andromeda reached out for Prudence's hand and squeezed it.

"I'm not seeking compliments." Prudence squeezed her sister's hand back. "But I felt the need to tell you. In fact, the more I speak of it out loud, the stronger I feel to battle it back. And"—she cleared her throat—"Annie, I am not quite above reproach. There is my second secret."

"After that powder keg, I'm not sure I want to hear." Lottie melted backward into her chair.

Prudence glanced toward the door. Marie would arrive any moment. She smooshed all the words together and spoke them as quickly as her tongue would allow. "I am in love with Mr. Bailey." She sucked in a breath and held it.

Another bout of silence.

Then Isabella broke it. "The American?"

Prudence nodded.

"How did this happen?" Lottie demanded.

"He was at Norton Hall. Came there to spy on me for Samuel."

Her sisters jumped to their feet in a flurry of skirts.

"Did he find anything out?"

"Has anyone punched him yet?"

"How can you love a low-down *spy*?"

"How could he?"

"Which he? Samuel or—"

"They're *both* despicable!"

The beloved voices overlapped, and Prudence waited until they fell into silence once more, turning to her for further explanation. Their passion convinced her better than anything could—no matter what happened, if she had her sisters, all would be well.

"Oh, Pru!" Andromeda wrapped her in a hug. "Do not cry!"

Then other arms embraced her, soft and light as feathers, yet strong as only women's arms can be, holding her up, beating back her sorrow.

If these women loved her like this, why had she been so scared for so long? She squeezed them more tightly, pulling them closer until they were a laughing tangle of limbs and skirts.

"Whatever is happening is all very nice and sisterly, but may I please have Lady Prudence back?" Marie's voice slurred a bit from the pins, but still held a note of command they jumped at.

Prudence returned to the pedestal, and Marie dressed her in the new ball gown. Once finished, she stepped back. "What do you think, my lady?"

Prudence, for what felt like the hundredth time this week, studied her reflection. It was the same sort of ball gown she usually wore—higher in the neckline than fashionable, the same white most unmarried women wore in the evenings, no embellishments, no surprises, virginal, boring, unsophisticated. She appeared the same as she ever did, and that felt wrong. So very wrong when she felt so very *changed*.

"It's boring, isn't it?" Imogen had not asked a question, no matter how she'd phrased her sentence.

"Im." Lottie scowled. "Marie has worked hard on this gown. Do not be rude. It is perfectly serviceable."

"Serviceable." Marie snorted, circling Prudence. "I agree with Lady Imobella." She'd long ago mushed the twins' names together, unable to tell them apart. "Serviceable is all well and good, but it is... boring. What do you think, Lady Prudence?"

"I think you and Imogen are correct. It is wonderfully made, Marie. Quite lovely. But I think I would like something a bit less... serviceable and a bit more... brazen for Lottie's ball."

Isabella clapped.

The gown had suited her before. It no longer did so. The wrong style and fit entirely for the sort of woman who ran off before dawn to find her friend and save her from trouble, for the sort who allowed herself to be ravished in a boathouse. Or the type of woman who compared dukes to the arse-end of a hedgehog to their faces.

"Will you be able to make some alterations in time?" Prudence asked.

Marie stopped circling and closed her eyes. "Not just alterations. An entirely new gown. Lower bodice, naturally. Puff sleeves. Square neck. And dusky pink tulle over..." She tilted her head to the side and tapped her lips. "Deep-blue satin, I think. Yes."

"I do not wish to trouble you," Prudence said, though she did not speak the truth. What she wanted. That gown, exactly as Marie described. It sounded spectacular, and Ben had told her to wear something just so. She wanted to wear something just so.

"I can see it now, my lady." Marie spit the pins in her hands and threw them in a nearby dish. "Just a moment. Let me make a sketch." She ran out the door.

"Did she spit out the pins?" Imogen asked, peering inside the small bowl.

"I've never seen her without them," Isabella whispered.

"It means she's quite serious." Lottie stood beside Prudence and took her hands. "As am I, Sister. You do not look so happy for a woman in love. Does he not reciprocate your feelings?"

What else to say but the truth? "I do not know."

Andromeda rested a hand on her belly and bit her lip. "And your feelings are unchanged even after learning about his machinations with Samuel?"

"Yes. No. I... cannot stop loving him, but it is all muddled together with anger now."

Lottie laughed, her breath puffing a curl out of her face. "I know that feeling all too well."

"What do I do?"

"Find out what you want and tell him. Then it is up to him. If he complies, and he shows you he can be better—every single day, he shows you—then you may begin to heal. With him. If he denies you. Or if he shrugs off your request as of no import, well... there are better men out there for you."

"I have already made a request of him." Prudence picked at a floret on the bodice of the ball gown.

"I assume," Andromeda said, "what you asked of him is not something trifling like a stroll round Hyde Park or a bit of jewelry?"

Isabelle swatted Andromeda's shoulder. "Of course it is not, Annie. Prudence wants more than outings and fripperies. She wants... What do you want, Prue?"

Prudence glanced at the empty doorway. Marie still sketched elsewhere. "I want him to publish the periodical I told you about, the one where we can hide all the information the ladies of the *ton* need to know about where to meet and when."

"And he said...?" Isabella prompted.

Prudence turned back toward her reflection, found herself smiling. "He's agreed." So easily, too, as if there'd never been a question in his mind, as if he'd always do as she asked, support her when she needed it. And not because he thought her incapable, but because... because... he admired her, didn't he?

Marie swept back into the room with a square of paper held high like a trophy. "I've got it. What do you think, Lady Prudence?"

Prudence took the sketch, and her sisters gathered round to look as well. Together they created a choir of approving hums and oohs and aahs.

"It's perfect." Prudence closed her eyes and imagined herself wearing it, imagined Ben seeing it. Yes, he'd admire it, admire her.

And she should admire herself.

Lottie nudged Prudence with her shoulder. "It's sure to make the men—"

"Or one particular man," Andromeda said.

"Absolutely mad with desire." Lottie finished with a wink. "She'll take it, Marie."

"My pleasure, my lady. Now." Marie found her pins and put them back between her teeth, eyeing the twins. "Which of you are up next? Lordy, I can never tell you apart."

As she worked, Prudence poured herself another cup of tea, and she sipped this one, slowly, letting the liquid warm her from head to toe. She'd decided to adore the gown, to feel like perfection itself while wearing it. No matter what happened, she would feel as if no man could look away. Every woman would want to work with Marie after.

She laughed. She could be spinning fairy tales. She might step out in her new gown and be as invisible as ever. But she would not decide before the day came that they were impossibilities.

She would dance with the London gentlemen and laugh with no other motivation than waltzing through an evening certain of her own worth.

Chapter Twenty-Four

The letter had arrived the very next day. Thick, creamy paper, lots of it, folded together with page after page of neat, even writing. Prudence's writing, curling in perfectly straight lines across the front and back of each page.

The London Lady's Almanac, she'd called it, and Ben had read it through three times, looking for the clues she'd hidden there. They seemed obvious to him, but perhaps only because he already knew the details. A piece on Lady Noble's upcoming ball, a note therein about how that lady planned to decorate her ballroom, how she'd commandeered a parlor downstairs simply to store more flowers so they could be refreshed throughout the night.

Ha. He'd bet his shop that was not the parlor's true purpose. Especially not when she'd included the bit about Lady Norton exclaiming "Utter perfection!" when she heard of the plans.

Not that he'd own the shop much longer.

He descended the stairs into the lower level of the warehouse, calling out, "Atkins." Ben waved the letter over his head. "I've got new work for you."

He found Atkins at the cylinder press where he always sat, waiting for his next print.

"Yeah?" he asked, looking up from a pamphlet inked by his own hands.

"I've got a new one for you. It'll be a semi-regular publication for us. You shouldn't have any trouble with the handwriting."

Atkins took it and looked it over, humming. "Not a bit. Clear as day. When?" He raised a brow.

"As soon as can be."

"How many copies?"

"The most you can produce."

Atkin's remaining brow joined the first high on his forehead, and he whistled. "The lovely Gabby Greta can give you five thousand."

Ben scratched his jaw. "Hm. Probably don't need that many, but let's have it. Why not? I'll shower her in the damn things." He turned. Had places to be. But he whipped right back around, walked backward toward the door, and called out, "Gabby Greta, Atkins?"

The man patted the cylinder press. "I knew a lady by that name who could produce more words than this here machine in less time using just her mouth."

Ben chuckled. "When they're done, send one to Lady Prudence at the Duke of Clearford's residence. Let her know her lady friends can pick them up here in the storefront." He waved and left. The walk to Mayfair offered plenty of time to rethink his plans, but by the time he reached Clearford's doorstep, they'd not changed.

He didn't knock, didn't wait for Jacobs, didn't have the patience to deal with the man at the moment. The door to the duke's study gave way with ease, and Ben didn't wait here, either, for an invitation.

A curse sailed through the air at the same time a knife did, both at the same time Ben flew into the room.

"Damn you, Bailey." Clearford pressed a hand to his chest. "You startled me. That blade could have ended up in your chest instead of the door."

A knife between his ribs would hurt less than the guilt currently ripping through him. Ben turned Clearford around and marched him behind his desk, sat him in that great big chair. Then Ben strode to the other side and steepled his hands on top of the desk.

"Let's talk business," he said as Clearford scowled.

"Not marriage?"

"Both. Hopefully. Depends on what Prudence has to say."

"I thought we were done being business partners."

"Yes. But I need your help one more time. Not for me."

Clearford twisted his mouth to one side. "What then?"

Ben settled into the chair across from him and folded his hands over the curved edges of its arms. "I want to give Prudence the shop."

Chapter Twenty-Five

Darkness, candlelight, a room of enraptured ladies, and the tall pillar of a veiled woman standing in the middle of the room, barely moving. Steady lines of poetry seemed to come off her in waves, holding the audience in thrall.

Prudence barely listened. She stood by the door, guarding the room's only entrance. They'd never held a poetry reading so close to a ballroom before. Faint strains of music from the string quartet wafted toward them. Had she made too much of Lottie's special flower storage room? Would someone wander about looking for it, to see the truth of what they'd read in the *London Lady's Almanac*?

She tried to focus on Cora, but her tale sped right toward tragedy, and Prudence wouldn't stomach sad endings tonight. She slipped through the door and into the hall. Better to keep watch out here. And better to focus on her victories. Not a month ago, she'd failed to organize just such a reading—caught first by her brother, then by Ben. Then everything brought to a grinding halt by Cora's ruination.

Could have been Prudence. She'd never been so grateful for another woman's loss. But she could not quite bring herself to wish she could trade places with her friend to alleviate her sorrow. Because then she could not have Ben.

Did she want Ben? She loved him, but...

She pulled the folded article about Lottie's ball she'd clipped out of the periodical Ben had printed. He'd done what she'd asked. And beautifully so. She'd kissed it when she'd first laid hands on it, had to wash the ghost of ink off her lips.

The door at her back opened, and Prudence swept to the side, allowing the ladies to spill into the hallway. They made a silent procession, eyes glassy with tears and hands clutching their hearts. Cora had gutted them. Hopefully that would please her.

Lady Templeton stopped next to her after everyone else had filtered down the hall and out of earshot. "Well done, Prudence."

"Well done, what?"

"The *London Lady's Almanac* is quite an ingenious idea. You've found a way to use that manly future baron of yours to great advantage."

Hers. She *had* tied that ribbon round his wrist.

Lady Templeton peered at the cut article Prudence held. "The paper is quite innocuous. Only those who know will guess its purpose. And now you do not have to bumble around during an evening trying to get everyone where they should be. You may, my dear, enjoy yourself. Now, go find your Mr. Bailey and do just that."

"I do not know if he is mine anymore."

Lady Templeton laughed, a high, cartwheeling thing that seemed to bounce off the walls. "Oh, my dear, I do apologize for laughing so, but he most certainly is yours."

"And how can you know?" He'd lied to her, after all.

"Because when I arrived at the specified shop on Fleet Street, a man was busy taking down one sign above the door and hanging a new one."

Prudence folded the bit of paper back into its neat squares, making each fold with careful precision. "That means nothing. He's just bought the shop. Of course he'd change the name. He told me what he wishes to change it to. Bailey's Prints. Just like his parents' shop in Boston."

"That is not what the sign said." Lady Templeton smirked as she walked away.

"Now what the..." Prudence ran after the older woman. "What did it say, then?"

"I think it will be more fun for you to find out for yourself." She winked, then disappeared down the hall and into the ballroom.

Before the door closed behind her, the sounds of merriment flooded the empty hallway, nearly drowning Prudence. If sounds could have color, these would be golden. And when the door slammed closed, cutting off that golden wave, Prudence floated toward it.

She hesitated, her hand on the door handle. Lady Templeton had told her to enjoy her evening. She'd never attended a ball with diversion in mind. Either she'd faced it with fear of rejection or with the steely purpose of a woman on a mission, ready to slay any distractions. To float among the dancing others, laughing and... falling in love... An impossibility.

She used to think that.

Now she chose to think differently, just as she'd chosen this gown which showed more of her collarbone and decolletage than usual, that shone pink and blue, dawn and the evening sky in the candlelight. Just as she chose to release her fears every time she looked in the mirror.

And she had another choice to make. About Ben.

She opened the door and stepped into the noise and chaos of the ballroom. Lottie had worked her magic, and millions of white blooms of all sizes decorated the walls and sconces and tables and chairs. Most organic, but many paper, folded with sharp precision. The curtains and tables had been draped in green velvet, and the furniture made of the same upholstery. The quartet wore green and white and gold, and every woman had been given a white bloom for their coiffure, every man one to pin to his lapel.

Prudence could not help but feel brave stepping into such a fairy land, pulled forth by the music as if by an enchantment. She ached to dance.

But first she must find Ben. She stepped into the throng, popping up on tiptoe, searching.

"Lady Prudence."

She whirled around. "Oh. Lord..." What was his name again? She could only ever remember he was The Heir. "Talls...by?"

He bowed, and when he popped back up, he said, "Yes, the Marquess of Northam's heir."

"Of course."

"You are looking quite lovely this evening, my lady. Nicer than I've seen you look before if you do not mind me saying. Quite transformed. For the better." She pursed her lips. She did mind, but he apparently could not tell. "I would be honored if you would dance the next set with me."

"Lady Prudence?" A tap on her shoulder. A gentleman stood behind her, one of the suitors who'd paid her court before Lottie's scandal last year. He bowed low and raked his gaze over her form as he straightened. "I, too, would be honored if you would dance with me."

"Why?"

He blinked. "Why... because... because you are a pretty lady."

"Did you think me pretty last Season? Do you think my sister well enough wed that you may court me anew?"

His mouth fell open. "I-I-I—that is to say... you looked just like all the ladies, and—"

"No, I do not think I will dance with you." Where was Ben? She popped up on tiptoe again. There—a flash of caramel-streaked hair moving out from behind a pillar, backing toward her corner of the ballroom. Ben. Her heart smiled. And then plummeted because as he backed toward her, two women followed. They batted their lashes and fluttered their fans. They laughed. And she could not know how Ben accepted their attentions.

She'd never seen women pay Ben attention before. She found it—

"Lady Prudence," Lord Tallsby said, "that dance? The quartet is striking up a waltz."

She faced him. "No, thank you. The last time we danced, you insulted me."

His turn to act the flopping fish. "I would *never* insult a lady!"

"You told me you courted me only because my sisters were not available. I call that an insult."

"I... well, I did not know you hid such bright plumage, my lady. I misspoke."

She rolled her eyes. "I'm not a bird, Tallsby, and I will no longer accept your attentions. You may leave."

He inhaled so deeply his nostrils flared alarmingly wide. But then he spun and left, so if his nostrils ripped to shreds under the force of his exhalation, Prudence would not have to witness it. Thank goodness. She had more important things to observe. Namely Ben's back ever toward her, two handsome ladies in clear pursuit.

She pushed through two gentlemen and ducked around a third, trying to get to Ben's side. He might need her help. Or he might not. Perhaps he enjoyed the ladies' attentions. Her stomach flipped. Oh, she did not like that a bit.

"Lady Prudence!" Another man's voice, jolly and high. A hand caught her wrist, whirling her around. Another suitor from last Season, and with him two other gentlemen, all looking at her with clear approval in their eyes. "I am delighted you returned to Town for the end of the Season. My friends have been hounding me for an introduction." He gave her their names, and they each in turn offered smoldering smiles above lingering knuckle kisses.

"Will you save a dance for me?" the jolly fellow asked.

"And I as well," the first knuckle kisser demanded.

"And the lady would not be so remiss as to leave me off her card, I hope." The second knuckle kisser batted his lashes.

And Prudence backed, slowly away from them, curling her kissed hand against her chest. She'd told Tallsby off, and she'd sent the other fellow packing for his bad behavior, but she could not be so rude to every single man in London. She did not possess a good enough explanation for that. Saying *I am in love with another* could not work because she could not announce that to the world when she remained unsure of the other's feelings.

The truth, though. He'd lied to her, and still she loved him. Because he was more than that moment, more than that bad decision. She only wished it had not built such doubt so sky-high inside her.

She retreated backward several more steps, ripping her dance card off her wrist. "Here." She shoved it all three gentlemen, and they lunged for it, three gloved hands wrapping round the slim gold chain at once, snapping it. They looked at each other in wide-eyed fright, then slowly turned dismayed gazes to her. They held the blasted bits of her dance card like holy relics.

"No matter," one said, clearing his throat. "Still works. See?" He tied the chain together.

"Bravo," another said. "You may write your name first."

"And you next," the third said, patting his comrade on the back.

They nodded, passing round her dance card, quite pleased with themselves.

A perfect moment to disappear into the crowd. Let them keep her dance card. She did not need it. Prudence took another quiet step backward. And ran into something. *Someone* because though the object at her back felt hard as marble, it was warm as well. She looked over her shoulder. At the same time, the someone looked over his shoulder.

"Ben!" she said.

"Thank God." He grabbed her wrist and tugged her toward the dance floor where dancers had begun to waltz.

"Mr. Bailey!" One of the women who'd been pursuing him waved her fan in the air. "You've still not signed my dance card!"

"Nor I, Mr. Bailey," the other called. "I'll save you a dance."

Ben groaned, wrapping a hand around Prudence's waist.

"Lady Prudence, your dance card!" Her previous suitor waved the ruined card above his head.

Another of the gentlemen snatched it away. "I'll just write my name twice if you do not mind!"

"I do mind," she growled.

But Ben took her hand and squeezed, and her frustration boiled away into nothing. She wanted to lay her forehead on his chest and breathe him in, but she looked up at him instead. Freshly shaved, hair perfectly coiffed, glinting more yellow than usual in the candlelight. His evening suit fit to perfection, revealing the breadth of shoulder and thickness of muscled limb she'd had the pleasure of calling hers for so very brief a time.

"My. No wonder you've collected admirers. You quite take the breath away, Mr. Bailey."

"Those women didn't care about me before. And what about you?"

His gaze roved down her form as he swooped her in a circle. "Spectacular."

"The gentlemen do seem to like it. I as well. I much prefer it to what I had planned to wear before."

"Not the gown, Prudence. You. The gown is pretty enough, but you, Lady P, you glow."

And she felt it, waltzing in his arms, felt strong everywhere he touched her, everywhere he didn't, too.

"How did the reading go?" He asked the question right next to her ear, his breath whispering across her neck and cheek.

After a shiver raced down her spine, making it difficult to speak, she said, "Perfectly. Thank you. For printing the almanac. May we count on you in the future?"

His grip tightened. "I'm afraid I can't answer that."

Her heart sank so low she almost tripped over it. "Ah. And why is that?"

"I've sold the shop. Only the new owner can say what is printed there."

She did trip now and over her own clumsy feet. "Ben, no! Why?"

He righted her so quickly no one likely noticed her stumble, and he danced her toward the edge of the ballroom, leaning low to whisper in her ear once more. "Because I love you."

She stopped dancing entirely to study his face. Not a hint of a lie or an omission there. But then she'd not seen it before. Should she trust him? Was trusting a choice, too?

"Two fellows are coming our way," he said, holding her upper arms. "They are no doubt intent on securing a dance. If that is your wish, I will release you and watch you dance every last set with fools I want to send flying through a window. I'd like to hear my bones crack against theirs, but more than that, I want you to see how wanted you are. How absolutely irresistible you are. So, I will stand here clutching my fists behind my back and watching every last time one of them touches you. If that is your wish."

"And if I do not want that?" she breathed.

"Then there is something I wish to show you." He took a step toward the open door that led into the front hallway and held out a hand to her. "The choice is yours."

The two gentlemen were almost upon them, and they knew they'd been spotted. Handsome, grinning, harmless, and finally, *finally* attentive to her.

She took Ben's hand, and together, they fled into the night. They ran past the line of coaches outside the house, and Ben hailed a hack. He settled on the opposite side of it from her, and she missed his touch. He'd said he loved her, but he sat so far away.

"What is it you have to show me?" she asked as the hack jerked into motion.

"I'd rather you see it, Lady P." He looked out the window. "What I said in the ballroom. I mean it. I know you cannot trust me right now, but I hope you will one day. And before one of those fools from the ballroom turns your head."

"If they are fools, Mr. Bailey, they cannot turn it."

"That I believe."

"They did not see me until I donned a pretty gown and held my head high." She looked out the window, too, at London dark and shadowy rolling by.

"And those ladies this evening did not see me before. But you... you said once, Prudence, after Norton's wedding, that you did not seek to change me. Do you remember?"

She tried to pull the moment, the words, from her memory, could not. Though she could not remember ever wanting to change him.

"I accused you"—he moved across the space between them to sit beside her, still not touching her—"of wanting to change me. And you said you did not wish to change me, but my schedule." He laughed. "I think I began to fall that very moment. It was clear from your tone you did not seek to placate me or flatter me. No lies in your curt words. How many others would have jumped at me with a list of things to rearrange on my person? Your brother and Norton certainly did. Not you. Hell." He lifted a hand, and she saw just in the periphery of her vision, how gently he touched and outlined the gauzy puff of her sleeve. "I'm a right arse. But I swear I speak the truth when I say I love you."

She closed her eyes and chose.

"I believe you."

Then his hands were on her, cupping her cheeks, pulling her away from the window and dragging her into a long, slow, sweet kiss. She tangled her hands in his cravat and kissed him back until the hack and the world outside the window disappeared. Languid and lazy, as if they had forever, deep and yearning, as if any second it might end.

And it did, the hack swaying to a stop, and Ben breaking the kiss with glassy eyes. He looked out the window. "Come along my passionate Lady P. We're here."

She tried to see where they were, but the dark square of the window held no answers, and she had to blink several times in the black night as he handed her out onto a quiet street.

"It's different at night, isn't it?" he asked, holding her hand and pulling her forward.

"Where are we?"

"Fleet Street."

The heady bustle of the daytime had stilled to a heavy hush. Even Fleet Street slept.

"But why have we come here?" she asked. The shadows began to take shape around her, the brighter colors coming into focus. She knew that blue rectangle. She'd banged on it until her knuckles were bruised the other day. "You've brought me to Bailey Prints."

"No."

"Yes, it is. I—"

"Look up at the sign." He pointed to where it swung in the wind. In the dim moonlight, she could just make out the words.

"Prudent Prints? I... I don't understand. Prudent?"

He looked down at her, taking both of her hands in his. "Yes, like *Prudence*, I sold the shop to your brother, but with one condition. It will go directly to you in your dowry. And that in any marriage contract you might have drawn up, it will stay in your name and under your control. As its new owner, you will have the final say over what pamphlets or broadsheets or books are published here. In fact, running it, organizing it, schedules—they are all yours to fine-tune and perfect as you see fit. Without any interference from me or anyone else."

A small sound like a strangled cry escaped her, and she clapped a hand over her lips to stifle it. What to say? He had given her what he'd wanted most in the world, and something undefinable welled within her, buzzing her limbs into lightness and pricking multi-faceted diamonds at the corners of her eyes.

"You will, of course," he said, "need someone who knows how the presses work, who has extensive experience in the industry to offer advice now and then, to help fix the machines. Preferably a man who already has a rapport with the workers. I hope you'll accept my application for the position."

She laughed, even as tears rolled down her cheeks. "Oh, Ben. Do not expect me to play favorites. You will have to interview with the rest of the highly competent applicants." But she dove into him, wrapping her arms around his body and laughing and crying into his chest. All the words that weren't right enough tumbled from her lips. "You should not have. You should take it back. How could you?" Words of denial which really meant *thank you* and *I love you* and *you are forgiven*.

He smoothed her hair and dropped kisses on the top of her head. "Because I love you. Because my parents ran their printshop together, and if I truly wish to honor their memory, I'd give myself entirely to love, to you, not to a business."

She sniffed and pushed out of his embrace, looked back up at the sign above the door. "I never knew I wanted to own a printshop."

"You like it?"

She cupped his face and drew him down so close he would not be able to doubt what he saw in her eyes and read on her lips. "I love *you*, Benjamin Bailey. And your schedule is about to run as timely as the watch in my pocket."

"Lord knows I need it. I don't even own a watch after I broke the last one." He wrapped his arms around her waist and pulled her tight against him. "I need *you*." He reached into his pocket and took Prudence's wrist, tied something round it.

She lifted it high so the moon could kiss it. Two ribbons intertwined, one pink, one black.

"Will you marry me, Prudence?"

She nodded and kissed her *yes* into his lips. She no longer needed a bruise or a ribbon to remind her she was loved, but she would wear these two always. "I love you." Each word a kiss he devoured. Each of his touches asking for more.

"'Ey!" The hack coach's cry broke them apart. "Should I wait here till you tup her or—"

"We're coming!" Ben bundled Prudence back into the hack and set her on his lap as it rolled back toward Noble's home. "There," he whispered near her ear. "Right where you belong. On your Prudence Perch."

"Oh, my best beloved Benjamin Bailey." She sighed.

He nipped at her ear. "Pretty Prudence."

"Beastly Ben." She pulled one end of his cravat loose.

"Mine."

He claimed her with a kiss, and she claimed him, too. When they entered the ballroom together half an hour later, rumpled and satisfied, no doubt remained in anyone's minds—they belonged to each other.

Epilogue

April 1821

The printshop held shadows, but Prudence tore through them, seeking her husband. He was late. The others had long since abandoned Prudent Prints, and he should have arrived home some time ago to change for the ball. Felicity's first ball. After her, only two more of Prudence's sisters would be left to join society.

"Ben!" Prudence cried, climbing the stairs to his office. "We must leave now!" He'd be a mess. He'd not shaved in the last several days, nor had he cut his hair in months. It curled up at his collar, shorter than it had been when they met, but longer than fashionable. The most perfect, most delicious length. She'd not be able to tug on it, even as she lectured him on punctuality. And if she didn't entirely ignore the rough scruff of his cheek against her palm, she'd never be able to usher him out the door and into the London evening.

The door at the top of the stairs flew open, and Ben appeared, wild and unruly, his waistcoat hanging open, cravat long gone. He reached out and grabbed her by the wrist, tugged her inside.

And kissed her like the first time. With need and longing, with delight and discovery, with a long stroke of fingers down her back that made her melt into his chest, clutch at his open shirt to remain upright. When he gasped an end to the kiss, she met his gaze, hot and happy. Time? What even was it? Why should they dance to its tune? Especially when she could get lost in his arms every minute and hour, present and future.

"I'm sorry, love," he said, his voice gravelly. He peppered her jaw with tiny little kisses like fireworks against her skin. "Got distracted. I've a suit to change into here."

"I'm aware. I put it there."

"I won't be long." He pulled her lips to his for another kiss.

And she gave into him gladly before pressing her palms into his chest and pushing distance between them. "Felicity. We mustn't let her down."

"Never." He tweaked her ear and threw open a wardrobe to the side of the office. He made quick work of stripping, muscles shifting and bunching beneath his skin, hair hanging just enough to hide his eyes from her.

Heat pooled low in her belly, and need made her fingers jump. A short touch. A short... tup. Surely it would not put them too far behind schedule. She'd merely toss her skirts up and lean over his desk. She ran her fingers across one edge of it. Ink-stained, it was, papers spilled across it from one end to the other. Her desk sat at the other end of the office, facing Ben's. It possessed a neat pile of papers stacked at the corner, on the opposite side of the blotter. Nothing else. Her desk would be less messy, but... something about seeing her spread across his papers made her husband a bit wild. She adored him that way. She enjoyed driving him to the edge of propriety, driving him over it.

She hopped up on top of his desk, pulling the edge of her skirt up past her ankle, revealing her stocking, and catching sight of something interesting inked onto a sheet of paper just peeking out from beneath her skirts. She freed it.

"Ben, what is this?"

Ben glanced over, half-dressed. He wore his stockings, breeches, shirt, and waistcoat, but everything undone. His fall only half-buttoned, his shirt untucked, and his waistcoat hanging loose about his shoulders. A length of linen wrapped around his neck but had not yet been tied.

He blinked at her. "What's what?"

"This." Prudence shook the paper at him. It looked much like the London Lady's Almanac they printed once a month or so. But it had a different title.

"You weren't supposed to see that. It's a surprise." He finished buttoning his fall and tucked in his shirt, then padded on stocking feet to her side. He hiked her skirts up higher and stepped between her legs, pulling her to the very edge of the desk.

She held the paper between them like a shield. "The Lady's Guide to Courtship?"

He tilted his head and scratched the back of his neck, a blush rushing across his cheeks with a fierce red. "I was thinking about your sister. Felicity is a serious young girl. And your brother's... advice has not proved particularly useful. For anyone. But it seems to me that you, your sisters, and your friends know more about what women want than your brother does." His lips curled into a mischievous grin. "I've been spying. To gather intel so I can print it up for you."

"Benjamin Bailey." She poked his chest, dropping the paper to her lap. "You know better. Spying?"

"I needed to find out what all of you women think, and you lot tend to know how locks work."

"Been listening at doors, have you?"

He shrugged, wrapped his arms around her waist and clasped them together low on her back. "Perhaps."

She reached up and finished wrapping his cravat around his neck. She tied it in the silence that settled between them like a body-warmed quilt, comfortable, lovely, and full of promise.

He picked up the broadsheet and held it to the side, reading it as she finished his cravat. "I'm not sure I got everything right. You will have the final say, of course, revising anything you'd like. This was merely a... proposal, to show you what's possible. Felicity should be armed with all the information she needs. As should your other sisters."

"As should all the women of London," Prudence said.

Ben nodded and pulled her so far to the edge of the desk that their hips met, kissed.

"Samuel will know we printed it," she said.

"Yes, well, Samuel has been silent with his own advice of late."

"For the best."

Ben kissed the tip of her nose. When Prudence took the paper from his hand, their fingers brushed, and as she passed the paper to her other hand, he wove their fingers together and kissed her knuckles.

"Do you like it?"

She skimmed the first several paragraphs and then opened it up. A bulleted list ran bold from edge to edge.

-Gentlemen, do not waste your time with a woman who does not spark your curiosity.

-Ladies, do not be scared to show your interest in a man if you think he might be interested in you.

-Gentlemen, do not be scared to ask for a kiss, and if the lady acquiesces, do your best to please her.

-Ladies, know your worth, for once you know how wonderful you are, then the right gentleman will see it, too.

Tears clouded her eyes, and she wiped them away, seeing only an item at the very bottom of the list before she dropped the paper to her lap and buried her face in her husband's cravat.

-Somewhere between courting and kissing is love.

His arms tightened around her, and when she lifted her face to his, smiling through the tears, he kissed her just as he had before and as he would again and again and again.

"It's absolutely scandalous," she breathed, wrapping her legs around his waist.

"Every bit of it true." He bit her bottom lip. "Far as I can tell." His hands became warm brands on her thighs, pushing up beneath her skirts, binding her hips, his naughty thumbs brushing streaks of fire on her belly. Lower.

Why had she just wrapped up his neck? She loved to nibble there. She feasted on his earlobe instead, tugged at that curling hair at his nape.

"Benjamin, Bailey," she whispered in his ear.

"Yes?" The word a mere pant. Of need. Of adoration.

"Love me."

"Right now?" he growled, slipping his fingers between her legs. "In all your finery atop the chaos of my desk?"

"Right." She rolled her hips against him. "Now."

"Pushy Prudence. As you wish."

He kissed her hard so many times they all rolled into one long embrace that made her body tremble. Her heart pounded loud enough to break through her ribs, and when he thrust inside her, scratching the desk back across the floor, she hung on tight, laughing as he loved her, smiling as her body fell apart in his arms. When he finished, he dropped to his knees with ragged breaths before her and kissed the insides of her thighs.

"I love you." A whisper. A truth.

She somehow stood on cloud-like legs and pulled him to his feet. "I love you." Another truth kissed into his beating heart.

They dressed with quick efficiency and slipped out of the printshop arm in arm. Prudence clutched the *Lady's Guide to Courtship* in her hand, and when they arrived at the ball, she snuck off to the lady's retiring room, left it like a powder keg on a table there, just before the flowers.

Ben waited for her in the ballroom, leaning against a column, his gaze roaming over the dancers. When she joined him, he straightened and said, "Now who's being sneaky, Mrs. Bailey?"

"Dance with me, Mr. Bailey?"

"I've got a better idea." He dragged her out into the deep shadows of the garden and pinned her against a tree, and in the moonlight of the night, to the sound of violins swinging on the evening wind, the wild Mr. Bailey taught her how to shine at midnight with every single kiss.

THE END

Thank you for reading *Between Courting and Kissing*.

How can Lord Norton win back his wife? By revealing his biggest secret, begging for mercy, and helping her write a happily ever after.

Make sure to pre-order book 4, *First Comes Courtship*, at a special pre-order discount!

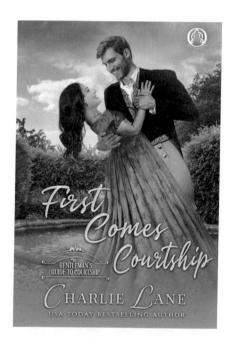

Also by Charlie Lane

A Gentleman's Guide to Courtship

#1 Never Woo the Wrong Lady

#2 How to Romance a Rogue

#3 Between Courting and Kissing

#4 First Comes Courtship

#5 Court a Lady with Care

#6 Dukes Court for Keeps

The Debutante Dares

#1 Daring the Duke

#2 A Dare too Far

#3 Kiss or Dare

#4 Don't You Dare, My Dear

#5 Only Rakes Would Dare

#6 Daring Done Right

Christmas novella: A Very Daring Christmas

London Secrets

A Secret Desire

Sinning in Secret

Keep No Secrets

Secrets Between Lovers

The Secret Seduction, A London Secrets novella

The Cavendish Family Series

Leave a Widow Wanting More

Teach a Rogue New Tricks

Bring a Boxer to His Knees

Three Kisses Till Christmas

About Charlie

USA Today bestselling author Charlie Lane traded in academic databases and scholarly journals for writing steamy Regency romcoms like the ones she's always loved to read. Her favorite authors are Jane Austen (who else?), Toni Morrison, and William Blake, and when she's not writing humorous conversations, dramatic confrontations, or sexy times, she's flying high in the air as a circus-obsessed acrobat.

Connect with Charlie: www.charlielaneauthor.com

f facebook.com/CharlieLaneRomance

📷 instagram.com/charlielaneromance

BB bookbub.com/authors/charlie-lane

a amazon.com/Charlie-Lane/e/B089G8541W